BACK FROM
THE DEAD

DENMARK

VEDBÆK

KLAMPENBORG

LYNGBY

ØRESUND

BISPEBJERG

VESTERBRO

AMAGER

COPENHAGEN

N

By the same author

Last Train to Helsingør
My Name is Jensen
The Girl in the Photo

BACK FROM THE DEAD

Heidi Amsinck

MUSWELL
PRESS

First published by Muswell Press in 2024

Typeset in Bembo by M Rules
Copyright © Heidi Amsinck 2024
by agreement with Grand Agency

Map copyright © Frederik Walkden

Heidi Amsinck has asserted her right to be identified as
the author of this work in accordance with the
Copyright, Designs and Patents Act, 1988

A CIP catalogue record for this book
is available from the British Library

ISBN: 9781739123857
eISBN: 9781739123864

Muswell Press
London N6 5HQ
www.muswell-press.co.uk

To my brother Henrik

June

Week One

1

Detective Inspector Henrik Jungersen squinted through his shades at the divers bobbing up and down in the harbour like seals. Behind him on the quay, by the gleaming spacecraft of the opera house, a crowd of passers-by had gathered with their bicycles, prams and dogs. They were held back by a handful of uniforms but unwavering in their determination to see what was going on. The many police cars suggested it was nothing good.

Henrik had rolled up the sleeves of his white shirt, but still the fabric clung damply to his back. The sun was beating down on his shaved head without mercy. 'Get on with it,' he said under his breath as the divers finished placing the body in a bag. He knew this meant the remains were falling apart. This unwelcome thought, along with the smell of diesel and harbour water, was putting him off his takeaway coffee, already lukewarm in his hand.

A couple of officers made a poor job of pulling the bag inside the dinghy. It took a third man to complete the

3

mission, the uneven weight distribution threatening for a moment to capsize the vessel.

The dead were heavy.

Especially those with watery graves.

The audience behind him, holding up their phones to film every bit of the action, knew nothing about such things, nor how difficult it was going to be to disentangle the mess that had brought the victim to this sordid end.

Who was he? Not some poor bloke who had drunk one too many in the interval of *La Traviata*. That much was clear. The fact that his head was missing was a major clue.

The sooner they had the body away to forensics and the crowd dispersed, the better.

Henrik was conscious of the empty space to his left on the cobbled quay. Having dithered for weeks, Detective Sergeant Lisbeth Quist, one of his two trusted wingmen, had finally accepted a move into a bigger job in organised crime courtesy of Henrik's boss, Superintendent Jens Wiese.

Why had the arsehole done it?

To show he could.

To gain Lisbeth's eternal gratitude.

To undermine Henrik by picking his team apart.

'You'll regret it,' he had told Lisbeth.

'My bank balance says I won't,' she had replied.

Another rung on the ladder, more money. Henrik got it, yet he was disappointed. Lisbeth still had more to learn, and who better to teach her than himself? Besides, though there were plenty of others to pick from in his team, Henrik couldn't be arsed to get to know someone new. Someone who would tolerate his foibles without running to the top brass to complain every five minutes. Someone who knew when to talk and when to let him think. Someone he could

4

stand pulling an all-nighter with when everything went to shit.

As everything invariably did.

To his right, Detective Sergeant Mark Søndergreen, his one remaining loyal foot soldier, was fidgeting nervously. Though Mark had got on with Lisbeth, Henrik suspected he had at first greeted her departure with relief. With the golden girl out of the way, Mark would finally be able to show what he was made of. But something in the dynamic had changed now that it was just the two of them. Despite Mark's best efforts at being cheerful, Henrik had felt himself turn sullen and forlorn: like Mikkel, his eldest boy, who barely spoke a word to anyone these days.

'I wish Lisbeth was here,' Mark had sighed as they had driven to Holmen in Henrik's car after the report had come in of a body floating in the harbour.

Henrik knew how unreasonable he was being, but as he stood there on the quay, watching the dinghy with the headless body turn and begin to chug towards them, he felt Lisbeth's absence as though he too were missing a crucial part of his anatomy.

It was bad enough that Jensen had paired off with another man. Jensen, the woman who didn't do boyfriends, was now shacked up with the billionaire entrepreneur Kristoffer Bro. She hadn't spent the night in her Christianshavn flat for ages.

He shouldn't know that, but he did. He told himself it wasn't stalking but making sure she was safe.

Kristoffer Bro.

A name he had hoped never to hear again. He had re-read the old police files and they had done nothing to change his view of the man, but Jensen was stubborn. She wouldn't want to listen.

('Remind you of anyone?' said his wife in his head.)

His wife. The mother of his three children, the woman he had spent his entire adult life with, for better or worse. All he had wanted, after she had thrown him out of their Frederiksberg home a few months ago, was for her to forgive him, so everything could go back to normal. At long last, she had relented, and it had felt great.

For about five minutes.

Until he had started to feel the pull of Jensen again.

He loved his wife.

He loved Jensen.

It was fucked up.

Sometimes, he thought of going back to see Isabella Grå, the psychologist with the pretty house in the Potato Rows with whom he had had a few sessions in the spring. 'Fix me,' he imagined telling her, throwing himself on her couch. He knew she couldn't, of course.

He was a lost cause.

'What have we got?' he asked the officers in the dinghy as they pulled up to the quay.

'A deceased male,' said one of them, looking distinctly green around the gills.

'I know that. Age? Ethnicity?'

'Not possible to determine at sight.'

Just then Henrik caught a whiff of putrefied corpse. The water in the harbour was warm this time of year. The body would have discoloured and distorted out of all recognition.

'But that was probably the point,' said the officer, speaking without breathing through his nose.

'Or they wouldn't have gone to the trouble of cutting the head off?' said Henrik, spitting away the vomit-heralding saliva that had run into his mouth.

The officer nodded. 'Or the fingers.'

'What?'

'All removed. Someone has gone out of their way to conceal the victim's identity.'

Henrik sighed. The murder had the hallmarks of a professional job. They weren't going to be able wrap this one up quickly.

'And I tell you what,' the sick-looking officer continued, 'it must have taken some heft to shift the body into the water, because this guy was built like a brick shithouse.'

2

Wednesday 10:14

Editor-in-chief Margrethe Skov towered above the staff who had assembled in *Dagbladet*'s canteen, sitting, standing, leaning, some shaking their heads in disgust, others struggling to hide their relief at having avoided the shoulder tap of death.

This time around.

But for how much longer?

Someone had opened the windows wide, succeeding only in admitting the traffic noise of central Copenhagen. If anything, the outside air was making the room hotter. Jensen fanned herself with a copy of yesterday's paper.

Margrethe was standing tall and broad-shouldered, hands at her waist like an overgrown Peter Pan, her eyes roaming the room behind thick lenses. Where her gaze fell, people looked away. 'I know this isn't what any of you were hoping to hear,' she said. 'But if we do nothing, we will all be without a job before the year is out. We have a chance to save *Dagbladet* by acting now. The ten colleagues affected have been informed, and I know you'll all want to join me in thanking them for everything they have done for this important ...' She paused, searching for the appropriate word. '... Danish institution.'

There was a commotion at the back of the room, a scraping of chair legs and clogs on lino. Frank Buhl, *Dagbladet*'s chief crime reporter until this morning was on his feet. '*You* are sleeping with the enemy,' he shouted, glaring at Margrethe, but jabbing his finger in the direction of the clean-shaven Swede standing behind her.

Hugo Persson, who appeared young enough to be Margrethe's son, and too young, certainly, to be CEO of a giant venture capital fund, looked horrified at the implication. Someone ought to explain to him the concept of a metaphor, thought Jensen.

Margrethe had briefly introduced Persson at the start. The Swede had made an anaemic speech that no one had listened to, before Margrethe had taken back the reins, determined to be the one breaking the bad news to her staff. She held up her hands in a vain attempt to appease Frank. Her light blue shirt was darkened at the armpits. Beads of sweat were running down her temples.

Jensen lowered her gaze to her own scuffed trainers. No one knew yet that Margrethe had passed Frank's role on to her, but some of her cannier colleagues would be guessing. Jensen felt their eyes stabbing into her back.

Her phone began to buzz noisily in her hand, startling her. It was Esben Nørregaard, member of parliament in the ruling party, the man who had given her the scoop that had launched her career. And his.

Not now Esben.

She declined the call.

Frank continued, tomato-faced in his lumberjack shirt,

saggy jeans and braces. 'How long have we two known each other, Margrethe Skov? And you couldn't tell me to my face?' He held up a letter, scrunched it into a ball, threw it on the floor and stamped on it.

His redundancy notice, Jensen assumed.

Did he have a family at home? She vaguely remembered him mentioning a grown-up daughter. At his age, he was unlikely to find another job. She couldn't see him making the leap to corporate communications somehow, and where else was there to go for newspaper hacks put out to pasture? A freelance bureau, run with diminishing hope from a spare bedroom?

Margrethe had given Jensen an ultimatum: 'Take the job or leave. Your choice. Either way, Frank is history.'

Jensen knew that the staff cull, the latest of many, was a condition of the Swedish mercy mission. The capital fund had deep pockets and vowed to safeguard the *Dagbladet* brand, but all the same the Swedes wanted things their way. The future was digital and mobile first, they said. Speculation was rife that they wanted to dispense with the printed edition of the newspaper altogether, though no one could quite bring themselves to believe that Margrethe would agree to that. Meanwhile, *Dagbladet* was getting a dedicated social media team. Its reporters would be expected to deliver across all platforms. 'It's the only way,' Margrethe had said.

Jensen wasn't going to argue. Everyone knew *Dagbladet* was years behind the curve and that its loyal print subscribers across the country were dying off, but why a rich Swedish investment fund would want to back a failing, leftist newspaper in Denmark was perplexing. Rumour had it that Margrethe and the Chairman of the Swedish fund went way back and that she had called in a favour. Jensen hadn't managed to get at the truth.

Yet.

Her phone buzzed again.

Fuck's sake, Esben, can't you just wait a minute?

The woman sitting next to her, one of the last photographers left on the newspaper's payroll, looked at Jensen angrily as though she had spoken out loud. Jensen felt herself blush. This wasn't the time to attract attention.

'And now you're going to let *Dagbladet*, our *Dagbladet*, be written by uneducated, unpaid, jumped-up . . .'

Jensen glanced up and caught Frank's eye. He faltered, unable or unwilling, despite his anger, to grasp the offensive noun that had been on the tip of his tongue a second ago.

When her phone buzzed again, Jensen felt as if the sound was being pumped out through giant speakers.

Call me now, Jensen, for the love of God!

Getting up, she mumbled an apology and pointed to her phone to show why she had to step away, realising too late that her gesture would only made things worse in the eyes of her colleagues.

She heard tutting behind her. Half-turning, she saw Henning Würtzen, *Dagbladet*'s ageing obituary writer, slumped on a chair in his beige suit with an unlit cigar in his mouth. He winked at her mischievously.

If the printed edition really *was* scrapped, how would Henning cope without being able to thumb through the pages, his fingers blackened by newsprint as he chronicled everything that happened to anyone who was anyone in Denmark? Jensen doubted he was even capable of using a laptop or smartphone.

Journalists of Frank Buhl's generation had learned to

adapt, but still there was a divide between them and the younger reporters who were digital natives. A decade, maybe two, and that divide would be gone. Would there be anything recognisable left by then of the news industry Jensen had joined as a teenager?

'Take the job, Jensen. What good would it do if both of you were unemployed?' Kristoffer had told her that morning as she had agonised over whether to refuse to step into Frank's shoes on point of principle.

He was right, of course, as Kristoffer often was. In many ways, the two of them were similar people: both loners with few friends, both absorbed in their work and driven to succeed against the odds, neither of them close to their family. 'I like having you around,' he had told her. 'You're the only person who doesn't want anything from me.'

She had hesitated before moving in, insisting on keeping the tiny flat in Christianshavn that she had rented from him in the spring. It had been an unnecessary precaution. Kristoffer had turned out to be great company and a good listener, so gradually she had moved most of her stuff into his cavernous waterside penthouse in Nordhavn.

He had humoured her as she had spent hours turning over the case of Carsten Vangede, the Nørrebro bar owner who had (allegedly) committed suicide after passing a USB with information on to her.

In case something happens to me.

Vangede had clearly thought his life was in danger, but the information on the USB had proved impossible to decipher. A bunch of invoices and documents and the address of a mystery property called Amaliekilde in Vedbæk, north of Copenhagen.

'Makes no sense,' Kristoffer had said. 'Besides, are your readers really going to care about a paranoid old drunk who thought he had been cheated by his accountant?'

'But what if his death wasn't suicide? The pathologist I asked said he couldn't be a hundred percent sure. What if he was killed because of what he had discovered?'

'Come on, Jensen. Can't you hear how far-fetched that sounds?'

She had passed the address of Amaliekilde to Ernst Brøgger, the source she had nicknamed Deep Throat, who had first encouraged her to investigate Vangede's claims. He had reacted dramatically, telling her to drop the story at once. Brøgger had evaded her calls and emails since, and Jensen had nothing else to go on.

Carsten Vangede had been a bankrupt alcoholic, estranged from his own family. The only evidence of the accountant who had allegedly siphoned money from his bank account was a pair of glasses in a case bearing the name of an optician in Randers, who had refused point blank to talk to Jensen.

What was it Vangede had found and thought important enough to save on a memory stick? Only Brøgger could tell them, Jensen had concluded.

She leaped up the stairs to her office at the top of the newspaper building, relieved to have escaped her role as villain in the canteen horror show.

Gustav, her temporary sidekick, was vaping menthol and staring idly at his phone. 'Is it over?' he said, pushing his headphones down and squinting at her through clouds of vapour.

'Bar the shouting,' Jensen said. 'And stop puffing on that bloody thing. I told you, no vaping in here.'

'Yes ma'am,' said Gustav.

She opened the dormer window as wide as it would go. The office felt like a sauna. The fan she had brought in earlier in the week merely redistributed the hot air, making the papers on her desk flutter like restless birds.

She braced herself for more questions, but Gustav had lost interest. The adult world of payslips, pensions and P45s was never capable of detaining him for long. 'They're pulling something from the harbour by the opera house,' he said, waving his phone at her.

'What is it?' said Jensen, frowning.

Gustav shrugged. 'Dunno. There's a bunch of people down there. Someone put it on Twitter.'

'Well, what are you waiting for? Go and check it out.'

Gustav jumped to his feet with a mock private's solute. His black jeans dropped below his hips, revealing three inches of underpants and one inch of hairless belly.

'Text me if it's interesting.'

She listened to his dragging footsteps disappear down the hall before calling Esben back. He answered on the first ring. 'Jensen, finally. What took you so long?'

'For God's sake, Esben, if I don't answer the phone, it's because I can't. I was in the middle of an important meeting.'

'It's Aziz,' said Esben, sounding breathless. 'He's missing.'

'Missing? What do you mean?'

The thought was impossible. The Syrian, who had worked as Esben's driver since he fled to Denmark in 2015, was at least six foot eight and built like the Hulk. He was as solid a presence on earth as a pile of bricks. People like Aziz didn't just vanish.

'He didn't turn up to get me when I arrived back from Brussels this morning. Never let me down before, so I went to see Amira, his wife. Floods of tears. Transpires Aziz hasn't been seen since shortly after taking me to the airport Monday last week.'

'That's, what, nine days ago? Why didn't she tell you sooner?'

'Said she didn't want to disturb me on my trip, but I'm not sure that's the real reason.'

'So what is?'

'Amira is afraid of what would happen to Aziz if they get sent back to Syria, and who can blame her. She doesn't want to attract any kind of attention to the two of them.'

'Is that a real possibility? That they'll be deported?'

'Not if I've got anything to do with it.'

Jensen recalled that Esben was the only politician in the governing party to have spoken out publicly against sending refugees back to Syria. 'Your stance is well known. Could this be some extreme right-wing thing? Somebody hurting Aziz to get to you?'

'Could be, but I doubt it. It's all a while ago now. Got a lot of abuse at the time but it has tapered off now.'

'So, what do you think has happened to him?'

'I don't know. That's why I'm ringing you.'

'You should be calling the police.'

'No.'

'Why not?'

'In case Aziz has got himself mixed up in something. I've got a bad feeling, Jensen.'

'I could tell DI Jungersen. He might be able to put a word out on the quiet.'

'Your cop Romeo, you mean?' Esben said.

'He *can* be trusted, you know.'

'It baffles me how you can say that after what that bastard has put you through.'

Jensen let it pass. It was a stale repartee. Henrik wasn't

good enough for her in Esben's eyes. 'My cop Romeo, as you put it, is history. I'm seeing someone else now.'

'Who?'

'None of your business,' she said. 'What do you want me to do about Aziz?'

'Meet me in half an hour. Usual place.'

3

Wednesday 11:03

The champagne bar at D'Angleterre was empty except for a couple of waiters polishing glasses and laughing at some private joke. Jensen guessed everyone was outside, desperate for a cooling breeze. They could have done worse than the air-conditioned stone and velvet cave at the back of the luxury hotel.

Esben wasn't on his usual perch by the bar, the King of Copenhagen with his Savile Row suits, flashing his irresistible smile at all and sundry. She found him in a dark corner, wearing a polo-shirt and creased chinos, nursing a bottle of sparkling water and brooding over his phone.

'No champagne?' she said, feeling his forehead. 'Are you ill, Esben?'

'Aziz going missing is no joke,' he said, recoiling from her touch.

The close bond between the Aalborg MP and the Syrian had always puzzled Jensen. Aziz was fiercely defensive of his employer, to the point of hero worship, after Esben had given him and his pregnant wife a home when they had first arrived in Denmark, intercepting them as they walked up the motorway towards Sweden.

Understandable.

But she knew less about the source of Esben's deep affection for Aziz. Whenever she had brought it up in the past, Esben had always changed the subject. She had assumed he was uncomfortable with discussing his role as Aziz's benefactor, but she could see now that there was more to it. In Aziz, Esben had found someone worthy of a profound respect that he bestowed on few others.

He looked pale under his suntan and had nicked himself shaving, leaving a pearl of congealed blood on his throat. For once, he was showing his age.

'I'm sorry,' she said, catching the eye of the waiter and pointing to Esben's sparkling water. 'Another one of those, please.'

Esben stared unseeingly at her, frowning as if in great pain. 'It's out of character for Aziz to do something like this without at least telling me, let alone his wife.'

'Going underground, you mean?'

'If that's what he's done, yes.'

'You think something might have happened to him?' she said.

Aziz was so strong as to appear invincible, like the marble gods on display at the Ny Carlsberg's Glyptotek museum. How was it possible that he could have come to harm?

Esben shook his head. 'I don't know,' he said.

Jensen remembered Aziz telling her that he had been a rich man's driver back home. 'Could it be related to something that happened to him in Syria? Do you think someone's after him?'

'Could be. I really have no idea,' said Esben, not meeting her eye.

'But you said that he might have got himself mixed up in something. What did you mean by that?'

'I just think … it might not be the best idea to involve the police at this stage, before we have an idea of what has happened. Aziz wouldn't thank us,' said Esben.

'There is something else. I can tell,' said Jensen, her voice hardening.

Esben looked around the bar, misery painted on his face. 'I didn't want to tell you over the phone.'

'What?'

'I started getting these threatening emails recently.'

'Who from?'

'Different Gmail accounts.'

'Saying?'

'Die.'

'That's it, "Die"?'

'No, I'm paraphrasing. They threatened to torture, rape and murder my wife, my children, me, in graphic detail.'

'Esben, that's horrible. You should go to the police. They can trace the address, find the bastards.'

'Actually, messages like that have been pretty standard in my time as an MP. Once you step into public life, all the crazies come for you. Might as well mount a target on your back.'

'All the same, you should have reported it.'

'I used to. Until I realised that I'd spend half my time running to the cops. No one actually carried out any of the threats, and over time you grow immune.'

Esben fell silent as the waiter brought Jensen's water and poured it over ice.

'So, what's different now?' she asked after taking a long, thirsty gulp.

'The fact that the emails coincided with Aziz's disappearance. What if they'd been threatening him, too?'

'I'm still not hearing a good reason for not going to the police.' Jensen studied Esben's face. He avoided her gaze.

'You think you know who it is, don't you?' she said.

'I can't prove it, but I think it might be linked to some approaches I've had from people wanting me to use my influence with the prime minister to plead their cause. Somewhat ironic, given I'm not exactly her flavour of the month. Well, not after the Syria thing.'

'All the more reason to report it, though.'

Esben looked at her with a meaningful expression.

Jensen frowned. 'You're worried what else they might find?'

'Well done, Sherlock. And the people in question aren't the most, shall we say, salubrious. Not the sort you'd want to be seen with in polite company.'

'Who is it?'

'I'll tell you another time. For now, I need you to find Aziz.'

Esben was no angel. A former salesman, he had transformed himself into a politician having been thrust into the public spotlight courtesy of Jensen's writing. He was certainly not above using his influence or charm with anybody to get what he wanted, including the prime minister, whose trusted inner circle he belonged to, or had done until recently. But one reason why Esben had always resonated so strongly with the electorate was his deep sense of justice. Jensen had only seen him truly angry a handful of times and always because of something he considered blatantly unjust. Shady people and dodgy deals weren't his style. 'You always told me the view is better from the moral high ground,' she said.

20

'And I still believe that. I've never gone along with any of that stuff, but that's not how some people might see it.'

'Not good for your image?'

'Something like that.'

Jensen sighed. 'What do you want me to do?'

Esben grabbed her hands, looking at her pleadingly. 'Talk to Amira. Find out what else she knows. Piece together what happened. You're good at that sort of thing.'

'Why can't you talk to her?'

'I already did, but I can tell she doesn't trust me.'

'Can't blame her for that.'

Amira would have picked up from Aziz or, more likely, concluded by herself that Esben was an incurable womaniser. This was his Achilles' heel, the one area of his life where his moral compass let him down.

'I think another woman might help loosen her tongue.'

'Just anyone with two X chromosomes?'

'No, Jensen, *you*. You're the only one I can trust. Please, will you do this for me? Talk to Amira and find out what's going on before I lose my mind?'

4

Wednesday 12:22

From Esben's description Jensen had expected a quivering wreck, but Amira Almasi was composed and calm when she opened the door to the apartment she shared with Aziz and their three children. The tall, slender woman in jeans, pink shirt and a white embroidered headscarf seemed determined not to let her anxiety interfere with her politeness. Only her red-rimmed eyes told of her fear for her husband as she waved Jensen inside. 'Come in,' she said in Danish, leading them down a tidy corridor to the lounge where the windows were open with white gauzy curtains dulling the glare of the sun.

The radio was on loud. According to the newsreader it was shaping up to be the hottest June in Denmark on record. On the dining table were books, a notepad with tiny, neat handwriting and a pencil case. 'I am studying to become a nurse,' said Amira. 'Have to use the time when the kids are out of the house, but to be honest I can't focus on it right now.'

'That's understandable,' said Jensen. 'How far have you got?'

'This year's my first. The summer break has started but I am behind, so I'm trying to catch up. The stupid thing is that I'd almost finished my nursing education in Damascus before we had to leave. Feels as though I'll never get there.' She shook her head, then appeared to gather herself. 'I'm talking too much, sorry. I will get us some tea. Are you hungry?'

'Always,' said Jensen, smiling.

The newsreader had moved on to a story about rising inflation and economic misery. Amira switched the radio off. 'Sorry,' she said. 'Only, I listen as much as I can. Helps with my Danish. Esben told me to when Aziz and I first arrived in Denmark.'

'Seems to have worked a treat,' said Jensen. While Amira was in the kitchen, she looked around at the couple's books, photographs and ornaments. There was a large flat-screen TV and a new-looking PlayStation, two controllers neatly stowed side-by-side on the shelf. Jensen imagined Aziz sitting on the sofa between his boys. She felt ashamed that she hadn't made more of an effort to get to know him. There had been plenty of opportunity back in January when he had chauffeured her around Copenhagen in Esben's car while she investigated the case of the young man who had been stabbed to death in the snow in Magstræde.

Her phone buzzed in her bag. Probably Gustav, reporting back on the harbour incident. Most likely it had turned out to be nothing. Gustav would be back at *Dagbladet* by now, bored silly and wondering where she had got to.

Jensen picked up a silver frame with a photo of Amira sitting next to Aziz on a sofa. The couple were cradling an infant, flanked by Esben and his wife Ulla. All four of them were beaming at the camera.

'Esben was good to us. We will never forget it,' said Amira, who had reappeared carrying a tray with two glasses of fresh mint tea and a plateful of something that was making Jensen salivate.

'This is *Qatayef*,' said Amira. 'You can find them all over Damascus.' She offered Jensen the plate of golden half-moons drizzled with syrup and pistachios.

Jensen took a bite of one, feeling the stickiness ooze down her hands. Her mouth filled with sugared nuts. 'Did you make these?' she said, licking her fingers.

'No,' said Amira. 'I'm a terrible cook. Aziz made them. I found them in the freezer and heated them in the oven.' She faltered and looked down at her glass, beginning to cry softly. Her thin shoulders quivered. 'Sorry,' she said, lifting a hand to her brow and covering her eyes. She wiped away her tears, got up and disappeared quickly into the bathroom.

Jensen walked up to the door. 'It's all right, Amira,' she said softly. 'Your husband is missing. No wonder you're upset.'

'Just give me a minute,' Amira said, blowing her nose noisily.

Jensen tiptoed down the hall. There was a bedroom with bunkbeds and toys all over the floor and a box room with a toddler's cot draped in pink, a four-poster for a princess. The master bedroom was at the end of the hall: tidy, bed made, no clothing in sight. Jensen looked over her shoulder before opening the wardrobe. His clothes to the right, hers to the left. Jensen recognised a jacket Aziz had worn in the winter. The hangers were full. Wherever he had gone, he hadn't been expecting to stay away for long.

Jensen heard the bathroom tap running and rushed back to the lounge, resuming her seat just in time before Amira rejoined her.

'My husband told me you're a good journalist: thorough, brave,' Amira said.

Jensen felt moved that Aziz had talked about her to his wife in such terms, despite the petulance she had shown him when they first met. 'I try,' she said. 'Sometimes I make mistakes.'

Amira waved her hand as if ridding herself of a fly. 'Esben says I can trust you.'

Jensen nodded. 'Completely,' she said. 'Tell me what happened, Amira, from the beginning. When did you last see Aziz?'

'Monday morning last week, so nine days ago. He left early to drive Esben to the airport then came back here to take the kids to school. I expected him to return afterwards, but he didn't.'

'Did he say anything before he left?'

'I've been racking my brain, but no. He just kissed me goodbye and headed out the door. He seemed happy, untroubled.'

'And when he didn't come back, what did you think?'

'I texted him and asked where he was, then heard his phone ping in the bedroom. I assumed he'd gone to the supermarket, or to see a friend and couldn't tell me because he'd left his phone behind, so I forgot about it. Until it was time to pick up the kids.'

'You went yourself?'

'Yes, but I was annoyed. We had agreed that he would get them, give me some peace to study. But because I hadn't seen him all day, I couldn't just leave it to chance, so I headed down to the school. I thought I'd see him there, flustered, apologetic, but to my surprise he hadn't turned up.'

'Then what did you do?'

'I got a neighbour to watch the kids while I went out searching for him.'

'Where?'

'His gym. A café he likes. Again nothing.'

'You must have been getting quite worried by this stage.'

'Aziz is not the sort of man you worry about. I just thought he had been stupid and inconsiderate. I fully expected to find him creeping into our bed in the middle of the night.'

'But he didn't.'

'No.'

'Yet, you didn't report it to the police the next morning. Why not?'

Amira lowered her voice, almost to a whisper. 'I remembered something he told me. Shortly after we arrived in Denmark. He said there might be people coming for him one day, from Syria, and that he might need to go away for a while if that happened.'

'You think he has gone into hiding?'

'Maybe. It's possible.'

'Esben tells me you and Aziz have been worrying about being deported?'

Amira became agitated. 'He can't go back to Syria, he just can't.'

'Why not?'

'It's too complicated to explain, but trust me, being sent back to Damascus would be extremely bad for Aziz, for all of us. What I can't understand is why he has gone without taking anything with him. No clothes, no phone, no passport. There's been no withdrawals by him on our joint bank account.'

'You're concerned something bad might have happened to him after all?'

Amira closed her eyes, nodded, heavy tears plonking onto her folded hands. Jensen reached out and rested her hand on top of hers. 'We'll find him,' she said. 'I promise you.'

'The thing is,' said Amira, sobbing her way through the words. 'I always thought I would know it ... if he was hurt ... I would feel it in my heart whether he was dead or alive, but I feel nothing. What do you think that means?'

Jensen squeezed Amira's hand. 'Don't torture yourself,' she said.

They finished their tea. Jensen had lost the appetite for her pancakes and Amira hadn't touched hers.

'You said his phone is here. Could I have it?' Jensen said. 'He might have left some clues.'

'I couldn't find any, but you're welcome to it,' said Amira. 'The passcode is his mother's birthday, may God rest her soul. Twenty-fourth of August nineteen-sixty-one. Aziz and I keep no secrets from each other.'

Not necessarily true, given that you don't know where he is, thought Jensen. While Amira went to get the phone, she pulled her own out of her bag and checked the message she had heard buzzing earlier.

It was Gustav, sure enough.

Body of headless man found in harbour.
Margrethe wants the story pronto.

27

5

Henrik and David Goldschmidt had exhausted their small talk about the heatwave and climate change, the number one topic of conversation in Copenhagen lately, aside from the ineptitude of the government, which was a constant. David and his husband had recently become vegan and joined Extinction Rebellion, and Henrik had used every means of ribbing the pathologist about his wokeness that he could think of.

'It's good to see you back to your normal unreconstructed self,' David had said, laughing and placing an arm around Henrik's shoulder.

Am I, back to normal, really? Henrik had thought.

Suited and booted, the two of them were now approaching the stainless-steel table where a pale-green sheet covered lumpy human remains. Henrik was grateful for the cold air in the basement, and for the fact that David couldn't see the involuntary grimace of disgust that he was making behind his mask.

'I don't need to tell you that we're dealing with an extraordinarily large individual, even allowing for the bloating that has occurred in the water,' said David.

'Meaning?'

'Meaning this one would have stood over two metres tall and weighing in at around 120 kilos,' said David. 'You ready?'

Henrik blinked in reply, unable to bring himself to say yes or even nod. When was anyone ever ready for being confronted with the putrefied, headless corpse of a fellow man?

Gently, all the while keeping his eyes on Henrik, David peeled back the sheet, exposing a heap of dark flesh. Henrik stood up a little straighter. It wasn't as bad as he had feared. The corpse had been robbed of its humanity along with its head and fingers.

There was a ragged gash the length of the torso, stretching from the hip to the shoulder, across the sewn-up chest. David saw Henrik looking at it. 'Sustained after death,' he said. 'Probably damaged by something in the harbour.'

'Tattoos?' asked Henrik. He couldn't see any, but the discoloured skin made it hard to tell.

'None,' said David. 'Which is unusual these days.'

'Cause of death?'

'Impossible to say without a complete body. No injury to the torso or limbs aside from the gash.'

'Shot in the head probably,' said Henrik.

David ignored him, never wanting to be drawn into speculation. 'Of course, we have to wait for the samples to be analysed, so I can't say much else. Though there is this.' He pointed to the man's wrists. 'Do you see these lines? Cable ties I reckon.'

Henrik nodded. Rope was fiddly and purchasing

29

handcuffs left a trail, whereas cable ties could be picked up for next to nothing from any DIY store. Even the police used them. 'How were the fingers removed?' he said.

'An axe. Same with the head. Quite cleanly. And posthumously.'

'A professional job, in other words,' said Henrik.

'I couldn't say,' said David. 'But I *can* tell you the body has been in the water for a week or so.'

'Can you be more precise?'

'You know I can't,' said David, his eyes above the mask smiling.

'So, we know nothing about the man aside from the fact that he wasn't shot or stabbed below his head.'

'Light-skinned. Black body hair. Somewhere between 30 and 40 years of age,' said David.

'Doesn't help much.' Henrik sighed. 'Anything noticeable about his clothing?'

'Levi's jeans, T-shirt, black leather jacket, Nike trainers,' said David.

Labels you could buy anywhere in the world. Henrik already knew there had been nothing in the victim's pockets to indicate his identity. 'Excellent,' he said, groaning inwardly at the thought of the case back in January when they had spent more than two weeks trying to identify a stab victim who had turned out to be a Romanian.

'What's on your mind?' said David.

The question hung for a while in the air between them. Henrik knew that the pathologist wasn't just asking about the case. He had never talked to David about his troubles with his wife and Jensen, but the man had a knack of sensing when Henrik was preoccupied by something personal. He decided not to rise to the bait. 'I'm thinking that this is something gang-related,' he said. 'Warring factions. Once we begin unpicking this crime, there will be more nastiness, mark my words.'

He had nothing to base it on, but the sad remains of the man lying on the table gave him a bad vibe. Copenhagen was at peak summer, at first glance transformed into a Mediterranean-style paradise, but as Henrik and his colleagues knew only too well, heatwaves brought spikes in violence. The high temperatures sent people crazy, evil was released all over the city, and now it had been manifested in this luckless corpse recovered from the harbour.

What would be next?

David's findings had confirmed Henrik's own sense that the murder had organised crime written all over it. Despite his foreboding, he felt his mood lift fleetingly. At least now he had an excuse to talk to one of three women in his life who had distanced themselves from him lately. And in contrast to Jensen and his wife, Lisbeth Quist might even be pleased to see him.

6

Thursday 09:30

'Shush,' shouted Margrethe, dumping her laptop and stack of newspapers on *Dagbladet*'s elliptical white boardroom table. The faces turning towards her were fewer in number and somewhat younger overall than yesterday when she had announced the latest round of redundancies, but the daily routine was reassuringly the same as always.

For decade after decade, all *Dagbladet* stories had officially begun and ended at the editorial meeting, and Jensen was glad that Margrethe had no intention of changing this fact. Nor would there be any messing with the newspaper's provocative political stance; Margrethe had made this abundantly clear to the Swedish venture capitalists. For all her bravado, however, Jensen couldn't help noticing how drained Margrethe looked. Her thick glasses were opaque with greasy finger marks, her features taut and grim. The negotiations with the Swedes must have taken it out of her, along with the accusations by several press commentators that she had sold out. Few had chosen to look at it from the alternative perspective: had it not been for Margrethe and her fighting spirit, *Dagbladet* would have shut its doors years ago.

Margrethe knew better than anyone that the battle was existential: no money, no newspaper, no validated purveyor of truth and scrutiny of the establishment. They would all regret it when *Dagbladet* was gone.

Yasmine, Margrethe's personal assistant, caught Jensen looking and shrugged briefly as if to say, 'What do you want me to do?'

Yasmine did her best to make sure that her boss was fed, watered and rested, but persuading Margrethe to prioritise her health above reporting on the news was a futile task.

'No one knows what Yasmine does,' Jensen had once heard someone say. She suspected that was because Yasmine did *everything*. Jasmine was Margrethe's gatekeeper, conscience, eyes and ears and social apologiser. Nothing happened at *Dagbladet* without Yasmine knowing about it.

In the early days, Jensen had wondered what was in it for the young woman who could have been a high-flying lawyer, but now she recognised that she and Yasmine shared a genuine affection for their boss and her giant brain.

As Margrethe began to run through the day's stories, Jensen felt Gustav growing restless on the seat next to her. She had just told him about Aziz's disappearance. He had instantly decided that the headless corpse found in the harbour was that of the Syrian and wouldn't be persuaded otherwise. Jensen knew he was impatient for the editorial meeting to end, so he could resume his plea. 'It's got to be him, Jensen. You must phone the police.'

'No, not the police, I promised Esben.'

'Call Henrik then. Jensen, you *know* who this is.'

Could it be Aziz? It was a possibility, but she didn't believe it.

Not really.

Didn't want to believe it.

Oh God.

Amira would have seen the news reports and be starting to wonder herself.

'Earth to Jensen,' said Margrethe, snapping her fingers. '*Hallo*.'

Jensen looked up to find everyone staring at her. 'Sorry, what?'

'I *said*, decent eyewitness accounts from the recovery of the body in the harbour yesterday.'

'Thank you,' said Jensen.

She stopped herself from adding that it was all Gustav's work. It wasn't just Frank Buhl who had moaned about the newspaper being written by unpaid teenagers. The staff representative from the Danish Union of Journalists had recently lodged a formal complaint. Margrethe had cut the issue dead by claiming adamantly that Gustav was merely shadowing Jensen to while away the summer months before going back to high school in August, something Margrethe still thought was actually going to happen.

Jensen had her doubts.

In the absence of any information beyond the fact that the body was missing its head, which had swept across Twitter in minutes, Gustav had acted quickly to interview a string of bystanders about what they had seen and how they felt about the macabre find. Nothing but feelings and guesswork, coming from people with no expertise or knowledge of the case whatsoever. Like wheel spin in the sand, but in the twenty-four-hour news cycle, every little piece of content counted.

'So now what?' Margrethe said.

'The police still aren't talking,' said Jensen.

'But we think—' Gustav began, stopping abruptly when she kicked his shin under the table.

'What Gustav is trying to say is that we tracked down the boat owner who found the body. He has promised *Dagbladet* an exclusive. We're seeing him later.'

'Good,' said Margrethe. 'Get him to take you out on the water. Show you how it happened. Film it.'

It was just more filler while they waited for some real news. Jensen knew there was no way around it; she had to call Henrik about Aziz. If for no other reason than to rule out the possibility that she couldn't bear thinking about.

She had looked briefly through Aziz's phone without finding anything suspicious. He seemed as square as they came: photos of the family, text exchanges with friends and messages from Esben, including a couple sent last Monday when he had waited in vain for Aziz to collect him from the airport. There were plenty of emails, but they were mostly official or spam. Nothing threatening that Jensen could see.

Perhaps Gustav would have more luck. She sensed him in the corner of her vision, scrolling through Aziz's WhatsApp messages under the boardroom table.

As the editorial meeting drifted on to other matters, Jensen looked outside the window at the hot sky above the city and felt something coming.

Something bad.

7

Thursday 09:57

The air conditioning in the office had broken down, leaving the incident room roasting and stinking of sweat and frustration after a long night, during which the team of investigators had got precisely nowhere.

'What's the point of having air conditioning if it doesn't bloody work when it's hot?' said Henrik, marching over to the windows.

'None of them open,' said Mark.

'Why the hell not?'

'Interferes with the air conditioning, apparently,' said Mark, prompting laughter from a couple of the detectives.

Henrik found it difficult to see the funny side. 'What a dump,' he said.

'At least the holidays start soon,' said Mark, ever the one to spot the silver lining. 'Should be glorious by the coast if the weather holds.'

'It won't,' said Henrik. 'Mark my words, the minute you set off for that summer cottage of yours the heavens will open. Hello to three weeks of playing Monopoly in the rain.'

'I like Monopoly,' said Mark. 'In any case, that's not something you need to worry about in Italy, is it?'

'No,' said Henrik miserably.

The weather in the Italian coastal resort to which he and his wife had travelled every summer since their first child was born was unfailingly hot and sunny with the odd brief storm to clear the air. It was everything else about the holiday that filled Henrik with angst. He hated flying, a fact he would have ample time to regret, and his wife to moan about, on the long drive down through Germany and across the Alps. And then there was the swimming pool full of screaming kids. The constant bickering and pizza dinners for five that you had to re-mortgage your house for. No sex, as everyone would be in a family room.

Not that he and his wife were finding it hard to keep their hands off each other these days.

Henrik would happily swap this scenario for a rainy holiday in their log cabin in the north of Zealand.

Watching football and drinking beer.

By himself.

'Been through missing persons yet?' asked Henrik.

'Yes. It helps that our victim was so tall. I quickly narrowed it down to two people.'

'And?'

'One is a blond nineteen-year-old, the other a white-haired seventy-four-year-old.'

'So?'

'Neither of them fit the profile as we're looking for a man between thirty and forty with black hair. Also, both are skinny.'

'Right. And you couldn't just have said that from the start?'

'What?'

'Just . . . forget it.'

Mark looked perplexed. 'Shall I check Europol then?' he said after a moment's pause.

'Once we have DNA,' said Henrik.

'So, what are we going to do now?'

'We're going to speak to Lisbeth. Ask her to meet us in the canteen.'

Mark hesitated. 'She's not going to change her mind about the transfer, you know. Don't you think—'

Henrik closed his eyes. 'Just. Get. Lisbeth.'

When Mark had left, he stood for a long while and looked out of the window. The new case was inconvenient, to put it mildly. He was already dealing with several tedious cases going nowhere, not to mention the mile-long paper trail from the harrowing Ordrup murder case where the prosecution was preparing for court. On the other hand, it meant he now had an excuse not to go to Italy.

His phone rang.

Jensen.

She came up on his phone as 'Garage', the word least likely to arouse his wife's suspicion, should Jensen happen to call at an inopportune time. It was a precaution he had made after his latest marital crisis. Wholly unnecessarily, as it turned out, for Jensen hadn't contacted him once.

Until now.

He felt the old familiar tug of warmth in his belly as he answered. 'Jensen. To what do I owe the pleasure?'

'Not what you think,' she said.

'And tell me, what is that?'

'I'm not calling for a cosy chat.'

38

'I'm sad to hear it,' said Henrik, and he was.

He knew it was absurd. He was the one who had called their relationship a non-starter. He had treated Jensen appallingly for years, this woman whom he loved like no other, and now he was flirting with her. It was unfair.

Wrong.

Exciting.

'The body in the harbour,' said Jensen, sending his mood back down into the basement.

'Jensen, how many times must I say it? I can't discuss my cases with you.'

'Hasn't stopped you before. Anyway, I'm not after information. More the other way around.'

She sounded hesitant. Not like her. What was this about?

'It's just that . . . Gustav persuaded me to call you. I don't think for a minute, but probably best to make sure.'

'About what?'

'Do you remember Aziz, the big guy who sometimes drove me around back in January during the Magstræde case?'

Henrik did, his mind reproducing a night-time image of a bearded giant, standing like a sentry by his black car as Henrik and Jensen talked in the alley next to the police building. He remembered that he had felt jealous. 'I knew it. There is something going on between the two of you, isn't there?' he said.

'What? No.'

'Ah yes, I forgot, you already have a boyfriend. How is Kristoffer Bro these days?'

Jensen paused for a second. 'How do you know about him?'

'I saw you.'

'Have you been following me?'

39

'No,' he lied. 'I was just passing the two of you in the street. You know how small Copenhagen is. Anyway, what is it about Aziz?'

'He's missing,' Jensen said, sounding hacked off.

'Oh.'

'Yes. And now you've recovered this body from the harbour, and I thought ... No, I'm sure it's not him. I can't see why it would be.'

Well, the size of the corpse would be a pretty good reason for suspecting, thought Henrik, though this wasn't yet public knowledge. If it had been, Jensen would not have managed to talk herself out of her worst fears so easily.

'How long has Aziz been gone for?'

'Ten days.'

Fits, thought Henrik. If the corpse really was the Syrian Arnold Schwarzenegger, they'd be a lot closer to wrapping up the case. He checked himself, keeping his tone even, knowing that Jensen would take such news badly.

'We'll need DNA. A comb, a toothbrush, that sort of thing.'

'I would have to ask his wife.'

'DNA will take time of course. Would be faster if she were able to identify him from the remains. Some distinguishing feature only she knows. Tell you what, send me the address and I'll go see her myself this afternoon.'

'No, not on your own. I'm coming with you. And you have to pretend to be my friend.'

But I am your friend, Henrik thought.

'If Amira gets even the slightest whiff of you being there in any kind of official capacity, she'll clam up. Also ...'

'What?'

'She'll have seen the news coverage from the harbour by now. She must be anxious it's him, so go easy on her.'

'You think I can't be sensitive to people's feelings, is that it?'

'I know you can't,' said Jensen. 'I'll be waiting outside *Dagbladet* at four p.m. Pick me up and we'll go and see her together.'

Henrik smiled to himself despite Jensen's dig. Now the day really *was* looking up.

8

'I wasn't going to give any interviews, though plenty of journalists have asked,' said the pensioner, whose name was Jørgen. He held out his hand to help Jensen on board his motorboat, a tricky operation involving a climb down a slippery ladder that clung to the side of the canal, followed by a leap of faith onto the gently swaying stern.

Jensen sat down, heart thumping. A tiny brown dog wriggled round her feet before finding its place next to Jørgen at the tiller.

Gustav jumped in last, with all the elegance of a baby elephant, sending the boat into a dangerous wobble that only Jensen seemed to notice. 'We're very grateful that you changed your mind,' she said, clinging onto the railing. Even short boat trips had been known to make her seasick and she wasn't exactly looking forward to their outing on the water.

Jørgen laughed. 'Your young apprentice here is very persuasive. I gather the two of you are quite the pair to help Copenhagen police with their cases.'

'Solve them more like,' said Gustav, eliciting another laugh from Jørgen.

'Gustav is being immodest,' said Jensen.

'Anyway, if I was going to do it for anybody, it was always going to be *Dagbladet*. It's the only newspaper I read. Please tell that editor of yours to save the printed edition for us oldies. I read that your new owners are thinking of going online only. Can't Margrethe Skov put a stop to that nonsense?'

No, thought Jensen, *not even the mighty Margrethe Skov can hold back the waves*. She decided not to shatter Jørgen's illusions. 'It's just a rumour,' she said, smiling. 'But even if it were true, we'd still be *Dagbladet*, only we'd stop felling so many trees,' she lied. The paper would still be *Dagbladet* by name, perhaps, but in all other ways it was changing dramatically, and replacing newsprint with ones and zeros was only the half of it.

'Tell us about yesterday morning. What happened?' she said as Jørgen untied the boat from its mooring and began easing it down the canal.

The water was dark green and slick, reflecting the boats, the tall townhouses and the pale blue sky, like the picture on a tin of Danish butter cookies. Jensen caught a smell of diesel from the chugging engine.

'Well, I got into my boat and set off, just like this,' Jørgen said, keeping his eye on the route ahead. 'Only, it was at dawn, so a lot quieter than now. It's been so hot these past few weeks that the only place to get some relief is out on the water, so I thought I'd head out a bit further than I normally do.'

'And this is the exact route you took?' said Jensen, gesturing to Gustav to begin filming on his phone as she chatted to the skipper.

Jørgen nodded. 'I'm not supposed to, really. There's a one-way system, but with a small boat like mine I can go against traffic.'

People were watching them idly from the cobbled quay, seated on benches in the shade of trees, nursing cans of beer, walking past with prams. Jensen tried to enjoy the temporary respite from the overheated newspaper building but the circumstances made it difficult. Henrik hadn't exactly disabused her of the notion that the body in the harbour could be Aziz. What if it really was?

Jørgen pulled over to allow a wide, flat harbour-tour boat to pass. What would the tourists staring at them be making of their strange little trio? A grandad with two grandchildren? A man with his daughter and grandson? Jensen was old enough to be Gustav's mother. Just.

The dog began to bark at something on the quay. Jørgen made no move to stop it. 'What is it, Max?' he said. 'Is there a cat?'

Jensen had liked Jørgen instantly, and not just because he had brought a thermos of coffee and offered her and Gustav a cup when they had first arrived. As she had drunk hers, trying not to frown at the bitter taste, Jensen had thought of Liron, the Israeli with his minuscule coffee van. It had been a while since she had seen him parked in his usual spot in Sankt Peders Stræde.

As they emerged into the inner harbour, Jørgen fell quiet for a while, navigating his boat past a couple of bigger vessels.

'I discovered the body on my way out,' he said. 'I'd planned to go past Trekroner, do a bit of fishing out there.'

Jensen nodded. She remembered the old island fort from a school trip an eternity ago. The Danes had placed canons there during the battle of Copenhagen to defend the city against the British fleet.

Not that it had done much good.

'Let me just turn her around,' said Jørgen, manoeuvring his boat with practised calm. 'Here,' he said, pulling up to a wooden post at the corner of a large area marked with a string of orange buoys. There was a yellow notice on the post saying: 'Military zone, keep out'.

Jørgen saw Jensen looking and pointed to a series of low buildings with red roofs at the edge of the water, a deep, dark blue sparkling with sunlight. 'That's the naval base in there,' he said. 'The body was outside the zone, sort of wrapped around this post. At first, I thought it was a bag, or an old coat or some rubbish dumped in the water. He was floating face down. Well, he had no head, but you know what I mean. You couldn't make out what it was. It was just this big, bloated lump.'

'What did you do?'

'I was curious, so I went right up close to it, turned it over, and that's when I realised it was a body.'

'Missing its head.'

'And its fingers.'

'Really?' said Gustav. 'Wow.'

The police had omitted to mention the missing fingers to the press. Jensen wondered why. Did they think it was significant somehow? She knew that lunatics sometimes confessed to crimes they hadn't committed, and that withholding information helped the police sort the wheat from the chaff.

'Anything else?' she said. 'What did the man look like?'

'Huge. Absolutely enormous.'

Aziz.

Gustav looked at her meaningfully. She shook her head at him. No need to share their suspicions with Jørgen.

Jensen was beginning to feel sick and trembly, but at

least out here on the open water far from the crowds that lined the canals, she would be able to vomit discreetly over the side, without making a spectacle of herself. 'You seem very ... sanguine about the whole thing,' she said, trying to keep her voice under control. 'Still, it must have been an awful shock, coming across a mutilated body like that?'

'I'm not squeamish, if that's what you mean,' said Jørgen. 'I worked as a hospital porter when I was a student. Used to see all sorts. You, on the other hand, look like someone who'd like to return to shore as soon as possible.'

No point in arguing. On the way back to Christianshavn, Jensen and Gustav quickly established that Jørgen didn't know any more than he had already told them. He remembered only that the body had been dressed in a T-shirt and jeans. 'To be honest, I didn't pay much attention once I realised it was a corpse. I called the police, and they were here in a few minutes. I gave them my statement and was back home shortly after,' he said.

'Just one thing,' Gustav piped up when, mercifully, they were back on terra firma and watching Jørgen fasten the boat to its mooring with thick rope. 'The harbour is busy today. Is it always like that?'

'Most days,' said Jørgen. 'Why?'

'Then why didn't anyone else spot the corpse all that time? The police said he'd been in the harbour for over a week.'

'It's a good question. I've been wondering about that myself,' said Jørgen. 'Of course, in the beginning the body would've been heavy, so it would've sunk out of sight. Only gradually as it bloated, it would have risen to the surface. There is also the possibility that others *did* see it, but assumed it was just some rubbish floating in the water. I'm retired. I have all the time in the world to investigate things that catch my eye.'

'Thank you, Jørgen,' Jensen said, shaking his hand. 'That was really helpful.'

'Did it give you any ideas?' he said.

No.

None whatsoever.

Except for unwanted ones about the body being Aziz.

'It's him, isn't it?' said Gustav as they walked away. His voice was agitated. 'It's got to be.'

Jensen said nothing, shuddering despite the heat.

A moment later Gustav got busy looking through the clips from the boat with the enviably short attention span of a teenager. 'I got it all,' he said. 'Margrethe is going to love this.'

9

Thursday 15:13

Perhaps it was Henrik's imagination, but Lisbeth seemed taller and broader somehow when she met him and Mark in the canteen at their usual table near the TV. Her white shirt showed off her suntan and short blonde hair. She looked pleased to see them.

'This is nice, isn't it?' said Mark, rubbing his hands together, before disappearing to get their coffees.

Henrik knew Mark had volunteered to get the drinks in the hope that any awkward tension might be gone by the time he returned, but to Henrik's relief, there was none. He was genuinely happy to see Lisbeth, and if Lisbeth had been annoyed that he had tried to talk her out of her career move, there was no signs of that now. It felt just like the old days, the dream team back together.

If only.

'So is organised crime all it's cracked up to be?' he said.

'There's a lot to learn,' said Lisbeth.

'Never ends,' said Henrik. 'How are you getting on with Biggie?'

Birgitte 'Biggie' Søndermark was Lisbeth's new boss. She had started on the force around the same time as Henrik and he reckoned she and Lisbeth, both straight-talking doers, would be getting on.

'Biggie's great. No issues there.'

'You mean there *are* issues?'

Lisbeth squirmed on her plastic chair but seemed to make up her mind not to elaborate. 'It's all just new stuff to get used to. I promise you I'm enjoying it. And then there's this,' she said, holding up her left hand and smiling broadly.

Henrik realised that he hadn't seen her smile like that in a long time. Smile full stop. Perhaps the job move was a good thing for her after all. 'What?' he said, pretending he hadn't noticed the silver band with a red stone on her ring finger.

'I'm engaged.'

'To Josefine? The hot doctor?'

Lisbeth nodded.

'Nice work, Quist. Congratulations.'

'With what?' said Mark, who had returned with three mugs on a tray.

'Lisbeth is getting married,' said Henrik.

'August and you're both invited,' said Lisbeth, beaming.

Henrik cut short Mark's effusive congratulations with feigned ill temper. 'Enough, enough, for Christ's sake.'

He turned to Lisbeth, his face serious. 'We need your help.'

'Oh?' Henrik saw that she was disappointed that he hadn't just wanted to check how she was getting on. She quickly composed herself, but her smile had gone.

'It's the headless body in the harbour,' said Henrik.

'And fingerless,' said Mark.

'Yes, and that. Doesn't match anyone reported missing, so potentially a foreigner. And the way the head and hands were separated from the body suggests it was a professional job.'

'What are you saying?'

'A liquidation, gang-related.'

Lisbeth nodded. 'We're interested in taking a look at it, that's for sure.'

'But it doesn't set any particular bells ringing?'

'To be honest, there's bells aplenty ringing the whole time in organised crime, but it doesn't fit immediately into any investigation that I'm aware of.'

Henrik nodded. It would have been too easy, he knew that.

'You've contacted Europol?' said Lisbeth.

'Not a lot to go on without a face. We're waiting for the DNA.'

'No identifying marks on the body? Scars? Tattoos?'

'Nope.'

Lisbeth sat for a while sipping her coffee in silence. 'This might be nothing, but you always said when something unexplained happened that we should look for other unexplained events occurring at the same time and try to find a link.'

Henrik was perversely pleased that she remembered, feeling his hopes rising again. 'Yes?'

'Well, there was that burning car last week, out at Refshaleøen, near where the harbour buses are moored. Was it Tuesday or Wednesday? Reported in the middle of the night by a private security patrol.'

'Loads of cars have been set on fire in the past year across the city,' said Mark, glancing nervously at Henrik.

'Yes, but this one went up in flames round about the time

that the remains of your victim must have been thrown into the harbour,' Lisbeth countered. 'Don't you at least think you ought to have a look?'

Mark glanced again at Henrik who nodded. 'We should check it out,' he said. His appointment with Jensen was less than an hour away. He had been good to his word and not told anyone about Aziz. Not that he had been tempted to do so. Present company excepted, there weren't many people on the force he truly trusted. More was the pity that Lisbeth had decided to move on. The three of them had always been a great team, arguing like fiends in private, while closing ranks on the outside world.

Walk on by. Nothing to see here.

Until Lisbeth had broken the circle by allowing herself to be lured into her new job by that bastard Jens Wiese.

'Arrange it for tomorrow,' he said, pushing himself up from the table by his knuckles. 'I'm busy this afternoon.'

10

Henrik listened to the soft-spoken Syrian woman opposite him by the dining table in the Nørrebro flat and sensed her immense pain along with his own powerlessness. He knew there was a good chance that the headless corpse David Goldschmidt had respectfully opened, probed and sewn back together was that of her husband Aziz.

How often had he sat like this, with a relative, knowing that the worst thing imaginable had already happened, and that his investigation, for all the importance of justice, would never undo it?

The afternoon hadn't panned out as he had hoped. His heart had sunk when he had pulled up outside *Dagbladet* to find the lanky figure of Gustav standing by the kerb alongside Jensen. This had robbed him of the opportunity to talk to her about Kristoffer Bro as they had driven to Nørrebro with Gustav strapped into the back, like some grotesque parody of a nuclear family.

'Do you think it's Aziz?' Gustav had wanted to know.

'Do I think what is Aziz?' said Henrik, being deliberately obtuse.

Jensen was looking out of the window as if she would rather be anywhere else. She was wearing a sleeveless black dress. He wanted to put his hand on her thigh, pull up the silky material and touch her tanned skin.

'The body in the harbour?'

Probably, yes.

'I don't know.'

'Jørgen said it was a very large man.'

'Jørgen?'

'Guy who found the body. We spoke to him. He took us out and showed us where he found it. He also told us the body's fingers had been cut off. You forgot to mention that in your statement to the press.'

'Didn't forget. Decided not to.'

'Why? You said—'

'For God's sake, Gustav, will you give it a rest?' Jensen had shouted, turning abruptly from the window. To Henrik's astonishment, her face had been wet with tears.

Now, he and Jensen were sitting at the dining table with Amira. After shooting them a long look of protest at being denied the excitement of the interview, Gustav had at long last taken the two Almasi boys into their bedroom to play with Lego. A restless toddler, a little girl not yet talking, remained on her mother's lap, pulling at her white headscarf.

At first, Amira had been reluctant to talk. Jensen had presented Henrik as a friend with contacts in the police, which wasn't technically a lie. Amira had remained sceptical until Jensen had told her how Henrik had once saved her from being stabbed to death. 'I trust him with my life,' she had said, and Henrik had felt a warm sensation spread across his body.

Amira fixed her gaze on him. 'I saw they pulled a body from the harbour. Is it . . .' she got no further but closed her eyes as the tears began to roll down her cheeks. She wiped them away impatiently. 'I want to know. I *have* to know if it's Aziz,' she said.

Amira was obviously the sort of person who would baulk at anything less than straight talk. He took a deep breath. 'There is a possibility that it is your husband,' he said, ignoring Jensen's angry stare. 'The body has been in the water for about the same length of time as he has been missing, but the only way we will know for certain is by doing a DNA test.'

Amira nodded and rose abruptly, putting her daughter on her hip. She left the room and returned with a toothbrush.

'Amira is studying to become a nurse,' Jensen said, by way of explanation, as Henrik put the toothbrush in an evidence bag.

'Thank you,' he said. 'And I need to ask, does Aziz have any identifying marks on his body? Like a scar, or a birthmark?'

'Yes,' she said, pointing to her left cheek. 'He has a small birthmark, here, like a teardrop.'

Henrik nodded gently. Jensen looked at Amira. Her voice was surprisingly soft when she started speaking. 'Amira, the only thing is . . .'

'No head,' said Amira. 'They said that on the news, too. How silly of me. In that case, I'm not sure.'

'OK,' said Henrik. They sat in silence for a bit. The little girl leaned into her mother's chest, sucking her thumb.

'Can I see him?' said Amira, suddenly, loudly, breaking the stillness. The toddler began to cry. 'I'll know if it's him.'

'Amira, are you sure you—' Jensen began.

'Please,' said Amira, over the rising wail of her child. She kept her eyes on Henrik. It was as if speaking the thought out loud had made her braver and more determined. 'I have seen a dead body before. You will not believe what I have witnessed.'

She got up again. 'Now, where is my phone? I'll get my neighbour to look after the kids. We'll go now, yes?'

Henrik had caught David Goldschmidt just as he was about to leave the Forensic Institute for the evening and asked him to organise an identification on the quiet. Jensen had sent Gustav back to the newspaper, on Henrik's insistence, but Amira had taken the boy's space on the back seat, and Henrik had quietly rued the fact that, for the second time in a day, he was prevented from having a frank conversation with Jensen about her choice of boyfriend.

As the four of them headed down the corridor to the post-mortem room, led by David Goldschmidt, Henrik noticed how Amira clung to Jensen's hand.

'We will make it as quick and painless for you as we possibly can,' David said, half-turning, his eyes full of sympathy.

'Don't worry about me,' said Amira. 'I trained as a nurse in a military hospital. It's just ... I never expected to have to do something like this.'

'No one does,' said David.

By the stainless-steel table, after swallowing several times, Amira nodded at David to indicate that she was ready. David had left a sheet over the gaping wound at the neck, and another over the legs and began by exposing the torso only.

Amira's hands flew up to her mouth as she looked. She began to sob uncontrollably, but when Jensen put her arm around her, she lifted her face, and Henrik saw the relief in it. 'It's not him. It's not Aziz,' she cried.

'Are you sure?' Henrik frowned.

What were the chances?

'Yes,' she said. 'Aziz is not hairy like that, and he has moles all over his body, just like me. Look,' She pulled up her sleeve to show them.

Then she composed herself and, before David could react, she had replaced the sheet neatly over the torso and nodded her thanks at him. 'Whoever this poor man is, he's definitely not my husband. And now I would like to go home to my children.'

11

Henrik was quiet for a while after they had dropped Amira off at the flat in Nørrebro. Jensen had accepted his offer of driving her back to *Dagbladet* so she could fetch her bicycle.

Amira's elation had quickly been replaced with renewed worry. The fact that it had not been her husband lying on the stainless-steel table did not mean that he was OK.

Far from it. The visit to the Forensic Institute had raised the spectre of Aziz's death and the multiple varieties of harm that he might have come to.

Jensen guessed Henrik would still be testing the DNA on Aziz's toothbrush and wondered whether it was doubt about Amira's testimony that was making him pensive.

'For what it's worth, I believe her one hundred percent,' she said.

'I do too,' he replied, surprising her. 'She's unlikely to be mistaken about something like that.'

'So what's on your mind?'

'You mean aside from the fact that I have a body whose

57

identity someone has gone to great lengths to conceal, and no bloody clue who it is?'

'There's no need for that tone. I'm relieved it's not Aziz. That's good news in my book and it ought to be in yours.'

'Sure, rather some poor bugger no one knows.'

Jensen ignored the provocation. 'What do you think has happened to Aziz?'

'How should I know?' Henrik said. 'He's a grown man. Strong. Fit. He'll turn up some time, I expect. Most people do.'

'So you'll do nothing to help?'

'Not as long as his wife won't report him missing, no. Or at least not at this stage.'

'For God's sake. She's scared, can't you see that? Of course she's worried about her husband, of course she wants him to be found.'

It was Henrik's turn to ignore *her*.

She sighed and looked out of the window as they crossed the lakes ringed by pretty, period apartment blocks and majestic trees. Not far from the Almasis', but a million miles out of their price range. The paths were heaving with people out for an evening walk, much like Copenhageners a century ago, only staring at their phones rather than eyeing up each other.

'What is it?' she said, without looking at him. 'Something's on your mind. I can tell.'

'Your new boyfriend,' he said.

'I knew it,' she cried. 'Aziz is missing, you've a headless corpse to deal with, and you're worried about who I'm seeing? You've no right—'

'I need to talk to you about him.'

She felt her face grow hot. 'No, Henrik, this isn't fair. For once, in all the time I've known you, I have a chance of building a relationship with someone else, someone I really like. You didn't want me, but you don't want anyone else to have me either, is that it?'

'No, it's not like that,' he said. 'Kristoffer Bro is not who he says he is.'

I don't want to hear it, she thought. *Whatever it is.* 'Do you know what? Stop the car, I'll walk back.'

'Don't be stupid, Jensen.'

'No, Henrik. I'm not going to sit here and listen to your crap. Let me out.' She began to pull at the door, ignoring his loud pleading.

They stopped at a red light. She undid her seat belt, unlocked the door and was about to get out when her phone rang.

Amira.

Shouting incoherently.

She felt Henrik looking at her quizzically.

'Amira, slow down, I can't hear what you're saying.'

The lights went green. Henrik stayed put, and the drivers behind him began to toot their horns. He yelled obscenities out of the window at them, but not until he plonked his blue light on the roof did the tooting stop, and they began to drive around him.

'What's happened, Amira?' said Jensen, putting the call on speaker. She gestured at Henrik to listen.

'Some people came while I was out. Men. They thought my neighbour was me. They asked where Aziz was. In English. Threatened her, hit her across the face when she couldn't answer.'

'And then?'

'They left when the children began to cry.'

'Amira,' said Henrik very slowly and deliberately. 'Does your husband owe money to anyone?'

Jensen thought of the new PlayStation and flat-screen TV in the living room. Were those things affordable on a driver's salary, with a family of five to feed? Perhaps they were gifts from Esben.

'No. Never,' said Amira. 'He wouldn't. Not without telling me.' She sounded certain to the point of being angry.

'And can you think of anyone who might want to hurt him? Someone he'd had an argument with, or a falling out?'

There was a short hesitation. Jensen suspected she was wrestling with whether she should tell Henrik about the people from Syria who might be after Aziz.

'Aziz may be a big man, and strong, but inside he is a boy,' Amira said. 'He always told me how he can't stand that other men assume he wants to fight them. And again, if there had been someone after him, he would have told me about it, you can be sure of that.'

'OK, Amira, listen to me,' said Henrik. 'We've got to get you out of that flat.'

'Why?'

'I don't think we can assume that you'll be safe, if those men were to come back.'

'I can't leave,' said Amira.

'Why not?'

'What if Aziz needs me and can't find us? Besides, the boys still have a week left of school.'

'Say they're sick,' said Henrik.

'I can stay in your flat while you're gone,' said Jensen. 'I mean, in case Aziz comes back?'

Henrik shook his head angrily at her, his mouth forming the word 'No'.

'If the men come back, I'll say I'm subletting the flat and have no idea where you are,' said Jensen. 'Go and pack your bags, Amira. We'll be there in ten minutes.'

'Unbelievable,' said Henrik, shaking his head as he turned the car around and headed back towards Nørrebro.

12

Henrik looked at the chicken pad thai that Jensen had fetched for him and found he had lost his appetite, despite her insistence that he would find none tastier in Northern Europe. On the one hand, he was delighted she would be getting away temporarily from Kristoffer Bro, on the other she was putting herself in harm's way, which meant that he wouldn't be able to rest for as long as she was staying in the Nørrebro flat. 'It's a bad neighbourhood. You won't be safe here,' he told her.

'Nonsense,' she said with her mouth full. Peanuts and sticky noodles plopped down the front of her black dress as she forked the food into her mouth. 'If it's safe for Aziz and his family, it's safe for me,' she said.

'Number one, unlike Aziz, you are not built like Rambo, and number two, that's precisely the point. We're here because Aziz and his family have turned out not to be safe.'

'But that's got nothing to do with the neighbourhood,' said Jensen, frowning.

'You're sure about that?'

'Shut up and eat, Henrik.'

He reluctantly took a small bite. There was coriander on it. He didn't like coriander, it tasted like soap. He picked at something that looked like a chunk of bread soaked in oil.

'That's tofu,' said Jensen, shaking her head at him. 'Jesus, I forgot how fussy you are. I should have bought you a burger.'

Their mutual efforts to get Amira and her family to safety seemed to have erased their clash over Kristoffer Bro from her mind. Henrik had overheard her as she walked out into the hall to leave a voicemail for him, telling him that she was working on a story and would be out for the night. She hadn't said where she was staying.

Good.

It wouldn't do the arsehole any harm to spend a few nights wondering what she was up to.

Lisbeth had been understanding and thankfully refrained from asking questions when she had arrived to take Amira to a safe house. As she led the family out of the flat, carrying their bags, she mimed for Henrik to call her. He would have a job persuading her to keep the incident under wraps. Lisbeth belonged to a new generation of cops who wanted to do everything by the book. Noble but impractical.

In the real world.

Amira had cried and made Jensen promise to contact her the minute she got any information on Aziz, no matter how small. She had also insisted on making up Jensen's bed on the sofa before leaving.

'Do you think the fact that bad people are out there looking for Aziz means that he's alive?' Jensen said to him now.

He set down his bowl and wiped his mouth on a napkin. 'Might just as well mean that he's dead.'

The fact that the Syrian had disappeared at around the same time as the headless body of another giant had been dumped in the harbour was a curious coincidence. He recalled what Lisbeth had said about looking for connections between unexplained events. The thought had crossed his mind that Aziz had something to do with the murder case, and this was why he had chosen to make himself scarce. His wife had spoken as if he wouldn't hurt a fly, but if he were provoked it might be another matter.

Henrik had feigned disinterest in Aziz up until now, but it would be helpful to know what the man had been up to. 'You need to establish his last known movements,' he said. 'Who saw him? What was he doing?'

'We have his phone,' said Jensen.

'Well, take a good look through it. Find his friends. Speak to them and ask what was on his mind. Was he struggling with something? Did he do or say things that were out of character?'

'Gustav and I are on it,' Jensen said.

Henrik got up, fished his car keys out of the pocket of his black jeans and looked straight at her. 'I know what you're going to say, but the second anything scary happens, I want you to call me. No matter what time it is.'

She nodded, surprisingly without protesting that she could look after herself. They both knew she was humouring him. 'Thank you, Henrik, for today. I appreciate it.'

He headed for the hall, tiptoeing in between Lego, a discarded princess costume and an assortment of colouring pens. The whole thing was wrong. He should be staying, to make sure she was OK.

'Wait,' Jensen said, stopping him in his tracks.

'Yes?' His voice betrayed the hope he felt that she would ask him not to go.

'What was it you wanted to tell me about Kristoffer?'

'It can wait,' he said.

'No, I want to know.'

He searched her face to check that she really meant it. She did. 'Ever heard him talk about his past?'

She narrowed her eyes, instantly on guard. 'Why are you asking that?'

'Have you?'

'No, but I know that his parents are dead. It might just be too painful to talk about.'

'I bet it is,' said Henrik, unable to keep the sarcasm out of his voice.

He sensed that Jensen was getting annoyed again. He wouldn't be able to retain her attention for much longer. 'Never mentioned his childhood, the school he went to, where he grew up?'

'Look, Henrik,' said Jensen. 'I like Kristoffer. A lot. If you have something to say, spit it out. I don't have time for guessing.'

She looked at the remains of her pad thai and began to pick at it with a fork but changed her mind and dropped the container on the coffee table.

'Just ask him. That's all,' said Henrik and headed for the front door.

He knew she was cross with him, but if there was one thing Jensen had never been able to do, it was to control her curiosity.

13

'How long did you say it's been here?' said Henrik, gesturing at the burned-out wreck.

The car had been reduced to a whitish grey hull. The windows had gone as had the number plates, along with anything else capable of melting. Only the chassis remained, sunken on its stumps.

'The fire was reported by a security guard the night between Tuesday and Wednesday last week,' said Mark, consulting his notebook. 'Not much car left by the time the fire service arrived.'

'So it's been ten days and it still hasn't been towed away?'

Mark shrugged. 'There's a backlog, apparently. They say the heatwave—'

'Heatwave, my arse. Fucking typical excuses.'

'I guess it wasn't considered urgent,' said Mark. 'I mean, it's not as if it's in the way or anything.'

That much was true. The car could hardly be said to lower the tone of the neighbourhood, a mixture of run-down industrial buildings and rusty old containers on broken tarmac and dry grass.

Only a hop, skip and jump away there was a street-food market where trendy Copenhageners and tourists would soon be gathering around picnic tables, quaffing craft beers and overpriced burritos, but this part of the area was ignored.

'Lucky for us that it's still here. I mean what if—'

'Yes, yes, thank you, I get it,' snapped Henrik.

He had slept badly for thinking of Jensen. Should he have kept quiet about Kristoffer Bro? Jensen wasn't stupid, and sooner or later the man was bound to reveal his true character. On the other hand, it pained Henrik to see her with someone so undeserving.

He had only given her a clue, knowing how she would react if he told her the whole story. He spat on the dusty ground and walked the short distance from the car to the edge of the harbour where he peered over the side at a couple of old-looking vessels.

'Do you think the guy could have been dumped in the water here?' said Mark.

'It's possible,' said Henrik. 'We'd have to check the currents and other conditions to see if he could have drifted as far as the opera house.'

It would have been simple enough for a couple of strong people to drag a body the short distance from the car to the water, even a heavy one. Any blood soaked into the upholstery would have burned off in the fire.

'They didn't exactly go out of their way to conceal their crime,' said Mark.

'They cut off the head and hands. I'd say that's going some way.'

'But why throw the body in the harbour in the middle of

the city, why not hide it somewhere, bury it in the woods, that sort of thing?'

'A man that size? You'd be surprised how hard it is to move a body more than a few metres by hand, even when there's more than one of you. And no matter where you hide them, bodies tend to turn up eventually,' said Henrik. 'They might have wanted the guy to be found. Just not right away, make it a bit harder for us.' *Either that,* he thought, *or the car had nothing whatsoever to do with the headless corpse and they were looking at the work of bored teenagers.* He sighed, looking around.

A tramp with a long white beard, pushing a bicycle, was busy picking beer cans out of a black bin bag some distance away. God only knew how many other people had been walking all over the area since the car was set alight. It had been over a week now. Too long for a search to yield anything useful, but they were going to have to try.

Something caught his eye in the footwell on the passenger side, a coin perhaps. He put on a glove and reached down for it, realising it was the rim of a shotgun cartridge. Had whoever killed the victim in the harbour tossed the cartridge in the car, hoping the fire would destroy it? 'Get a forensics team out here now,' he said to Mark.

'Yes boss.'

'There would have to have been more than one of them,' he said, looking around.

'Two bad guys?'

'At least. One to drive the car with the body, one in a getaway car. Two to heave the corpse over the side into the harbour, and then the pair leave together, having set the evidence on fire.'

'Or maybe they came by the same car and left on foot.'

'No,' Henrik said. 'Too risky. Wouldn't have wanted to run the risk of getting caught. Any CCTV?'

'Not right here. It's a blind spot, which is presumably why they chose it.'

'Plenty of cameras along the road leading into this area, though. Get what you can, let's try to reconstruct what happened.'

'On it,' said Mark.

Henrik wondered if Aziz would turn up on the film. He fished his phone out of his pocket to check for news from Jensen.

Radio silence.

He felt a cold spike of panic in his blood.

What if something had happened to her? What if she was lying somewhere, helpless and needing him?

Don't be so stupid. Jensen can look after herself.

If anything, she was probably sleeping, having been up all night researching Kristoffer Bro. Trouble was that the man had gone out of his way to erase his own digital footprint. Jensen would find an online record that was scrubbed to within an inch of its life. That in itself ought to worry her, if she was as good a journalist as he thought she was.

He turned back to Mark. 'Get the team to seal off the area and comb it for any evidence. Cigarette filters, chewing gum, scraps of rubbish, footprints in the dust. I want it all.'

'Consider it done,' said Mark. 'By the way, I checked out the chassis number.'

'And?'

'Black Audi Q7. Almost new. Registered as a hire car.'

'Oh yeah?' Henrik spun round to face Mark. 'Why didn't you say that before?'

'I was going to. Look here.' He held up his phone.

Henrik quickly scanned the message with the name of the rental firm and began to walk resolutely back to his car.

'Wait,' said Mark. 'Where are you off to?'

'The airport. To speak to the hire company. If this car has anything to do with our headless corpse, I reckon they can tell us who he is. You coming, or what?'

14

Friday 10:06

'I told you. We have to map Aziz's last known movements. Go back to the morning he disappeared. Speak to his daughter's nursery and his sons' school. Talk to his friends, find out who he saw, who he was with, what he did,' said Jensen into her phone.

She was in her favourite spot, on the dormer windowsill in her office under the eaves of the newspaper building, her legs folded, her head resting against the wall.

'And when you say *we*, you mean *me*,' said Gustav.

She could hear him sucking on his e-cigarette. She wondered what Amira and Aziz would make of him vaping in their home.

'I do have a job to do, Gustav. There was another stabbing last night, out at Ørestaden.'

She hadn't started the story yet, still had to go and look at the scene, speak to the family of the fifteen-year-old victim now fighting for his life in a bed at Riget, the national hospital in the centre of Copenhagen.

As soon as she had finished thinking.

The view presenting itself from her window was not of the cool, Nordic capital she knew, but some imitation southern-European city. A golden light rested over the red-tiled roofs, holding the promise of another hot day. The air smelled of dusty tarmac, rubbish and exhaust fumes. Even this early, the heat was making her sweat. It felt wrong, almost enough to make you long for the rain and the cold. Danish summers weren't meant to be this good.

The night in Amira and Aziz's flat had passed uneventfully once she had got used to the street noise. It had taken her a while to persuade Gustav to come and babysit the flat while she went to work.

'Do I have to?' he had whined.

'Yes. I promised Amira in case Aziz comes back.'

'But it's stupid,' said Gustav. 'Even she would have had to go out now and again, do the shopping, take the kids to school.'

'Just do it, Gustav. I'll figure something out. It's only for today. You can use the PlayStation.'

'I'm seventeen, Jensen, not five.'

'Anything happen so far?' she asked him now.

'Like what?'

'Seen anyone? Heard anything unusual?'

'No, it's just a dumb, empty flat.'

'Made any progress with Aziz's phone?'

'Not really. He didn't speak to that many people by the looks of things. Amira. Esben. Guy called Abdul. That's about it.'

'Abdul?' Jensen recalled seeing the name in Aziz's contacts.

'Yeah. Seems like they do weights together. Most of the messages are about meeting at the gym. Apparently,

71

they were meant to meet at one p.m. on the day Aziz disappeared.'

'He never showed?'

'Not according to the messages Abdul sent later that day. He seemed pretty pissed off.'

'I'll go chat to him.'

Her phone pinged. A message from Gustav with the address of the gym. She jumped down from the dormer sill and was scooping her bag up from the floor when she heard shuffling footsteps approaching.

'Hello Henning,' she said.

The old man grunted a reply and made a beeline for her coffee machine, a used paper cup in his hand. She recognised it as one he had scavenged from her office some weeks ago. At least the coffee was relatively fresh. She had been craving one of Liron's brews that morning, but there was still no sign of the Israeli and his van. Maybe he was on holiday. Maybe there was a new girlfriend on the scene.

'So you're the new chief crime reporter,' said Henning as he filled his cup without asking.

'It's not official yet,' said Jensen.

Henning chuckled to himself. 'Everyone knows.'

Jensen looked at the old editor, wondering whether Margrethe would be the same when her time came. Unable to stand retirement and begging to be let back into the newspaper, even if it meant taking what was literally the graveyard shift: the obituary page.

Henning's skin was parchment thin and blue-veined, his hands trembling. To most people, he was a man whose time had come and gone. Yet, his astonishing brain held more than sixty years' worth of *Dagbladet* stories. Perhaps he had come across Deep Throat, the most elusive man in Copenhagen, AKA Ernst Brøgger?

'Ever heard of a man named Ernst Brøgger?' she said.

Henning stared at the ceiling, the cogs turning in his mind. 'Solicitor. Polymath. Entrepreneur. A finger in every pie. Why do you ask?'

'I'm trying to find him.'

'That's going to be hard.'

'Why do you say that?'

Henning didn't reply but left his paper cup by the coffee machine and went back to his office. After a few minutes, he returned with a slim paper folder from his filing cabinet, dropping it on her desk.

There was one article inside, a tiny column of yellowed newsprint. It noted Ernst Brøgger's sixtieth birthday and was written by Henning himself.

'That's all there is?' she said.

'Yep. Brøgger always shunned the limelight. No one even knows where he lives.'

'Then how come *you* know him?'

'He has a reputation. Knows everyone who is everyone. A good source, back in the day.'

Still is. When he bothers to get in touch, thought Jensen.

'I need to ask him something,' she said. 'He gave me a tip-off but as soon as I got somewhere with the story, he told me to drop it, and now he refuses to answer my calls.'

'Heh, heh,' said Henning. 'Brøgger is as slippery as an eel.'

Her desk phone began to ring. She stared at it. Anyone who knew her had her mobile number and switchboard calls were usually bad news. On the other hand, what if it had something to do with Aziz?

'Jensen,' she said warily, lifting the receiver.

Henning was already walking out of her office, waving a trembling paw as goodbye.

She waved back.

'Oh, thank you for picking up,' said Markus, the receptionist whose sarcasm could always be relied upon. 'Your boyfriend's here.'

'Tell him I don't want to talk to him,' said Jensen. She wasn't ready for another of his attempts to spoil her one opportunity of building a relationship.

With someone worthy of her, for a change.

'You kept that one quiet,' said Markus.

'What do you mean?'

'You. Dating a celebrity.'

'Oh.'

Kristoffer. Not Henrik. Henrik wasn't her boyfriend. Never had been.

Nice Freudian slip, Jensen.

'Be right there,' she said.

15

Friday 10:37

'Forgive me for saying so, Jensen, but you don't seem that pleased to see me,' said Kristoffer.

They were sitting under a parasol outside a café in the King's Garden. Around them, people had sought refuge from the sun under the trees, leaving the beige, tinder-dry lawns almost empty.

Kristoffer had taken his sunglasses off and was waving them at her over his espresso and bottled water. He was wearing navy blue shorts, slip-on shoes and one of his collarless pale blue linen shirts, buttoned down with the sleeves rolled up as far as they would go. His eyes sparkled with intensity.

Handsome.

Deadly.

People were looking at them, recognising Kristoffer from the magazines. A smiling woman approached holding up her phone. 'Can we get some peace here?' Kristoffer spat at her, sending her scurrying away.

On past occasions, he had happily posed for selfies with complete strangers. It was one of the reasons why Jensen preferred hanging out in his flat, just the two of them.

What had got into him?

'I'm just surprised,' said Jensen, gulping sparkling water straight from the bottle. 'You've never turned up at the newspaper before.'

'And while we've been together you've never spent the night away from me. I wanted to check that you were OK.'

'As you can see, I'm absolutely fine.'

'You could have answered my texts.'

'I'm sorry. I've had a lot on my mind.'

'Where were you last night?' said Kristoffer.

He was smiling but seemed tense, perching uncomfortably on the tiny, green-painted folding chair, like an adult at a children's tea party. He hadn't touched his coffee.

Was he worried that she was seeing someone else? It was unlike him to be jealous. 'What's this about, Kristoffer? What do you want?'

'See what I mean?' he said as if she had proved a point for him. 'What kind of question is that? As if I must *want* something.'

'All right,' said Jensen. 'I'll tell you, if it's so important to you, but on one condition. You must promise me to keep it to yourself.'

'Have I ever betrayed your confidence?'

'No,' Jensen admitted.

Esben, Gustav, Amira, Henrik and his colleague Lisbeth all knew about Aziz by now. One more wouldn't make a difference. Besides, she was interested in what Kristoffer would make of it.

'You know Esben Nørregaard, the member of parliament?'

'Doesn't everyone?'

'He and I are friends. It's a long story, I'll tell you someday. Anyway, his driver Aziz went missing eleven days ago. He's from Syria. At first, we thought it was him the police dragged out of the harbour on Wednesday, but thankfully it wasn't.'

'So where do you think he is?' said Kristoffer.

'We don't know. He took nothing with him, not even his phone. Anyway, some people came looking for him yesterday when his wife was out and a neighbour was watching the kids. They weren't friendly, so we've moved his wife to a safe house. I'm staying in the flat in case Aziz makes contact.'

'What's your theory?'

'A few different options. Something might have spooked him to go into hiding. Apparently, he once told his wife not to worry if he ever disappeared for a bit. Or he might owe money to a loan shark.'

'All sounds plausible,' said Kristoffer.

'Or it has to do with some death threats Esben has been receiving.'

Kristoffer glanced up at her in surprise. 'I thought politicians got those all the time?'

'Yes, but the timing of the most recent ones means there could be a connection.'

'As in?'

'As in someone has harmed Aziz to get at Esben.'

Kristoffer laughed.

'What's so funny?'

'Your imagination,' said Kristoffer, knocking on her forehead. 'First someone fakes the suicide of a drunk, and now this mafia theory.'

Jensen pulled back from him, anger making her cheeks flush. 'You wanted to know what I was working on. If I'd known you'd be like this, I wouldn't have told you.'

'Sorry,' said Kristoffer. 'It was just … your face. You looked so serious.'

'OK, your turn,' she said, folding her arms across her chest.

'What do you mean?'

'Your turn to share something with me.'

Despite his questionable motives, Henrik's missives about Kristoffer's past had struck home. Aside from his rags-to-riches story, she knew very little about the man in front of her.

'Me?' said Kristoffer.

'Yes. I mean about your childhood, where you're from, your mum and dad, that sort of stuff.'

'My parents are both dead, and I was an only child. I've told you this already. Several times,' said Kristoffer.

'What was it like? Were you close? I mean, your parents can't have been that old when they passed away?'

'Leave it Jensen, for Christ's sake. It's not as if I quiz you about *your* family, is it?'

'You can if you want, but there isn't much to say. My mum lives in North Jutland. She's a painter. I don't see her very often, and I don't have any siblings.'

'See? Boring. Just like my life story. Let's not be like this, Jensen, raking over each other's past with a thousand questions. Let's be different.'

Jensen emptied her bottle of water and reached for her bag. 'I'm a journalist, Kristoffer. It's like asking me not to breathe. Speaking of which, I ought to get back to work. Thank you for …' she gestured at their drinks.

'Jensen,' Kristoffer said, slamming his hands on the table

and rattling his coffee cup. The people at the neighbouring tables stared at them. 'Do you find me attractive?'

'Yes.'

'Good company?'

'Yes, except right now.'

'Good in bed? Attentive?'

'Why are you asking me that?'

'Because I'm racking my brain here. Most of my adult life, I've been able to pick and choose when it comes to women. Beautiful women. Young. Keen. Every day I receive messages. You should see them. Or, actually no, they would make you uncomfortable. Google my name and you will see that "Kristoffer Bro wife" is the most common search term people use for me.'

'*You* obviously did,' she said.

'Women want to know if I'm married, who I'm with, if the position is free.'

Jensen felt her cheeks grow hot. 'Are you saying I ought to be more grateful that you picked me?'

'Of course not, but it seems it's not enough for you. You want more. You want to know every little thing about me.'

'You were the one who pursued me. I wasn't interested, but you insisted.'

'You're saying I forced you? Oh, I am terribly sorry.'

'That's not what I'm saying. It's just—'

'Do you know what, Jensen? I'm not sure what we're doing here any more. Maybe you shouldn't bother coming back at all, once your little nocturnal stake-out in Nørrebro is over.'

Nørrebro? Had she mentioned Nørrebro?

'Maybe I shouldn't,' Jensen shouted.

She watched him stomping away. What was happening to him? He had clammed up when she had pushed him about his past. What was it that was so bad that he would rather pick a fight than tell her about it?

It was time to talk to him. Properly.

As soon as he apologised.

16

When Jensen asked after Abdul at the gym, saying that she had to see him urgently on a personal matter, the fitness trainer at the desk pointed to the free-weights area at the back. The room smelled of rubber mats and sweat. A big TV on the wall was showing an American football match with the sound off.

She found a heavily tattooed man in his thirties reclining on a seat, lifting dumbbells with weights the size of small tyres. He was wearing combat trousers, black boots and a sleeveless top that showed off his bulging muscles. There was no one else there. The rest of the clientele had probably decided it was too hot for exercising.

'Abdul?'

'Who's asking?' he said, making no move to get up. He grunted faintly with exertion until he had completed the set.

Then he put the dumbbells on the floor, wiped his hands on a towel and looked at her for the first time. He seemed taken aback to find someone not wearing gym clothes.

'My name is Jensen. I'm a ... friend of Aziz,' she said, not wanting to scare the man by telling him that she was a journalist. 'Aziz Almasi?'

'Yeah?' Abdul narrowed his eyes at her as if he considered such a friendship highly unlikely. 'What do you want?' he said.

'Aziz has disappeared.'

Abdul said nothing, his face blank and unreadable.

'His wife gave me his phone. He left it behind. That's how I found you. See?'

She showed Abdul the screenshots of his texts to Aziz that Gustav had sent her earlier, feeling the man's resistance soften.

'Shit,' Abdul said. 'I thought ... we were supposed to train together last week, but he didn't show. To be honest, it annoyed me that he didn't even bother returning my calls,' he said, wiping his forehead on a towel.

He seemed genuinely surprised. Jensen's heart sank as she realised that he was unlikely to know anything. 'I'm looking for clues, any clues, as to where he might have got to. When did you last see him?'

'Sunday last week. I'm down here most days, Aziz almost as often. We spot for each other on the bench press. Aziz is a monster. He can do more than 200 kilos.'

'How did he seem?'

'Normal. Said he had a week off work. We arranged to meet on the Monday, but like I told you, he never showed.'

'That's it?'

'Pretty much.'

'Do you ever see him outside the gym?'

'Never. We're not friends like that. Aziz keeps himself to

himself. We just talk about our wives, our kids, sports, that sort of thing. I don't even know where he lives.'

'Did he ever mention to you that he was worried about being sent back to Syria?'

'All the time.'

'Had he received any letter, or heard anything, that made him believe there was an imminent threat of this happening?'

'No, I don't think so. It was nothing new, just something he mentioned often. He didn't say what, but I could tell there was something he was really scared of, back home.'

Jensen nodded. This chimed with Amira's story. 'Any other worries?' she said. 'Do you know if he owes money to anyone, for instance?'

'If he does, he hasn't told me.' Abdul looked at her more closely. 'What do you think has happened to him? I mean, he can definitely handle himself ... I can't imagine him lying in a ditch somewhere.'

Me neither.

'I honestly don't know. I wonder if this is linked to his past. He once told me that he worked as a chauffeur for some rich man back in Syria. Perhaps it was someone who was in trouble with the regime and that's why Aziz fled?'

'More the opposite. I don't think the guy he worked for was someone he admired.'

'What makes you say that?'

'Just something he said once. Look, it's not something I ever heard him talk about, but some of the other Syrians who come here reckon he might have been a White Helmet.'

'A White Helmet?'

'Like I said, he never told me himself,' said Abdul, shrugging. 'Where do you think he is?'

83

Aziz, a Syrian Civil Defence volunteer, risking his life to save the lives of others? It felt plausible. When Amira fell pregnant, he must have decided it was too risky to stay.

'I don't know,' said Jensen. 'But I'm going to do everything in my power to find out.'

17

Henrik's nerves were jangling. He was bitterly regretting the fried hotdog with the whole shebang that he had wolfed down at a sausage stand on the way to Kastrup Airport. The raw onion and pickled cucumber kept repeating on him as he and Mark marched through the terminal to the car-hire desks. He needed to get back into some sort of routine with food. Like Mark, who brought a packed lunch to the office every day: four half slices of rye bread; two with salami, remoulade and fried onion; two with liver pate and pickled beetroot; packed with greaseproof paper inside a kid's green lunch box with a rainbow on the lid.

OK, not quite like that.

The airport was making him nervous, with its milling masses and departure boards listing far-flung destinations. As if, by some false step, he might find himself dragged to an aircraft and forcibly strapped into a seat.

Last time he had been to Kastrup was over a year before when he had gone to collect his wife from a conference in

Munich. It had been a disaster. The plane was delayed and Henrik thought it a good idea to calm his nerves by getting drunk in a bar in arrivals, which meant that his wife, when she eventually showed, had to drive them both home to their house in Frederiksberg, with him snoring in the passenger seat.

The few times in his life that he had flown on an aircraft, he had done so in a state of extreme drunkenness as close as possible to total oblivion. This was many years ago now, before he had realised that owning up to his fear of flying was preferable to experiencing near-death sensations at 38,000 feet. How people willingly got on planes, even enjoyed themselves, was beyond him. Even this side of security he was getting the heebie-jeebies. It didn't help that it was the last day of the school term and Denmark's big annual getaway had begun. The noise level in the place was deafening.

There was a queue at the car-hire company, where only one of the three chairs behind the desk was occupied. An employee who looked not much older than Henrik's eldest son was busy staring gormlessly at a screen while an English-speaking woman tried to have a conversation with him about a child seat. Behind her were at least three separate parties who looked close to losing the will to live.

Mark pushed his way to the front but was too polite to interrupt the conversation. The adolescent employee kept typing and staring at the screen, as if hoping that would make the woman and everyone else go away, like figures in a computer game.

'Fuck's sake, who's in charge here?' said Henrik, muscling in next to Mark.

'Excuse me?' said the car-seat woman. She looked him up and down with contempt. The child on her arm began to cry.

This made the boy behind the counter wake up. 'I'm serving a customer. Join the queue,' he said in Henrik's direction, vaguely gesturing.

'I don't care,' said Henrik, shoving his badge under the boy's nose. 'DI Jungersen, Copenhagen Police. You need to check a car for us. Now.'

'What the hell is going on here?' said the woman to the clueless boy. 'Where is your supervisor?'

'This is a police matter. Step back,' Henrik snarled at her.

Mark held up his hands and tried to intervene when the door to the back room opened and a dark-haired member of staff in her thirties stepped through. Her ponytail was scraped back from her face so unforgivingly that her nose was pinched, the heavily made-up eyes slanted and hard. She was picking at something in her teeth.

'Sort out your customer, Kasper,' she said to the boy, before taking her time to acknowledge Henrik's presence.

'Good to see there are adults at work here after all,' he said.

'If you have a police matter with us, you need to call our head office.'

'Yes, but where would the fun be in that?' Henrik said.

'We don't tolerate rudeness to our staff,' she said, pointing to a sign on the desk.

'Oh really?' said Henrik. 'How about rudeness to your customers?'

'What do you want?' said the ice queen.

Henrik held his phone screen under her nose. 'I want you to look up this registration number and tell me who rented it.'

The woman typed, her talon nails clicking furiously on the keyboard. It took an age. 'What's taking so long?' said Henrik.

Big mistake. The woman stopped typing, her eyebrows shooting up towards her hairline. 'Do you want to know, or don't you?'

'My colleague didn't mean it,' said Mark. 'Do carry on.'

'You ought to put him on a lead,' she mumbled, resuming her typing. 'A muzzle might be an idea too.'

'All right, you've made your point. Now get on with it,' Henrik said.

At length the woman spoke. 'Seems the car was hired by a Christopher Michael White.'

'When is it due to be returned?' said Mark.

More furious typing.

'Yesterday,' said the woman. She frowned. 'Seems it wasn't, though.'

No, thought Henrik. That might have been because someone decided to use it to transport a mutilated corpse before torching it. Was Christopher Michael White their headless corpse?

'I want a copy of his passport,' he said, dropping his card on the desk. 'Today.'

He began walking towards the exit, leaving Mark to smooth things over with the angry brunette. Mark was good at making amends, his boss having given him a lot of practice over the years.

Henrik wasn't proud of himself, but one minute longer in the airport and he couldn't be held liable for his actions.

18

'Thank God this week is over,' said Jensen, flopping onto the Almasi family's three-seater sofa.

It was still hot outside, far too hot for comfort. Through the open windows came the sound of thumping car stereos and drunks shouting at each other, along with the smell of fried food, cigarettes and beer.

Gustav wasn't listening. He was busy unpacking cartons and plastic boxes from Sticks 'n' Sushi, wrenching chopsticks apart and mixing soy sauce and pea-sized amounts of wasabi with the practised moves of someone living off takeaways.

Jensen hadn't spoken to Kristoffer after his meltdown in the King's Garden. She checked her phone but there were no messages from him. 'This doesn't feel right,' she said, cooling her forehead with a bottle of Carlsberg.

'What doesn't?' said Gustav with his mouth full of crispy prawn.

'Us, stuffing our faces in Aziz's flat while he's out there on his own, in trouble, or worse.'

89

'We've got to eat,' Gustav shrugged. 'Can't help Aziz if we starve to death.'

No chance of that, Jensen thought, watching Gustav pour a liberal measure of treacly sesame sauce over a tray of roasted cauliflower.

All around him, the flat bore the signs of the allegedly 'deadly boring' day he had passed there while Jensen had been at work. He appeared to have spent part of it lying in the middle of the floor on a pile of cushions he had assembled from the bedrooms. His laptop was there and his headphones, a half-empty bottle of Fanta next to crisp packets and sweet wrappers.

She decided not to give him a hard time, grateful that he seemed relaxed and untroubled these days, no longer snapping whenever the subject came up of him resuming his studies after the summer break. It was as though the episode in Aalborg that had seen him expelled from school had lost its sting now that she knew about it.

'Do you ever think about those boys in Aalborg?' she had asked him once.

'Who?' Gustav had replied, squinting at her through a cloud of chocolate vape.

'You know who.'

'No, never,' he had yielded. 'Should I be?'

He had already been through enough. She hadn't wanted to confront him with what she had learned from the pupil who had been too scared to tell her his name: that the Aalborg boys hadn't forgotten Gustav, that they wanted revenge.

Perhaps the few times recently when Jensen had felt she was being watched were down to those boys. Perhaps they were following her and Gustav, waiting for their chance.

In that case, Jensen reckoned Gustav might not see them

coming. He had deleted his social media accounts, the source of so much pain, and she had never heard him speak to anyone from the Aalborg days, or even anyone his own age. Another reason why it was high time for him to return to school.

'So,' she said, succumbing to hunger and pinching a piece of salmon sushi with her chopsticks. She dipped it into the pot of soy and wasabi that Gustav had stirred just the way she liked it.

'What do we know about Aziz's movements, before he disappeared?' she said.

'Took Esben to an early Brussels flight and got back to Nørrebro in time for the school run. Left Amira at ten past eight with all three kids. Took the boys to school and, according to one of the teachers, waved to them from the school gate just after twenty minutes past eight.'

'Did the teacher say anything about how he seemed?'

'Normal, apparently. She noticed Aziz because Amira usually brought the boys. She said Aziz seemed to be in a good mood, though he isn't the most talkative of parents.'

That sounded about right, thought Jensen. 'Then what did he do?'

'Arrived at the nursery with the little one after half past eight. Chatted to one of the nursery teachers about a teddy bear's picnic planned for the end of term. Nothing unusual about his behaviour. He seemed relaxed.'

'OK, and after the nursery?'

'Nothing. We only know from Abdul that he never showed at the gym.'

Jensen thought about it for a while. Aziz had dropped Esben off at the airport and was supposed to have collected him after his trip. She frowned. 'Where's the car?' she said. 'Esben's car? The expensive black one.'

'Dunno,' said Gustav.

Jensen got out her phone and dialled Esben's number.

He answered almost immediately, his voice anxious, if slurred with drink. 'Any news?'

'No, but listen, Esben, I thought of something. What happened to the car?'

'What, my car?'

'Yes, the black one Aziz drives you around in.'

'It's in the garage, here in Klampenborg.'

'You sure?'

'One hundred percent. I saw it myself this morning.'

'So, when you go away on your business trips, Aziz never uses the car for himself?'

'Well, yes. Aziz and that car are—'

'Inseparable?'

'Precisely.'

'So why is it at your place now? Did your wife need to use it while you were away?'

'No, Ulla has her own car. Besides, she's in Tuscany for a month. I guess that, for whatever reason, Aziz must have taken it back here after he dropped me at the airport when I went to Brussels.'

'But how would he have got back to his own place?'

'Must have taken the S-train.'

'Why would he have done that when he would normally use the car while you were away?'

Esben was quiet for a while. 'My God, Jensen, you have a point. It doesn't make sense. What do you think it means?'

'I don't know yet. We'll come and see you tomorrow. Take a closer look at the car. See if he left some clue behind.'

She hung up, rubbed her face.

Gustav homed in on the last California roll and she gestured at him that he could have it. He wasted no time cramming it into his mouth.

92

'So,' she said. 'That's all we've got. A normal morning. Except sometime after eight thirty, Aziz vanished into thin air.'

Gustav rolled onto his back, burping beer and raw fish. 'Not quite,' he said.

'What do you mean?' said Jensen.

'There's this guy Kemal across the street, in the kebab shop.'

'I thought you said you stayed here all day.'

'For God's sake, Jensen, I was famished, so I popped over for, like, ten minutes.'

'And?'

'I spoke to Kemal who works there and asked him about Aziz. He said everyone knows Aziz. Called him a gentle giant. Didn't know he was missing, and don't worry, I didn't tell him anything, but Kemal insisted that he saw Aziz the other day.'

'Where?'

'Outside his shop.'

'Why didn't you say so sooner?' said Jensen. 'That could be really important.'

'Because he's obviously mistaken. I mean, it can't be true,' said Gustav. 'Not when Aziz hasn't been home for all that time. Can it?'

19

Friday 19:33

The meal was over, and the kids had dispersed in search of their iPads and PlayStations, leaving a trail of debris in their wake. On the table were the remains of chicken fajitas that only his wife had eaten as the recipe intended. Henrik had eaten his without cheese, his youngest, Oliver, had been given a version without peppers and onions, Mikkel, his eldest, now a vegan, had made his with meat-free sausage, cucumbers and tomatoes, whereas Karla, his daughter, hated fajitas, so had been given a piece of salmon with rice.

Henrik couldn't remember the last time all five of them had eaten the same meal. He looked at his wife as she poured herself another large glass of white wine. The bottle was nearly empty.

He wasn't drinking, having already flagged the possibility that he had to return to the office later to work on the new case. A coward's option in case the evening turned sour. Highly likely, given the mood his wife was in.

'Shouldn't you . . .' he began.

'Shouldn't I what?' she replied with her nose in the glass.

She had thrown off her headmistress heels, opened the top buttons of her pink sleeveless top and unzipped her white trousers. Her mascara was running and her pinned-up dark hair was starting to fall around her face. She was still beautiful, but the years had hardened her. *He* had hardened her, and there was now a permanent look of scepticism and defiance in her brown eyes.

'Hold back a little?' he said, softly, feeling himself sliding into a trap.

'The fuck I will,' she said, pointing at him with her glass. 'Do you know what kind of day I've had? Running a school, running this house, the children, all while you're out doing your own thing? No? I didn't think so. So if you don't mind, I've had a shit day and a shit week, and to top it off, I have just had to cook five different meals, because no one in this fucking family will eat the food that's put in front of them, so if it's OK with you, I'm going to have as much to drink as I bloody well like.'

'I guess I asked for that. I am sorry you have so much to deal with and that I'm not around more to help.'

He truly *was* sorry and had learned over the years to own up to it, rather than argue. Had he been a useless husband and father? Yes. Did his wife have part blame for that? Yes, he had always thought so, though he would never say it to her face. The problem was that she was good at running things, really good. She was better than him at pretty much every aspect of life except fitness training and policing. Helping someone like his wife meant becoming her dogs-body, her factotum; only one of them could be boss and Henrik had never been any good at playing second fiddle, so he had made himself absent from home, and his wife had assumed the martyrdom at which she also excelled.

'Yeah, yeah,' she said. 'I've heard it all before. But nothing changes, nothing, and guess who'll have to do all the washing and ironing and packing for our holiday.'

'Ah,' said Henrik. 'About that . . .'

His wife looked at him sharply. 'Oh no,' she said. 'You're not doing this to me again.'

He held up his hands. 'I didn't say anything. Only, there's this case.'

'The body in the harbour.'

'Yes. I think we might have got hold of something big.'

'For Christ's sake, can't someone else take it for once?'

Yes.

'I don't know,' he said. 'Only we have to prepare for the ... eventuality that I have to stay behind. Just for a few days. I've been thinking, you said your sister has been complaining about having no one to go on holiday with. Why not ask her? You could share the drive, and then I'll be along in a few days.'

'Charlotte? She wants to party all night in Ibiza. You seriously think she'd share a family holiday with her big sister and her three kids?'

'If you ask her nicely. A free trip to Italy? My guess is she'll bite your hand off,' said Henrik.

His wife narrowed her eyes at him. 'You don't want to go, do you? You've always hated our holidays, can't wait to get back.'

True.

'That's not true, we've had some great holidays.'

'You're forgetting that I know you, Henrik,' said his wife, emptying her glass.

Her unspoken question hung in the air between them: is it her again?

Jensen.

Henrik sensed neither of them had the energy to go there. 'I can assure you, there's no ulterior motive. It's simply that I'm working on this new case and don't know if I'll be able to drive to Italy on Monday.'

He checked his phone. Still no messages from Jensen. He wanted to see her, to make sure she was all right. 'Speaking of which, I need to get back to the office. Leave the dishes, I'll sort them when I get back.'

'Yeah sure,' said his wife, emptying the bottle into her glass. 'Do you know what? Maybe I *should* go to Italy with Charlotte. Sure as hell, she'll be more fun than you.'

He opened his mouth to speak but didn't know what to say that he hadn't said a thousand times before.

'Go,' she said. 'Just go.'

He felt the weight of his failures on his shoulders as he let himself out without saying goodnight to the kids. They wouldn't look up from their screens anyway, accustomed as they were to him leaving.

Outside the day had barely cooled. People were in their gardens, having barbecues, playing football. Normal families, doing normal things with each other.

He got into the car, thinking that he would drive to the office via the Almasi flat in Nørrebro, and was just about to pull into the road when his phone rang.

Lynn Walker, Detective Inspector in the Metropolitan Police. He had met her in London at a conference fifteen years ago, on the same trip when he and Jensen had first locked eyes at the Danish Ambassador's residence in Sloane Street and his fate had been sealed.

Lynn, a no-nonsense Mancunian, had stayed in touch. They understood each other and shared a love of policing. Henrik had never asked, but he suspected that for Lynn, too, the job, with its seductive routines, was a way of escaping a difficult private life. 'Lynn, really appreciate you calling me back.'

'My pleasure, Jungersen.'

'Did you get the passport photo I sent you? Christopher Michael White?'

'Yes.'

'And?'

'It's fake. Christopher White died twenty-one years ago of a brain tumour, aged ten.'

'So, who is the guy? Is he British? We know he flew in from London.'

'We don't know. I'm trying to have some image analysis done for you.'

'Thank you, Lynn. Call me back as soon as you hear.'

Fuck.

Back to square one. That was policing. One step forward, two steps back.

Henrik pulled into the road and headed for Nørrebro.

20

The rush hour was on and the kebab shop was a furnace. Customers were shouting at the top of their voices to get heard, jostling each other out of the way. Behind the counter, there was a production line: four people slicing meat and topping up the filled breads with chopped salad before wrapping them.

The smell of the grilled lamb and garlic sauce was making Jensen salivate and she looked with envy at the people carrying away their grease-stained bags.

A bald man in his forties was manning the till, ensuring that everyone got served in some sort of order. He was wearing a white cap and a long white apron over a black T-shirt, using his expressive eyes to communicate with the customers, while barking orders at the chefs behind him.

'That's Kemal. He's the boss,' shouted Gustav at Jensen as they pushed their way to the front.

'Maybe we should come back later when it's less busy,' said Jensen.

'No, Kemal is a good guy, he'll talk to us. Gave me a free kebab and everything when I came round earlier.'

'You're terrible,' Jensen laughed.

People were forever giving Gustav food, as if they saw in him some poor, mistreated child who needed feeding up and looking after. It was an illusion he encouraged whenever he wanted something. Jensen had to admit that once or twice it had come in handy.

'Hey Kemal,' Gustav shouted.

'Gustav, my friend,' replied Kemal and the two of them launched into some complicated handshake.

'Well,' said Kemal, ignoring the customer immediately in front of him who looked annoyed at having been interrupted mid-order. 'Are you going to introduce me to your friend?' he said.

'Kemal meet Jensen,' said Gustav.

They shook hands. 'Delighted to meet you. Now, what can I get you two?' said Kemal, eliciting another angry stare from his customer, who nevertheless knew better than to voice his frustration. Kemal's food was obviously too good for anyone to want to argue with him.

'Oh, we don't need anything,' said Jensen, shaking Kemal's hand. 'I'm a journalist at *Dagbladet* and Gustav here is my trainee.' She noticed a wary look enter Kemal's eyes, and immediately realised her mistake. 'But that's not why I'm here. I'm a friend of Aziz and his wife. Is there somewhere more private we can talk?'

Kemal's eyes became warm again. 'A friend of Aziz is a friend of mine,' he said.

He called to someone in the back room to come out and take over at the helm, then opened the counter and let Gustav and Jensen through. The tiled floor was spattered with salad and grease.

They were led into a room with bright, yellow-painted walls and white plastic furniture. A teenage boy in a baseball cap and over-ear headphones glanced up from his phone as they entered. Kemal looked at him and pointed at the door with his thumb. The boy left without a word, closing the door after him and shutting out the clamour of the shop.

With a fan running and the back door open, the room was pleasantly cool. Kemal offered them bottles of cold water. 'Have a seat,' he said. 'What's this about?'

'You remember what you told me today, when we were chatting?' said Gustav, taking a long gulp.

'About the history of the shop? About my father and how he founded this place with my uncle?'

'That was a lovely story,' said Gustav. 'But I was thinking of what you said about seeing Aziz the other day?'

'What about it?' said Kemal, frowning as his eyes roamed from Gustav to Jensen and back again. 'What's going on?'

Jensen looked at Kemal and decided they could trust him. He seemed genuinely concerned. She cleared her throat. 'Aziz has been missing for almost two weeks. No one knows where he is, not even his wife.'

'Fuck,' said Kemal, rubbing his face hard. 'For real?'

'Yes,' said Jensen. 'So, when you told Gustav that you'd seen him, we didn't know what to think.'

'It's true, I swear to you on my son's life.'

'When exactly was it?' said Jensen.

'Monday.'

Jensen's heart sank. Kemal would have spotted Aziz as he took his kids to school on the day he disappeared. They were back to having nothing. She sighed. 'Monday last week, you mean.'

'No, no, this week, because it was the day they got our delivery wrong.'

'What time was it?'

'Not long after the lorry left. Half past eight in the morning, that sort of time.'

'Aziz had not been home for a week by that point,' said Jensen. 'Are you sure it wasn't someone else?'

Kemal looked insulted. 'Have you *met* Aziz? He's the biggest man I've seen in my life. You wouldn't mistake him for anybody.'

Jensen nodded. This was true. 'What was he wearing?'

'I don't know. Normal clothes, I guess.'

Jensen thought of the smart suit Aziz always wore when he was driving Esben around town. 'Work clothes, or more like the weekend?'

'Weekend, I suppose.'

'Anything else?'

'He wore a blue baseball cap. And sunglasses.'

'Right.'

'It was weird,' said Kemal, scratching his bald head. 'He'd usually come in and say hello, have a coffee, or a bite to eat. That's what I thought he was going to do, but he just walked past really fast. Like he was late for something.'

'And you haven't seen him since?'

Kemal shook his head. His eyes widened. 'You think something's happened to him?'

Gustav began to speak, but Jensen spoke over him. 'Nah. I'm sure he'll turn up soon, wondering what all the fuss is about.'

She emptied her bottle. 'Thanks for the water, Kemal, and for your time.'

'And let us know if you see or hear anything else,' said Gustav, making the universal sign of a phone call with his finger and thumb.

'Wait,' said Kemal, as he was leading them out of the room. 'I just remembered. There *was* something else.'

'What?' said Jensen, feeling a familiar tingling sensation in her palms.

'I have never seen Aziz without a full beard before. But on Monday, I did.'

'What do you mean?' said Gustav.

'No beard. I don't know why, but he'd shaved it all off.'

21

'Christ, Henrik, you scared me. What are you doing here?'

Jensen looked cross, stopped a few steps below him in the dingy stairwell, and Henrik briefly lamented the fact that it had been ages since she had greeted him with a smile.

He had known it was her the minute he heard the street door being opened, followed by light, running footsteps on the stairs. Jensen moved at a different speed to normal people.

His knees creaked noisily as he got up. 'Making sure you're still alive, what do you think I was doing?' he said gruffly, trying to hide the relief he felt on seeing her.

He had panicked at first when no one answered the door, even considered breaking in for a moment. Instead, he had sent Jensen a stream of text messages asking where she was. 'Do you ever look at your phone?' he said, keeping his tone light.

'I was busy,' said Jensen, pushing past him as she fished

the keys to the flat out of her bag. 'Besides, if you're going to carry on about Kristoffer, I'm not interested.'

She entered the flat, dumping her bag on the floor. She didn't exactly invite him in, nor did she shut the door behind her.

There was a paper bag by the rubbish bin in the kitchen, full of empty takeaway containers. Jensen was by the sink, her head under the running tap.

'How is Gustav?' he said.

'Oh, you know, his usual self. He seems to have forgotten about Aalborg.'

'That's good, isn't it?'

'I'm not sure the boys he hurt see it that way.'

'The scumbags got what was coming to them. I checked it out. It's true: they don't want to press charges, and I'd say that's pretty wise, given the bullying they subjected him to.'

She turned to face him, her face and hair streaming wet. 'You did that for Gustav?'

He shrugged. It was partially thanks to Gustav's tenacity that his last big case had been solved, and besides, he liked the lad. More importantly, he knew Jensen liked him. 'So,' he said. 'Where were you this evening?'

Jensen leaned against the kitchen counter, kicking her shoes off. 'Not that it's any of your business, but there's this guy who told us he saw Aziz on Monday passing by in the street. Gustav and I went to see him just now. His name is Kemal.'

'People think they see stuff all the time. Doesn't mean it's true. As a journalist you ought to know that,' said Henrik.

'Gustav and I believe him. He was quite specific about how Aziz looked. Said he was wearing a baseball cap and sunglasses and that he'd shaved off his beard.'

'Had he done that before?'

105

Jensen shook her head. 'I assume he was trying to disguise himself.'

'Yet your man Kemal was positive it was Aziz he saw.'

Jensen nodded. 'Said he'd know him anywhere by his size.'

Plenty of big men out there, thought Henrik. Their headless corpse, for one. He decided not to argue. 'OK,' he said, holding up his hands. 'If you say so.'

Jensen grabbed a pile of circulars from the kitchen counter and fanned herself with them. 'God, I'm so hot,' she said. 'Isn't it just unbearably hot in here?'

'Not really,' said Henrik.

Jensen pushed past him and went into the living room where she plonked herself on the sofa and closed her eyes.

Henrik walked over to the window. 'You shouldn't be staying here,' he said, without turning. 'Whoever it is who is after Aziz, they're bound to come back here sooner or later. And if he hasn't turned up, they'll be pretty desperate.'

'I'm fine,' said Jensen. 'If something bad happens, I'll call the police.'

You may not get the chance, thought Henrik. 'Besides, I don't believe Aziz would be stupid enough to come back here, so there really isn't any point in you staying. I'm sure Amira would understand if you explained it to her.'

'I wonder how she's holding up,' said Jensen. 'Did that colleague of yours say anything?'

'Lisbeth? No. Which I think you can take as good news.'

Jensen nodded.

'Tell you what,' said Henrik. 'Why don't *I* stay here tonight. You go home, get a good night's sleep.'

'I can't let you do that,' Jensen said.

'Yes, you can. I'll be fine on the sofa.'

'No, I'd rather stay, in case something happens.'

'Can I ask you a question?' Henrik said.

'What?'

He kept his voice soft. 'Don't bite my head off, but if I were to wager that you don't want to go home, would I be right? Has it got something to do with what I told you about your boyfriend?'

Jensen opened one eye. 'You told me nothing.'

'I'd be wrong?'

'Yes, completely wrong.' Jensen lay down on the sofa, wriggling to make herself comfortable, and folded her forearms over her face.

'I know you won't believe me, not after ... well, the whole debacle with my wife throwing me out, but I do know the feeling. Of not wanting to go home,' Henrik said. 'In fact, right now I can't think of anything less appealing.'

'I'm not talking to you about it,' Jensen said.

For all her bravado, he could tell that something was worrying her, something she wasn't telling him. He knew her, better than he knew himself.

Every inch of her.

He would have to ask her about it another time. She had closed her eyes and begun to snore gently.

Henrik fought an urge to kiss her, finally giving in to the temptation. *May God forgive me*, he thought as he tiptoed to the sofa, sat down on the edge of it and touched his lips to hers.

He woke at 3:14 a.m., having slumped over Jensen's legs, one hand resting on her belly, her hand touching his head. His phone showed three messages from his wife:

Thanks a bunch for letting me know where
you are.

I'm taking Charlotte to Italy. Don't bother coming.

You utter bastard.

22

Saturday 11:24

'This had better not be some wild goose chase, Mark. I've barely slept,' said Henrik as he and Mark headed out through Copenhagen's suburbs towards the summerhouse district at Roskilde Fjord.

'Case keep you awake?' asked Mark, whom Henrik had permitted to drive for once in the hope of catching some sleep on the way.

'Something like that,' he said, taking a sip from his takeaway latte and leaning his forehead against the car window as the summer-scorched city passed by in a golden-brown blur.

There weren't many people he would happily hand the wheel to, besides Lisbeth and Mark. Mark was solid. A good driver, fast but careful. Fit. Didn't mind hard graft. Not a great brain, nothing like Lisbeth, but a plodder, and plodders, too, got results.

Eventually.

In truth, Henrik was glad to have somewhere to go.

Anything other than returning home and facing the full force of his wife's anger.

He had finally left the Nørrebro flat just after 6 a.m. when hot sunshine began to flood through gaps in the white gauze curtains.

After waking up practically on top of Jensen, he had spent what was left of the night in an armchair opposite, with one hand on his service revolver, snapping awake at every little unfamiliar noise.

Jensen had stayed asleep throughout, now and again moaning a little.

I would kill for her, he had thought.

Once, only a few months back, he almost had.

Jensen hadn't stirred when he had got up and let himself out, after standing over her for a good minute while debating whether to wake her up and say goodbye.

She was as slight as a child in her torn denim shorts, her slender legs tanned and covered in mosquito bites and scratches, her parted lips revealing her gappy front teeth. Not a conventional beauty like his wife, and not his type at all.

It was her energy that drew him to her, he decided. That and her dark blue eyes which seemed to see through you. No sign of any of that in her sleeping form, which gave off an air of helplessness that made Henrik feel protective.

He was aware this was an illusion. Jensen didn't need, didn't want, looking after. She wasn't that type of woman. None of the women in his life were.

He closed his eyes, feeling dead. In his youth, he had regularly pulled all-nighters and still been able to function the next day. Now, he found himself incapable of doing so without needing several days to recover.

'Tell me again what your mate said?' he asked Mark.

'He said they'd had reports from a dog walker who'd seen a couple of men throw something into the water.'

'What was it?'

'They couldn't see exactly, but it was like a small white bundle. They thought it was odd, so they phoned the police.'

'Who did nothing about it?'

'Correct. You know what it's like. There was nothing else to go on. Besides, what were they supposed to do? Send divers out?'

'Right. Still, your mate remembered the report.'

'Yes. When he saw the news about the body we found in the harbour.'

'And did the person who reported seeing the men hear them talk to each other?'

'Yes. Apparently, the men were Danish. Big men, and youngish, the witness said, but unfortunately that is all the description we have to go on. We have an appointment with her this afternoon, so we can ask her again.'

Where was Mark going with this? 'So, two big, young Danish guys throw something in the water, and this is linked to our case how?' said Henrik.

'My mate heard on the news that our victim was thought to be a foreigner.'

'And?'

'He thought . . . well, before he knew that, he'd gone to a shop near the beach where the two men were seen and asked if they'd noticed anyone unusual stopping by lately.'

'And they had?'

'No big Danish guys matching the description of the men on the beach, no.'

'OK, so . . .'

'But they *did* say that an English-speaking guy had come

111

to the shop a couple of times. Which they thought was strange as the holiday season hasn't really started yet.'

'When was that?'

'Twelve days ago. Anyway, when my mate heard the news from Copenhagen, he managed to trace the guy to a local summerhouse. That's where he's going to meet us.'

Some guys throwing a package in the water. A foreigner turning up in a seaside convenience store out of season. It wasn't much, but people noticed such things, their instincts telling them that something was off.

'Good work, Mark,' said Henrik.

Mark's phone began to ring.

Lisbeth's voice came through the loudspeakers. 'Where are you?'

'On our way to Roskilde Fjord to investigate a tip-off. Why?' said Mark, a note of irritation in his voice.

'Jungersen with you?'

'He's trying to sleep.'

'Right here,' said Henrik. 'What do you want?'

'That headless corpse of yours?'

'What about it?'

'I think we may have found its head.'

23

Saturday 11:41

Dagbladet was quiet as always on a Saturday. Most of the journalists had the weekend off, bar the unlucky few who had to put Sunday's paper to bed. Jensen parked her bike in the courtyard and took the back staircase to the reporters' floor under the roof of the building, carefully balancing two paper cups. She had been relieved to spot Liron's coffee van in its usual spot in Sankt Peders Stræde. The man himself had been fast asleep on a folding chair, his head tipped backwards into the warm sunshine, a thin line of saliva glistening in his goatee.

She had tiptoed up to him from behind, covering his eyes with her hands. To her surprise, Liron had jumped up, grabbed her by the wrists and shouted aggressively in a language she assumed to be Hebrew.

'Chill, Liron, it's me, Jensen,' she had said, twisting herself free and rubbing her arms. His grasp had been strong enough to inflict pain.

'Fuck me, lady, don't do that again,' he had said, hands on

his knees and panting as if recovering from a sprint. Then he had begun to laugh, and the old Liron was back. 'Come here, give us a fucking hug,' he said. He pulled her close and they stood for a long while, a static human form among the passing Saturday shoppers.

Jensen had often wondered what Liron had done for a living back home in Israel before meeting a Danish girl and deciding to emigrate to this tiny kingdom in the north. His violent reaction, though it had lasted no more than a few seconds, had done nothing to dispel her disquiet about his past. What had happened to a person to make them react like that?

'How's business?' she said.

'Slow as hell,' said Liron, pouring beans into a grinder and turning it on. 'Copenhagen's as fucking hot as Jerusalem and no one's buying coffee. Why, Jensen, why? Do they not drink coffee in Jerusalem? All this time I've been teaching these fucking people about coffee and they've learned nothing.'

Jensen laughed, noticing that he had described her fellow citizens in the third person. After her fifteen years in London, even Liron regarded her as a foreigner.

He set out a paper cup in front of him as he tamped the ground coffee into a silver scoop, ready for the beaten-up espresso machine he had bought second-hand in Milan.

'Whatever you're making, I'm going to need two,' she said.

As usual, Liron hadn't asked her what she wanted, but made what he thought she needed. 'Think of me as your coffee sommelier,' he had once told her.

'Fuck, you look tired,' he said, grinning. 'Hot new lover kept you up all night?'

'Thanks a bunch, Liron,' said Jensen, pretending to be annoyed.

She had woken up to find dozens of texts from Kristoffer, ranging from the contrite (*I'm so sorry, I've no idea what got into me*) to the pleading (*Please, please, Jensen, come back to me, I'll tell you everything you want to know, anything at all*) to the desperate (*Jensen, are you still alive?*)

Had she been unfair by not replying? Probably. She had wanted to punish him, but now it felt like she had been unreasonable. She would return to his Nordhavn penthouse tonight. Henrik was right. There was no point in her staying on in the Nørrebro flat, and she and Kristoffer needed to talk.

Liron had picked up on her brooding. 'Something wrong, Jensen?'

'Do you remember Aziz, my Syrian friend? I brought him here once, back in January.'

'The giant? How could I fucking forget? Almost broke my hand when he shook it. What about him?'

'Hasn't been home for almost two weeks. I'm worried something bad has happened.'

Liron laughed. 'To the fucking terminator? I don't bloody think so. It'll be something to do with a woman.'

'A woman?'

'It's always to do with a woman when men do stupid things.'

'He didn't take his phone, or his passport, or any clothes.'

'Because he doesn't want to be discovered in his little love nest.'

'Aziz is devoted to his wife, Liron.'

'In that case I'm sure he will be back soon, with his tail between his legs. Don't worry Jensen, everything will be fine,' he said, putting one arm around her as he operated the espresso maker.

You don't understand anything, Liron, Jensen thought, but there had been no point in going on.

'My mate Alessandro from Alba taught me how to make a proper cappuccino. You make the espresso at a higher pressure, so you extract more of the taste,' Liron said, finally handing her two lidded cups.

'And remember, cappuccino is for breakfast. The rest of the day, the milk is for the baby's bottle. In Italy, never order cappuccino after noon.'

'It's good to see you, Liron,' she said, pecking him on the cheek and walking away.

She went straight up to Henning's office, the two cappuccinos cooling in her hands. The retired editor was asleep by his desk, still holding the ornate silver scissors he used for cutting out articles.

She spoke to him gently. 'Henning? I brought you a coffee.'

That woke him up. He opened one eye and reached out for the paper cup, immediately raising it to his mouth.

'What do you want?' he said after a while, smacking his lips.

'Must I want something?'

'It's a Saturday. No one comes here on a Saturday, not even you.'

'You're here.'

'I am no one.'

'So you say. Anyway, I wanted to talk to you. Yesterday, I asked you about Ernst Brøgger.'

'And I told you what I know.'

'The article mentioned he was born on Bornholm?'

Bornholm. The name of the rocky island in the Baltic Sea snagged at something in Jensen's subconscious. She tried but failed to grasp the connection.

'Yes.'

'Any family?'

'A brother, but you won't find anything about him either.'

'Why not?' she said, her eyes straying to the filing cabinets at the back of the room.

Henning noisily drained his cup, then removed the lid and tipped the leftover milk foam down his throat. 'Because, if possible, he's even better than Brøgger at keeping a low profile.'

Henning had finished talking and closed his eyes. Jensen knew that she wasn't going to get anything else out of him.

She left him in his office, slumped into his chair, asleep. He was still holding the empty coffee cup. Behind him on the bookshelf stood a dozen more assorted cups, donated by colleagues or scavenged from abandoned desks.

Jensen's phone pinged as she was about to enter her office. Esben.

> Come immediately. There's something you
> have got to see.

24

The officer from North Zealand Police had been making himself comfortable on the terrace of the summerhouse, an attractive log cabin on a large plot of well-kept land, distant from its neighbours. As Henrik and Mark approached the house along the gravel drive lined with wild rose bushes, the man jumped up from the sun lounger he had been reclining on, quickly tucking away a thermos flask and lunch box in his black rucksack. 'Dinesen,' he said, shaking Henrik's hand.

Dinesen had white-blond hair. His eyebrows and lashes were almost white and stood out against his blushing face. His breath smelled of rye bread and cheese.

'Sorry if we kept you waiting,' said Mark.

'Not at all,' said Dinesen. 'Glad to help.'

Henrik guessed Dinesen would be dealing mostly with burglaries in his district, and perhaps the odd incident of antisocial behaviour. Holding a possible clue in a major Copenhagen murder investigation had to be exciting.

Henrik had wanted to turn around and head back to the

city as soon as Lisbeth had ended the call, but Mark had dug his heels in. 'My friend's come all this way out here to meet us. The least we can do is show up.'

'Our missing head has just been found and you're worried about letting a mate down?' Henrik had said.

'I really think he could be on to something. Let's hear him out,' Mark had said. 'I'll have you back on the road in fifteen minutes, twenty tops.'

Dinesen spoke as he walked them around to the front of the summerhouse. 'It was luck, really. The wife of one of the local constables works for a company that cleans holiday homes in the area, including this one. When I mentioned the foreigner who had been spotted in the shop, he remembered something odd his wife had told him.'

Henrik moaned to himself, wishing to God that Dinesen would come to the point.

'The cleaners work in pairs. Once a rental has ended, they go in, change the beds and clean the place, ready for the next occupants. Anyway, they turn up here and find the place has already been cleaned. Totally spotless.'

'So, the people cleaned it before they left, so what?' said Henrik.

'That's what they thought,' said Dinesen. 'Easy money. No need to tell the owner it wasn't them who straightened the house.'

'But the constable remembered, and he told you about it,' said Mark, his eyes flicking nervously between Henrik and Dinesen.

'That's correct. So, I decided to do a little investigating. I found out that this place is owned by a Copenhagen doctor. He confirmed that he'd rented the summerhouse to an English family. They had asked in advance if the property came with a highchair and cot.'

A child. A wife. Not good. Were they about to make a nasty discovery inside the house?

'Did anyone notice any children with the British guy when he called into the convenience store or see them around the area?' said Henrik.

Dinesen shook his head. 'I asked around. No one remembers seeing any foreign family with kids. But then this house is somewhat isolated from its neighbours.'

'Under what name was the house rented?' he said.

If it was Christopher Michael White, they would have the connection they needed.

It wasn't.

Of course not.

That would have been too easy.

'Smith,' said Dinesen.

'And you're completely certain that no one has been inside the summerhouse?'

'Not to my knowledge,' said Dinesen, unlocking the door. 'I have the owner's permission.'

They were hit by a strong smell of cleaning products. The house was abandoned. The beds were neatly made, the fridge empty, no toothpaste stain in the sink.

The place was scrubbed clean.

Too clean.

If Christopher Michael White or whatever his name was had ever stayed here with his family, someone had cleaned up after them, and very recently, too, judging by the smell of chlorine and pine needles.

'Weird,' said Mark.

Henrik bent down to inspect the floor in the kitchen where it met the skirting board under the cupboards. There was something there, a tiny dark patch. It was a hunch, nothing more. 'Fetch the Luminol from the car,' he said to Mark. 'And Dinesen, close the blinds, would you?'

That was the thing with murder, you couldn't get rid of all the evidence. No matter how hard you tried, there was always something left.

Mark returned with the spray can, panting from exertion. Henrik sprayed the skirting board, then held up his torch, watching the dark patch turn a fluorescent blue.

Blood.

Not a lot, but enough.

'Bingo,' said Mark.

Henrik guessed the killers had used plastic sheeting as the head and hands were parted from the body, and the patch on the wood was an accident. 'No one touches a thing. I want forensics up here now.'

25

Saturday 12:45

Three tiny white dogs crowded around Esben's feet as he greeted Jensen and Gustav at his front door. 'Any news?' he asked, his voice full of hope.

Jensen shook her head and Esben's shoulders fell.

Meanwhile, Gustav dropped to his knees and within seconds had the three yapping balls of fluff whipped into a frenzy.

'Get off,' Esben shouted aggressively. It wasn't immediately apparent if he was talking to Gustav or the dogs. He looked dishevelled in a crumpled T-shirt and faded red shorts. He hadn't shaved and the dark rings under his eyes told of a restless night.

She had never been to Esben's villa in Klampenborg before. Whether it was because he still considered her a potential conquest (*dream on, Esben*) or was afraid that his long-suffering wife Ulla would come to that conclusion, he hadn't invited Jensen home once since she had moved back to Copenhagen.

The villa was more luxurious than she had imagined. Not opulent, but classy and old money, like an English manor house, covered in vines and surrounded by fragrant roses and a lawn that looked like it had been trimmed with nail clippers.

Inside the cool entrance hall there were Persian rugs on the parquet flooring, Chinese vases and old paintings in gilded frames. A vast bouquet of pink lilies spread their scent across the room. The walls were dappled with sunlight coming through from the back of the house.

Jensen was dying to take a closer look, glimpsing a white sofa arrangement and a grand piano through open double doors, but Esben wasn't offering a tour. He walked her and Gustav into an enormous kitchen where a cleaner, a smiling Filipino woman wearing bright pink Marigolds, looked up from the sink. Jensen lifted her hand in greeting, but Esben didn't stop or as much as acknowledge the woman's presence. Despite Gustav's protests, he shut the three dogs away in a utility room to one side. They continued to bark excitedly behind the closed door. 'Bloody ankle biters,' he said. 'And she had to go and get three of the damn things.'

Good on you, Ulla, thought Jensen, who had always suspected that she would get on well with Esben's wife. The daughter of a wealthy property developer, Ulla was the one with the money, and it was clear that she wore the trousers too. It was nice to know that Esben's home, at least, was one place where he wasn't able to get his own way. Did Ulla know about his infidelities? She seemed too smart not to.

Esben led them into an untidy office facing the garden where a sprinkler was keeping the lawn tropically green, despite the scorching heat.

Obviously, this was Esben's man cave. The walls were lined with books: novels next to volumes about sailing, golf

123

and fishing. There was a Corbusier recliner in one corner and a black leather desk chair that looked fit for the commander of a Nasa space mission.

In amongst the detritus of papers and receipts on the desk were several coffee cups, an almost empty bottle of red wine and a plate of pizza crusts. Jensen guessed the cleaner wasn't allowed in this room. 'What's this about?' she said, as Esben closed the door behind them.

'Just wait,' he said, sitting down in front of an enormous flat monitor. The screen saver was a loop of Nørregaard family photos. 'Talking to you last night got me thinking.'

Esben clicked the mouse a few times and the screen changed from a picture of himself, Ulla and their four kids smiling on the deck of a yacht, to grainy black-and-white split-screen footage of the Klampenborg house from four different angles.

'Security cameras?' said Jensen.

'Yes,' said Esben. 'Remember those cranks I told you about? Well, I might not be running to the police every five minutes, but that doesn't mean I'm prepared to take chances with my family's safety.'

Jensen nodded. When she and Gustav had first arrived, Esben had buzzed them in from the street through a serious-looking iron gate. The Nørregaards weren't exactly welcoming visitors with open arms.

So far, nothing was happening on the screen. 'Look at the date,' said Esben, pointing to the top right-hand corner where the time showed 09:20 a.m.

'That's the day Aziz disappeared,' said Jensen.

'Correct. Now watch.' He pointed to the bottom left-hand screen, which showed a slice of his front drive. After a few seconds, a black car slid into view and stopped in front of the double garage to the left of the house.

What they saw next made both Jensen and Gustav shout out in unison. 'Aziz!'

Getting out of the car and opening the garage with a key.

'The remote control isn't working. Aziz had been meaning to get the battery changed,' said Esben.

He pressed a few buttons and the time fast-forwarded. 'Now keep watching,' he said.

The picture had changed and was now showing the inside of the garage. The bonnet of the black car was open and Aziz was leaning over it. The time was showing 10:13 a.m. They watched him for a while, coming and going from the engine, picking up and setting down tools on a work bench running along the back wall.

'What is he—,' Gustav began, but Esben held his finger to his lips and pointed to the screen.

Aziz was bent over the car again. After a few seconds, he jerked upright, hitting his head on the bonnet as he did so. He raised one hand to his scalp, while craning his neck as if to catch sight of something outside in the drive. Then suddenly he crouched down, hiding behind the car.

'Fuck, someone's out there,' said Gustav.

'Shush,' said Esben. 'Keep watching.'

Twenty seconds passed and Aziz stayed where he was. Then he began to crawl forwards on all fours, eventually disappearing from view down one side of the black car. Esben hit some more buttons and the view changed back to the drive.

After a while, Aziz could be seen back on his feet, edging away from the garage with his back to a tall hedge. He looked over one shoulder, then quickly ducked.

'Who's that?' said Gustav, pointing as two men came into view, their faces concealed with baseball caps and scarves.

'I don't know. I've been through all the footage from that morning. This is the first time they appear.'

Cornered with his back to the hedge, Aziz came out of his hiding place and confronted the men. At first, they were talking, then Aziz shoved one of the men hard on one shoulder. The other man shoved back. A third man appeared. There was a scuffle between all four, which Aziz appeared to be winning and then, in a split second, he fell to the ground, and one of the men started beating down on him with a baseball bat, until one of the others dragged him off.

While Aziz was lying there, seemingly unconscious, one of the men looked up and around, his gaze stopping when he was looking straight into the camera. Quickly he walked up to it, pointed a gun and the screen went blank.

'That's it,' said Esben. 'The bastards took the cameras out one by one.'

'You must have footage showing the three men arriving?'

'None whatsoever and, believe you me, I have looked.'

'How is that even possible?' said Gustav.

'They must have come in from the neighbour's property, through the shrubbery and into the front garden that way. That's the only entry point that won't set off the alarm, which means they must have been staking out the property beforehand.'

'They would have known about the cameras then,' said Gustav.

'Perhaps they didn't care,' said Jensen.

'The old boy next door is deaf and more or less blind. People could just walk up his driveway and hop over the fence,' said Esben.

The three of them sat for a while and looked at the black screen. Jensen felt sick.

The way Aziz had fallen to the ground had looked unnatural, frightening. Had he been stabbed? Or shot? Or injected? Questions flooded her mind. 'You told us last night that the black car was in the garage. You didn't suggest there was anything unusual about it, so I assume that means the men tidied up after Aziz, then closed the bonnet and the garage door.'

'They must have done. I've been all over the place, but there is no sign that anybody was even here.'

'What about your cleaner, did she notice anything unusual?'

'Maria was in Vejle visiting a cousin last week, as both Ulla and I were away.'

'What about the dogs?' said Gustav.

'Kennels,' said Esben.

'Does Aziz normally come here while you're travelling?' Jensen asked.

'I didn't think he did. Ulla prefers to drive herself, so there is nothing for Aziz to do if I'm not here. And he is free to use the car. On the other hand, I never told him *not* to come here, and obviously he had the keys, so he could come and go as he pleased. I'm assuming something on the car needed fixing and he wanted the space and peace to look at it.'

He looked at her miserably. 'Oh God, Jensen, what am I going to do?'

26

Ida Kaurup was a professional busybody, the type that Henrik had come to both love and loathe during his career.

'About time you showed up,' she said, before Henrik and Mark had even got out of the car. 'It's been ages since I reported those men. No wonder crime is rampant in this country.'

Instead of inviting them into the neat, white-rendered bungalow with a red Toyota Yaris parked in front, she stepped out and locked the front door.

'Are you going out?' said Mark. 'We were hoping to have a word with you.'

'I know that, dumbo. Now are we going in your car or mine?'

'What?' said Mark.

'Well, do you want to see the place or not?'

The short journey to Roskilde Fjord, with Ida in the back seat, was a trial in patience. She insisted on telling

128

them her life story, including how she and her husband had found the house of their dreams just eight weeks before he had died of leukaemia. How she had got the springer spaniel panting noisily on the seat beside her, to fill the void he left behind. How she always walked the dog by the same beach, a place her husband had loved, twice a day.

'I can't sleep nowadays, so I'm up and out by five thirty every morning.'

The three of them and the dog walked a sandy path that forged its way through the vegetation. Ida was marching at the front with considerable speed, Mark was bouncing alongside her spaniel, like a human dog, and Henrik was at the rear, wondering what they were all doing there.

He and Mark had already been to the local shop where they had picked up hours of CCTV recordings which some unfortunate soul on the investigation team would now be tasked with watching. The shop assistant could not remember the exact day or time that the English-speaking man had come in talking on his mobile phone. The man had been wearing jeans, a T-shirt and a baseball cap, and was described as 'short and thin'.

Those three little words had made Henrik's hypotheses crumble. What did they have? A spot of blood in a summerhouse and a short, thin, English-speaking man in a grocery store.

Not a six-foot-eight human mound of flesh.

He was anxious to get back to the city and see David Goldschmidt at the Forensic Institute about the head.

It was Mark who had persuaded him that they might as well go and talk to Ida Kaurup now that they were here.

Ida had stopped at a point on the path where it overlooked a wide stretch of the beach. 'Here,' she said. 'This is where I was when I saw the men. Tuesday last week, just before six a.m. They were at the other end of the beach from me.'

'Did they see you?' Henrik said.

'No. I was crouching down, and besides they wouldn't have expected anyone to show. Not if they had done their research. I almost never meet anyone on my morning walk. The afternoon is a different matter. Sometimes, especially in the summer, it can be crowded, but in the morning, never.'

'So, they were quite far away from you,' said Henrik.

'Nothing wrong with my eyesight,' she said, looking at him sharply. 'I could see perfectly well.'

'Could it have been fishermen? Throwing their catch back into the water?' said Mark.

'I don't know about you, but I've never seen men fishing wearing leather jackets with those patches sewn on the back,' she said, looking at him sceptically. 'They were bikers, for sure, and it wasn't fish they were throwing into the water. It was something bundled up in a white cloth, a sheet maybe, and it must have been heavy, because it landed not all that far out.'

The body and the head had been dumped elsewhere, so if this had anything to do with their case in Copenhagen, it might be the murder weapon, thought Henrik. 'How big was it?'

She made a shape with her hands. 'Like this. Oblong. The size of a large holdall.'

'Do you think you could give a description of the men?'

'Of course. One of them had a beard and a ponytail and was wearing something white on his left hand, like a glove or a bandage.'

'Did you see their faces?'

'Quite clearly. I told the police when I reported it, but no one was interested.'

130

'I am sorry about that. We'll ask our local colleagues to bring you down to the station,' he said. 'Now, Mark here and I must return to Copenhagen. But first, I want you to show us precisely where those men were standing.'

27

Saturday 13:21

'I'll tell you exactly what we're going to do,' said Jensen. 'Two things. Number one, you're going to tell me absolutely everything.'

She and Esben were sheltering from the sun under a large oak tree, while Gustav ran about the garden with the dogs.

Esben was pacing up and down. 'I've told you everything already,' he protested.

'No, you haven't. You refuse to involve the police because you want to protect Aziz. Fair enough, but I don't believe that's the whole story. What are you afraid of?'

'Public association with bad people.'

'Who?'

'What about the recordings I just showed you? What do you think happened to Aziz?'

'Don't change the subject,' said Jensen. 'And will you bloody sit down? You're driving me mad.'

Esben sat down next to her. He sighed deeply and rubbed

his face with both hands as if trying to scrub himself clean. She could see the fear in his eyes.

'Remember that I don't know whether what I'm about to tell you has anything to do with what happened to Aziz,' he said.

'Got a better theory?'

'No,' Esben admitted. 'OK. Years ago, before I got into politics—'

'After we met in Aalborg?'

'Some months after that, someone offered to introduce me to a few people. I didn't think anything of it. Especially not after I won my seat in parliament later that year. Networking has always been part of politics.'

'You scratch my back, I scratch yours?'

'You make it sound dirty.'

'Isn't it?' said Jensen.

'Not in my case. I was simply introduced to a few influential people who helped to boost my profile in the party. Couldn't see the harm. Except . . .'

'Except?

'The people in question seem to have a different version of events. They appear to be under the impression that I owe them a favour.'

'They told you that?'

'Not in as many words. They first got in touch a couple of months ago. In the beginning the emails were quite benign, friendly even. They were asking me for introductions.'

'To?'

'All sorts of people. The mayor of Aalborg, the chair of the planning committee, the prime minister. The three of them are personal friends, having studied political science together in Aarhus many years ago.'

'And did you do as they asked?'

'No.'

'Why not?'

'Because I didn't agree with their intent. There were some plans on the table for a big golf resort in North Jutland. Hundreds of jobs, luxury holiday homes, the works.'

'What's wrong with that?'

'It was in an area of outstanding natural beauty. Besides, we're not talking about nice people here. The money would be of dubious provenance to say the least.'

'You still haven't told me who *they* are.'

'It's complicated. Companies within companies within companies. I haven't got to the bottom of it yet.'

'But you know they're bad people.'

'They threatened me and my family. They trolled me, and now Aziz is missing. I have been trying to tell myself that there could be another explanation, but now I think they came here that morning to look for stuff they could use to blackmail me with. Only Aziz got in the way. They must have known I'd gone to Brussels and probably thought the house would be empty. To be completely honest, I only arranged the trip to try and get away from the threats for a bit, cool the whole situation down.'

'Did you tell Aziz about the threats?' said Jensen.

'No. He would only have got worked up about it. I can see now that I ought to have done, so he would at least have stood a decent chance.'

'You think Aziz was kidnapped?'

'I fear it's far worse than that.'

'Killed?'

Esben nodded miserably, looking down at his feet.

'But Gustav and I spoke to someone who claims to have seen Aziz in the street on Monday. I believe him. I think Aziz could still be alive.'

'Then you're more optimistic than I am. You saw what happened on the film. They did something to him, Jensen, and it's all my fault.'

There was a loud commotion and both Jensen and Esben turned to see Gustav running towards them, chased enthusiastically by the three tiny balls of fur who thought he was playing a game with them.

Gustav was holding up his phone, a serious look on his face. Jensen glimpsed a black-and-yellow 'Breaking News' headline.

'They found the head,' he shouted. 'We've got to get back. Come on!'

'What in God's name is the lad talking about?' Esben said.

'The body discovered by the police in the harbour by the opera house a few days ago. It was headless.'

Esben looked alarmed.

'And before you ask, it's definitely not Aziz,' said Jensen, getting up.

Klampenborg S-train station was less than ten minutes away from Esben's house. If she and Gustav were lucky, they could be back at the newspaper within the hour. 'Stay here,' she told Esben. 'I haven't finished with you yet.'

Jensen began to run for her bike, followed swiftly by Gustav.

'Wait,' Esben shouted after her. 'You said there were two things I had to do. What was the second?'

'You have to tell the police everything. If you won't, I will.'

28

'What do you mean, it's not the same man?' said Henrik, staring at David in disbelief.

Between them on the stainless-steel table was a severed head placed next to the corpse they had pulled from the harbour. The head had been found by Lisbeth's colleagues in a dustbin during a raid on some business premises. It had been wrapped in clear plastic. The owner of the firm had denied all knowledge of it, as had his staff. It was the sort of business where people came and went in lorries all day long, and the bin had been in an area easily accessible by a determined intruder.

'I mean the cuts don't match,' said David, pointing to the body parts.

'Look,' he said, with his usual patience. 'Both cuts are made with an axe, but the angles are completely different. Besides, it's obvious this head belongs to a much smaller man.'

Henrik looked at it. Amira had said that Aziz had a

teardrop birthmark on his cheek; the head in front of him did not. The unknown man had brown hair and pierced ears but no earrings, perhaps a fad that he had left behind along with his youth. He reminded Henrik of the pig heads on display in the butcher's window when he was a boy.

'The DNA will give you further proof, of course, but I can say categorically, that this isn't the head you're looking for.'

'Whose is it then?' said Henrik.

David shrugged. 'As I said, the DNA should tell you more, but for now we don't have a lot to go on, except that the head is from an adult white male, black hair and brown eyes.'

'How did he die?'

'I'll tell you when you bring me the rest of him,' said David.

'In other words, we've got fuck all,' said Henrik.

'For now, yes,' said David. He covered the body, removed his Latex gloves and crossed the floor to the sink where he began to wash his hands.

'How come you're still working on this case?' said David. 'I thought you were going to Italy on holiday?'

'I was,' said Henrik.

'There must be someone who can take over from you?' said David, drying his hands.

'You sound like my wife.'

'And that's not a good thing?' David laughed.

Henrik forced a smile. He wasn't going to get into all that with David.

Not now.

'What about you?' he said. 'Off somewhere?'

'Monday,' David replied. 'My husband's family own a holiday home on Bornholm. Bucket and spade. Ice cream from the kiosk by the harbour. Friends stopping by for a few days here and there.'

Fuck, Henrik thought. He always dealt with David whenever he needed something at the Forensic Institute. David understood him, gave him the benefit of the doubt, was quiet when he needed to be. 'Nice for you,' he forced himself to say.

They shook hands and Henrik headed for the door with a grunted 'Thanks'.

'Wait,' shouted David. 'How's that journalist friend of yours?'

'Who?' said Henrik, but he wasn't fooling the pathologist, who merely smiled at him by way of reply. 'I assume she's fine. I haven't heard from her in a while,' he said, as casually as he could.

'It's just . . . back in the spring she was asking me all these questions about whether it's possible to fake a suicide,' said David. 'She was referring to a specific case. Guy called Carsten Vangede who killed himself in January this year. I looked up the notes and told her that in my opinion a faked suicide couldn't be ruled out. But since then, I haven't heard from her. I guess I'm curious. Do you know if she got anywhere with it?'

Henrik remembered Jensen mentioning the case to him. She was convinced Vangede wouldn't have killed himself. He also remembered shutting the conversation down. 'Haven't got a clue, mate,' he said.

'Oh well,' said David, smiling. 'Maybe she's forgotten.'

Henrik thought about it as he climbed the stairs to the exit. The very idea of Jensen forgetting was preposterous. When she first got a notion into her head, there was no way she would let it go voluntarily.

Fuck, Jensen, couldn't you just have left it?

He would have to speak to her. It was no distance at all from the Forensic Institute to the Almasis' in Nørrebro.

As he got into his car, his phone pinged with a text. Jens Wiese, his boss.

Meeting in 30 mins. Monsen's office.

29

'Knock, knock,' said Jensen, approaching Margrethe's desk, which was piled high with books and papers.

'Ah, our star reporter,' said Margrethe, squinting at Jensen through her thick lenses. 'Come in.'

Jensen took the seat that was normally reserved for roastings when Margrethe was angry about something, but nothing of that sort appeared to be on the way.

'Fantastic piece you wrote on that young stabbing victim.'

'Nice of you to say so, but he is still dead,' said Jensen. 'And it will happen again.'

'True,' said Margrethe. 'But by showing the humanity of victims, the tragic scale of their loss, you have perhaps just made it that bit less likely that we'll see a repeat.'

'I don't think many teenage boys read *Dagbladet*,' said Jensen.

'No, but they might watch television. TV1 has just told me they're doing a documentary after reading your piece.'

Jensen looked at her boss. Something had changed. What was it? Margrethe had a new haircut, shorter, which suited her, and her blue dress was new, but it wasn't that.

Margrethe was happy, as impossible as it seemed. 'We have turned a corner,' she beamed at Jensen. 'This week alone we added five hundred and thirty-three new sub-scribers. The viewing figures for our videos are through the roof, including your interview with that boat owner in Christianshavn.'

'You've changed,' said Jensen. 'I thought you felt all that digital candy floss was a distraction from the real news?'

'Well let's just say that the scales have fallen from my eyes. Finally, the newspaper has a future. But what we need now is something altogether more analogue. An old-fashioned scoop. Something to shake the very foundations of the establishment.'

Jensen laughed. 'Oh, is that all? You should have said. I'll have that with you by five o'clock.'

She decided not to mention Aziz, knowing that Margrethe would ask her to write the story immediately. 'There's the body they found in the harbour. I know the lead investigator. Could turn into a big story,' she said.

'There you go,' said Margrethe.

Jensen laughed.

And stopped laughing.

'I'm serious,' said Margrethe. 'I'm counting on you. You may be the last person left in this place who's able to do it.'

30

When Henrik stepped into the office of Chief Superintendent Mogens Hansen, better known as Monsen, at almost the appointed hour, Lisbeth and her boss Biggie had the look of naughty pupils who had just been given a telling-off by the headmaster. Wiese had his back to the window and was hovering by Monsen's shoulder to make it clear whose side he was on. As if there was ever any doubt. Everyone at the station knew that Wiese coveted Monsen's job and considered himself the crown prince of the outfit. Henrik hoped to God some knight in shining armour would turn up before Wiese got anointed. Wiese's campaign of sucking up to the top brass made him want to vomit.

Monsen looked livid at having had to come in on a Saturday. He was in home clothes: beige chinos and a red polo shirt which stretched dangerously over his gut. 'Jungersen, you're late,' he scowled.

'Sorry,' said Henrik leaning his behind on a low

bookshelf, his arms folded across his chest. 'It's the heat wave. Traffic's fucked all over the city.'

Lisbeth sent him an unhappy glance, cheeks flushed. He winked at her.

'Seen the news?' said Monsen.

Henrik hadn't. Apart from the football coverage, which he followed religiously as a die-hard Brøndby FC fan, he usually did his best to avoid the news. Whatever they wrote about criminal investigations was pure garbage, he knew that for a fact, and what did that say for the rest? The news couldn't be trusted. The only exception he made was for Jensen. Over the years, her articles had become a means of staying close to her.

She had just written a piece on a young boy who had been stabbed to death on a night out with his friends, somehow managing to maintain a sense of objectivity in her words, which had made them all the more powerful.

Her coverage of the harbour murder had been sober so far, though it was clear that she had absolutely nothing to go on and was treading water by interviewing witnesses who were as clueless as she was.

Oh no.

He went cold all over.

Had he inadvertently given her a clue about the case that had now ended up on the front page of *Dagbladet*? Was that what this awkward gathering in Monsen's office was all about? 'Which particular news are we talking about?' he said warily.

'Then you haven't,' said Monsen. 'Lisbeth, why don't you enlighten Jungersen?'

Lisbeth looked down. Her new engagement ring sparkled on her left hand, a source of joy now all but forgotten. Henrik felt sorry for her, wondering if she was regretting her career move.

She cleared her throat. 'The head we found?'

'Yes,' said Henrik hesitantly.

He didn't like where this was going.

'Well, we intended to keep it under wraps, so to speak,' Lisbeth said.

'I'll take this,' said Biggie, placing one hand on Lisbeth's arm.

A skinny, freckled redhead, Biggie was a hoot, as well as a great cop, and had done well as head of the organised crime unit. Henrik was happy to see that she was protective of Lisbeth. Team members covering for each other, the way it should be.

Monsen was the same. No matter what was said inside the four walls of his office, he could be relied upon to take the flak from the Commissioner if anyone in his unit came under attack.

Obviously, Wiese hadn't read that particular memo.

'As Lisbeth said, we wanted to keep it quiet. Partly to give you guys some time to sort yourselves out, and partly to not screw up our own operation, which is at a delicate stage.'

'Don't tell me,' said Henrik. 'Someone talked to the press.'

'Got it in one. Probably one of the staff. Despite our severe warnings. A severed head in a bin ... I suppose that was too exciting a secret to keep.'

'Another fucking cock-up. Can't this department get anything right?' said Monsen.

He was being unfair. A press leak was virtually par for the course these days. Everyone had a phone, which made them a broadcaster to the world. Not that the leak was going to help their investigation, but that was beside the point. The real issue, as Henrik knew to his cost, was that Monsen, at his advanced stage of life, wanted things tidy: the kind of detective work that allowed you to be home for dinner at six every night.

The kind that didn't exist.

'Fucking vultures are ringing the phone off the hook now. We're going to have to call a press conference, set things straight. And Jungersen, I want *you* to take it.'

What?

'But I don't do them any more. Not after . . . Wiese takes them now. Or I suppose Biggie may as well.'

He knew that the four people in the room were aware that he was referring to the incident, more than a year ago now, when he had lost his rag and called a female reporter a cow on live TV. Either Monsen had forgotten, or he reckoned enough time had passed for the world to forgive and forget.

'Monsen, I don't think—,' Wiese began.

'Shut up,' said Monsen. 'Jungersen's case, Jungersen's press conference. At least we've now got a more or less complete corpse, so we should be able to identify the poor fellow very soon, am I right?'

Henrik squirmed.

This was going to be awkward.

'There's just one thing,' he said, looking at his boots. They looked rough on Monsen's posh carpet.

'Spit it out,' said Monsen.

'The head. It doesn't belong to our man in the harbour. DNA isn't in yet, but Forensics are positive that the head isn't his.'

After a few seconds' silence, Henrik looked up to find Wiese, Biggie and Lisbeth staring at him open-mouthed.

Monsen was holding the palm of one hand to his forehead, as if checking if he had a fever. 'Excuse me, what did you say?'

'I'm saying that it seems we have two different victims whose deaths may or may not be connected, though if they're not, it would, to put it mildly, be an unbelievable coincidence.'

'Two beheaded men, not one?' said Monsen.

'Posthumously beheaded, yes. We don't know yet how either victim died.'

'Why behead someone who is already dead?'

'To make it harder for us to identify them. To fuck us up. I'd say they've pretty much hit the bullseye. We have a lead, though. We think that a car set alight on Refshaleøen around the time of the murders may have been hired by one of the victims.'

'Oh?'

'Only a theory so far, but a promising one,' said Henrik.

He decided not to tell Monsen about the blood in the summerhouse until it had been analysed. He knew that the link between that and the body in the harbour was tenuous at best.

'Theory, my arse. This whole case is a total farce,' said Monsen. 'Headless corpse in the harbour, head in a bin. No fucking clue. We'll be a laughing stock. Again.'

'Which is why we can't have a press conference, not yet,' urged Henrik.

'Henrik is right,' said Biggie.

Monsen took his time to respond. 'Very well,' he said, finally. 'We'll delay the briefing for twenty-four hours. And meanwhile, you find those missing body parts if it's the last thing you do. Now set to it, before I change my mind.'

On his way out of Monsen's office, Henrik had a call on his mobile from reception.

'There's something for you down here.'

'What?'

'Best come and see for yourself.'

He spotted the large cardboard box as soon as he stepped into the foyer. It was dwarfing the receptionist who was trying his best to hide a grin. 'From your wife,' he said.

Henrik flipped open the box and was greeted by a rank smell of cheese and tomato sauce. Inside were the dishes from Friday night's dinner. The ones he had promised his wife he'd do.

Before Jensen had distracted him.

Shit.

31

Saturday 17:03

Jensen stood side by side with Esben and his three white dogs, like a welcome party at a country estate, and watched Henrik roll up the gravel drive in his black car. She had insisted on him coming, brushing aside his excuses about being too busy. 'It's important. You can spare me one hour,' she had told him.

On his part, Esben had shown no great desire to meet Henrik, appalled as he was at Henrik's treatment of her over the years. However, he had finally accepted that they needed Henrik's help and insider access if they were to make any headway in their search for Aziz. 'Henrik is the only option we've got. And he owes me big time,' she had said.

Henrik looked tense and in a bad mood when he stepped out of the car in his black jeans and white shirt, shades resting on top of his sunburned head.

The white dogs greeted him excitedly but snuck off when he didn't pay them any attention, unusually for him, the self-proclaimed great lover of man's best friend. Jensen knew that it was his fascination with police dogs that had first made him join the force. 'It was either that or a life of crime,' he had always told her, seemingly only half joking. He had wanted to be a dog handler but finding out, to his surprise, that he was good at solving murders had sent him down a different path.

'I've heard so much about you,' said Esben, unsmilingly, as the two men shook hands, sizing each other up.

'Likewise,' said Henrik. He looked around, taking in the house, the garage, the lush garden and the pretty windows through which Ulla's artworks, and her impeccable taste in furnishings, were on display. 'Nice gaff,' he said. 'I didn't know being a member of parliament paid so well.'

'It doesn't,' said Esben, offering no further explanation, including the inherited fortune of his wife.

The two men glared at each other.

'Oh, for Christ's sake grow up,' said Jensen, clapping her hands loudly in their faces. 'Can I just remind you both that we're here because a man has been missing for almost two weeks and could be in grave danger?'

'I can't stay for long,' said Henrik.

'What a shame,' said Esben under his breath. He led the three of them around the house to the chlorophyll-green lawn and garden furniture with cream cushions arranged under a giant parasol. His laptop was open on the table.

'Now, Esben, I want you to tell Henrik everything you told me. From the beginning,' said Jensen when they had sat down.

'Must I? I'm not sure it's—'

'Esben, if those bad people don't kill you, then I swear I will,' she said.

'What bad people?' said Henrik, suddenly alert.

149

Esben rubbed his face and glanced up at the house as if considering making a run for it.

Jensen spoke for him. 'Esben received some threatening emails.'

'It was nothing,' said Esben. 'Just the usual crap you get in my position.'

'Oh, and what's that?'

'Death threats, that sort of thing.'

'Who from?'

'Anonymous,' Esben shrugged. 'We can all be brave behind a screen.'

'You don't seem too worried about it,' said Henrik.

'That's because I'm not.'

Henrik turned to Jensen, frowning. 'So why are we here talking about emails?'

'Because there was a particular batch of them just before Aziz disappeared,' said Jensen. 'Esben suspected they might be related to an attempt to blackmail him into seeking favours with the prime minister.'

'And?'

'He now thinks this might have something to do with Aziz's disappearance.'

Esben turned his laptop so the screen was facing Henrik and pressed play. Henrik watched attentively as Aziz was floored and the screen went black.

'That was recorded the morning he disappeared,' said Jensen. 'He never came home.'

'Well, what do you think?' said Esben.

'I think I'm looking at a crime being committed,' said Henrik, removing his shades from the top of his head with a theatrical flourish. 'You should have reported it immediately.'

'I didn't know about the recording till yesterday. I had

150

no reason to believe that Aziz would come back here after dropping me at the airport.'

'Why did he?'

'The recording seems to suggest that he was working on my car.'

'Why?'

'How should I know?'

Jensen put a hand on Esben's arm and turned to Henrik. 'Esben is trying to protect Aziz.'

'Oh yeah? And how is that working out for you?' said Henrik.

Esben, normally a picture of calm, was turning bright red, his hands bunched into fists.

'Esben is worried about Aziz's status as a Syrian refugee. He's always wanted to keep a low profile in Denmark. You saw how reticent Amira was to tell you anything at all.'

'The last thing we want is a big fuss,' Esben spat.

'No, I can imagine that wouldn't be good for your image,' said Henrik.

'It's got nothing to do with me.'

'That's not the impression you gave me a moment ago. Let's talk about your emails again, shall we? Who are the people putting pressure on you?'

'I don't know exactly.'

'Oh, I think you do.'

'There are loads of different companies, go-betweens, representatives.'

'Who?'

'I think it's . . . at the heart of things . . . it might be some-one called Leif Kofoed.'

'What?' said Henrik.

Jensen turned to Esben. 'Why didn't you tell *me*?'

Henrik was frowning to himself. 'I'd heard the old man popped his clogs, somewhere in South America.'

'Well, in that case he has a doppelganger,' said Esben.

'Wait, you know him?' Jensen turned to Henrik, astonished. The name meant nothing to her.

'Yes, I know him. Or let's say he's known to the police. Also known as Mogens Mogensen or Hans Hansen or Niels Nielsen. I could go on.'

'Who is he?' said Jensen.

'No one good. He's a conman, a parasite. Whenever something bad is happening, something really bad, Kofoed is never far away.'

'Is he wanted for something?'

'You could say that, but we can never make anything stick. Not since he ended up in prison as a juvenile. It hardened him, taught him how to evade justice, how to hide while others do his dirty work,' said Henrik. He had recovered from his surprise and was smirking at Esben. 'So, you're mixed up with Leif Kofoed, are you? I can see why you wouldn't want *that* to become public knowledge.'

'In no way am I mixed up with him, but he may be under the false impression that I owe him a favour.'

'And do you?'

'Not as such, only ... about fifteen years ago when I began my career, he introduced me to a few people.'

'Who?'

'Leif Kofoed is well connected. He's never happier than when he's able to do someone a favour. It was all quite innocent I can assure you.'

'Except now he wants you to reciprocate.'

'You could put it that way.'

'What does he want?'

'To go legit. He wants to build a golf resort in North

Jutland, by the coast. He's getting old. Wants to move back to Denmark, entertain the great and the good, royalty, aristocracy. He's got the cash. All he needs is something as mundane as planning permission.'

'Wait, Leif Kofoed is in Denmark right now?' said Henrik, leaning forward in his seat.

'I don't know where he's staying or where he lives. It's not as if he hands out business cards.'

Henrik went silent for a moment. 'I need those emails you mentioned. If we can establish a link to Leif Kofoed that way, we can . . .'

'You can't,' said Esben. 'I deleted them and, even if I hadn't, you couldn't possibly pin them on him. He wouldn't make an error like that. I don't even know for sure if there is a link, it's just a hunch.'

'Did Kofoed call you, or email you?'

'Never. He's not stupid.'

'So how did he put pressure on you?'

'It wasn't an outright thing. Kofoed is always impeccably mannered. He did what he used to do all those years ago and just appeared out of nowhere. I was out walking the dogs in Dyrehaven, and suddenly he was there, standing on the path in front of me, smiling.'

'What did he say?' said Jensen.

'He asked me how I was, asked about my wife, my children. Then he told me about his plans and asked me if I'd get him a meeting with the prime minister to plead his cause.'

'And?'

'I said no. I said the local authorities, the community, would never agree to his scheme anyway.'

'What did he say to that?' said Jensen.

'OK.'

'That's it? OK?'

'Pretty much. He tried to persuade me. Talked about all the jobs the scheme would create and what a boost it would be to the local tourism economy. We exchanged a few more pleasantries, and then he walked to this chauffeur-driven car, got into the back and left.'

'And the threatening emails are connected to him how?' said Henrik.

'Started coming a few days later.'

Henrik pointed to Esben's laptop. 'I'll take that,' he said.

'I *said* I deleted the emails.'

'Nothing is ever fully deleted.'

'No,' said Esben, slamming the lid shut. 'I refuse.'

'Something to hide?' said Henrik.

'I'm not accused of anything, you're not conducting a formal investigation, and I've a right to privacy same as anyone else,' said Esben.

'Actually, I *am* investigating. I've no choice now that you've shown me what's happened. And if you want to help your friend Aziz, I suggest you hand that laptop over.'

Esben clasped the laptop to his chest. 'No.'

'For God's sake, how old are you two?' said Jensen. She wrenched the laptop from Esben's hands. 'I'll take this, find out who sent those emails. What else are you going to do about this, Henrik?'

'I'll put some people on the case. We need to get forensics to take a look.' He turned to Esben. 'And *you* need to find somewhere else to stay. You're not safe here.'

'I'm fine, thank you.'

'No, you're not. I noticed someone in a car staking out your property when I arrived. They drove off when I approached. I got the number plate, a fake.'

'Why didn't you say?'

'I'm telling you now.'

'I'll go and stay at D'Angleterre.'

'In full view of everybody? Do you think that's wise?' said Jensen.

Esben shrugged. 'In a luxury hotel in the middle of Copenhagen with loads of people around, what could possibly happen?'

32

'Don't rush off, give a man a chance,' said Henrik, watching Jensen as she strapped on her bike helmet for the ride back to Copenhagen.

They were surrounded by tall hedges, from behind which came the sounds of affluence: ride-on lawnmowers, sprinklers, a slow game of tennis.

They had left Esben Nørregaard to his packing. The insufferable arse had refused a lift to town in Henrik's car, insisting on calling a taxi.

'You were a total prick in there,' Jensen said, her face red, her eyes sparkling with fury. 'I should never have called you. Esben is my friend.'

'I'm sure that's what he tells you. Sadly, the man has a reputation with women.'

'See? I can't talk to you,' said Jensen, preparing to get on the bike.

Her legs were deeply tanned under her short white dress,

her hair tied in a ponytail. He wanted to free it from the elastic band, run his hand through it.

Things he had no right to do.

'Wait,' he said. 'I promise I will be discreet, but that CCTV footage of Aziz being attacked is not something I can ignore.'

'So now we're getting the formal police investigation that Esben expressly didn't want,' said Jensen.

'Have you asked yourself *why* he doesn't want it?'

'Because like me he's anxious not to put Aziz in any more danger than he already is. *If* he is still alive.'

'And that's the only reason? I don't trust the man. I bet there's a lot more to this story than he's letting on, the smarmy git.'

'OK, I'm going,' said Jensen.

'Hold on,' said Henrik, grabbing the handlebars of her bike. 'Jensen, I'll help you, and I'll keep the enquiries under the radar, but please promise me that you won't go back to that flat in Nørrebro. I don't like you being there. Whoever's after Aziz, they're not your nice, friendly uncles.'

'Oh, don't worry, I'll be sleeping at Kristoffer's from now on. I'll be safe with him; his apartment block is virtually a fortress. Now would you take your hands off my bike?'

Something brittle and sharp snapped inside him. The thought of Kristoffer Bro's grubby mitts all over Jensen was intolerable. He couldn't hold it in. 'Have you asked him yet? About his past?'

Jensen freed herself from his grasp and began to cycle away.

'Did he tell you how his father died?' he shouted, desperate to stop her.

It worked. Jensen's bike came to a standstill, her thin shoulders dropping in a way that moved him profoundly.

He had made a misjudgement. He shouldn't have brought up what he knew, not like this, in the street, with her being so angry.

When she turned, she was staring at him with a look of disappointment. 'Wow. You really are something.'

'Ask him. Ask him what happened to his father.'

'You're pathetic, Henrik,' she said, in a low sad voice. 'And now I'd be grateful if you'd butt out of my private life. Perhaps you should concentrate on your own for once.'

She began to pedal away furiously. 'No,' he shouted. 'Jensen, it's not what you think.'

But this time she didn't stop. 'Fuck,' he said, slamming his hand hard on the roof of his car. It was burning hot, scalding his palm. 'Fuck.'

An elderly woman on a mobility scooter with a front basket laden with artificial flowers rolled around the corner, staring at him angrily.

'What?' Henrik shouted at her, got in his car and drove off in the direction of Copenhagen, tyres screeching.

33

'Doughnut?' Mark tipped the box of fat, chocolate-coated wheels under Henrik's nose.

He had to summon all his strength not to grab one and take a giant bite out of it. 'I don't know how you can eat that rubbish and not gain weight,' he said.

'My mother says I have hollow legs,' Mark laughed.

Henrik didn't join in the mirth. His own mother had said the same thing to him before she died. He had been like Mark until he turned forty, but keeping his weight down was now a daily battle and even his punishing fitness routine was no guarantee of victory. His legs were still weak and trembling after his hour on the spinning bike that morning, and the small tub of yogurt and granola that he had picked up from Ole & Steen along with his coffee on the way to the office had left him starving. 'Take them away,' he said, gesturing at the doughnuts. 'They're making me sick.'

At least the air conditioning had been fixed and the room

was pleasantly cool. It was almost enough to make you long to spend time in the office.

Not that Henrik needed persuading. He had wanted to be anywhere but home this morning, with his wife still giving him a hard time for not joining her on the drive to Italy.

On his insistence Mark had agreed to come to work for a few hours before he left for his summer holiday. He was bouncing with nervous energy, rambling on about packing and the price of nappies and whether he could fit his inflatable canoe in the back of the family car.

Henrik had never gone anywhere near the holiday packing for his own family, at most chucking his own stuff in a bag at the last minute and sometimes not even managing that.

Wiese had tried to talk him into going on his family holiday as planned, which would mean handing the case to another lead investigator, but Henrik had stood his ground. 'I think we're onto something big,' he had said.

There was also the delicate matter of Aziz, which he needed to handle personally. He couldn't break his promise of discretion to Jensen, even if she *did* hate his guts right now.

('Oh yeah? You're keeping promises to people now?' said his wife in his head.)

'Who is that?' said Mark, pointing to a photograph of Aziz that Henrik had been given by the Syrian's wife.

'Oh, just someone I'm looking into. Nothing to do with our case,' said Henrik, shoving the photo under some papers. 'Is there anything back from forensics yet on our second victim?'

'Not yet,' said Mark, wiping chocolate from the corner of his mouth and licking his fingers. 'We're speaking to an expert to determine where the headless corpse might have drifted from, given the prevailing currents.'

Henrik nodded.

'Where do you think they are?' said Mark. 'The missing body parts?'

'No idea, but I intend to find them,' said Henrik, getting up and grabbing his leather jacket before remembering that it was blisteringly hot outside and leaving it on the back of his chair.

'Where are you going?' said Mark, wide-eyed.

He had picked up another doughnut, his third, and was about to take a large bite. Henrik felt himself salivate. 'I've got an appointment with Lisbeth at the business premises where the head turned up. You could come along. Unless you'd rather stay here and work on your diabetes?'

Mark dropped the doughnut back in the box and got to his feet, wiping his mouth on his sleeve. 'You sure?' said Henrik. 'You don't need to go back home or anything? Iron your wife's knickers?'

Mark was silent the length of the corridor. Henrik didn't come to his aid. He knew he was being unfair by suggesting that Mark was slacking by going on holiday, but he couldn't help it. What was he going to do without him?

'I promised my wife,' Mark said when they reached Henrik's car. 'I have a right to take—'

'Yes, yes, I know all that,' said Henrik, starting the engine and reversing out of the parking space. 'Leave entitlement, the rules, the nice way things ought to be. But this isn't an ordinary job, Mark. There is everyone else and then there is us.' He had gone too far but there was a nugget of truth in it.

Mark said nothing on the rest of the journey.

34

Jensen was woken by the sound of Kristoffer's expensive coffee maker grinding the beans for his morning espresso. She reached out with her eyes closed and patted the empty space on the sheet next to her. It was still warm.

Slowly, she blinked her eyes open. The sunlight was already bright on the edge of the blinds.

She would never get used to the size of Kristoffer's place. The ceiling several metres above her, the oversized lamps and hotel-lobby interior design. The two of them were forever roaming the vast spaces searching for each other.

'Kristoffer?'

There was no reply. She set her feet on the floor and reached out for the nearest piece of clothing: a light blue shirt of Kristoffer's. It looked like a dress on her in the big mirror beside the bed. She padded out to the kitchen, smelling coffee. The room was flooded with light, sparkling on the gleaming surfaces of Kristoffer's ovens, wine fridges and gold taps.

'Good morning,' he said, putting his phone away. He was already dressed in shorts and a linen shirt, his hair wet from the shower. 'I didn't want to wake you,' he said. He folded her in his arms, reaching up under the shirt.

'I'm glad you're home,' he said, kissing her neck. 'Coffee?'

'Yes please.' He handed her a tiny white cup and she buried her nose in it, reflecting on the fact that for all the thousands of kroner Kristoffer's espresso maker must have cost, the coffee still wasn't as good as Liron's.

'I'm sorry if I was a bit . . . off with you on Friday,' he said.

'You were,' she said, snuggling up to his scented body.

'It's just . . . something going on at work. I guess I was stressed and took it out on you. I shouldn't have done that. Friends again?'

'Friends,' she said, feeling a wave of affection for him. Henrik's clumsy attempt to warn her off was having the opposite effect: it had made her realise just how little she knew about Kristoffer and what he had been through, losing his parents when he was young. 'I'm sorry I've been pushing you to talk about your past. Occupational hazard, I guess. Like I said, I'm professionally nosy.'

'It's OK,' said Kristoffer, looking down at her intensely. 'Did I tell you that you have astonishingly blue eyes?'

'Only about a million times,' said Jensen, laughing.

'Look, my past is complicated, and quite sad,' said Kristoffer. 'I find it difficult to talk about, even after many years of therapy.'

'I'm a good listener,' said Jensen. 'Would you tell me?'

Kristoffer looked at her as if deciding whether he could trust her. She met his gaze, encouraging him.

'Maybe some other time, but not now. I must work,' he said.

'On a Sunday morning?'

163

'I told you. Entrepreneurs don't keep regular hours.' He kissed the top of her head. 'We will talk, I promise. Soon.'

The door phone rang. They both stared at it. Jensen couldn't remember a single instance when it had rung before. No one ever came to the penthouse, aside from the cleaners, but they never worked on the weekend. 'Who is that?' she said.

'I'm not expecting anyone,' said Kristoffer, frowning.

He pressed a button, and the voice of the concierge came through the speaker. 'I've got a teenage boy down here, insisting on coming up. Shall I tell him to get lost?'

'I don't know any teenage boys.'

'He's rather persistent,' said the concierge. 'Says his name is Gustav?'

35

Sunday 09:58

Lisbeth was waiting by the loading bay of Copenhagen Food Distribution, checking her watch as Henrik and Mark parked up. She was in shorts and trainers and a sleeveless top, ready for the trip to the beach that she had allegedly been promising her fiancée Josefine for weeks. 'You've got me for fifteen minutes, then I'm out of here, or she'll cancel the wedding,' she told them, smiling in a way that wasn't altogether convincing.

Behind her a uniformed police officer was guarding the entrance, which had been taped off. The yard was hot as hell and dusty. Even the weeds were dying, lying limp and brown where they had emerged through cracks in the tarmac.

Henrik doubted the company would ever reopen. A severed head in a bin wasn't exactly great advertising for a food business.

The owner was still in custody, although, according to Lisbeth, he was denying all knowledge of the macabre find and had no idea why the head had turned up on his premises. 'My instinct says he is telling the truth,' said Lisbeth, sighing deeply.

'What prompted the raid?' said Henrik.

'We had a tip-off that the company was a cover for a major drugs operation.'

'Who said so?'

'Anonymous. But the things they said ... it was clear they knew stuff.'

'So, you decided to raid the place and then what?'

'No drugs in evidence, but of course we conducted a thorough search, and that's when we found the head.'

Henrik nodded to himself. Whoever had tipped off Lisbeth's unit had obviously known about the head and wanted the police to find it.

Why?

Who?

Where was the other head?

It made no sense.

The uniformed officer held up the police tape for them as they entered the warehouse. It was cool and dark with a vaguely noxious smell. Lisbeth led them through what looked like a temporary storage area to a dingy corner with two large wheelie bins, one red, one blue.

'It was in there,' she said, pointing to the red one. 'Apparently, this is where the food waste is kept.'

'What happens to it?'

'It gets taken away and destroyed.'

'When?'

'Wednesdays and Saturdays.'

'So, the head would have been placed in the bin sometime between the collection on Wednesday and yesterday morning.'

'No. Apparently, the collection on Wednesday didn't happen. It could have been any time in the past eight days.'

Mark went over to the second wheelie bin and opened the lid, stepping back at the rank smell. 'What's this one for?'

'General waste. Apparently, that one *was* emptied as planned last week. On Thursday.'

Mark looked at Henrik as if expecting him to explain how everything fitted together. He shrugged.

No idea, mate.

He had already checked twenty times, but still there was no reply from Jensen to his apologetic text messages.

Nor was there anything from his wife, though she must have noticed the row of clean dishes he had left on the kitchen counter by now.

He had headed to work before she got up, giving her a chance to calm down before they spoke again.

'Any CCTV?' he asked Lisbeth.

'Not in here,' said Lisbeth. 'There's a camera in the loading bay. We're looking through the recordings, but to be honest I'm not holding out much hope. Only ten people work here permanently but loads of lorry drivers come and go through the day. Technically, only the staff have access to the inside areas, but there's a toilet back here and the drivers often ask to use it. They're not meant to, but apparently it happens all the time.'

A dingy room. Ten seconds alone to throw a plastic bag in the bin.

'And the staff?'

'We're checking, but so far nothing,' said Lisbeth.

'It would have to be someone who knew this place, including the location of the bins,' he said. 'How long has the business been running?'

'Twelve years.'

'We'll need a list of all past and present staff members,' said Henrik.

'And any lorry drivers who come here regularly,' Mark chipped in.

Lisbeth nodded. 'We should be getting that tomorrow. I'll share it with you as soon as it comes in. And now I really must go, or Josefine will blow her top.'

'I bet the owner is lying,' said Mark when they were back in the car with the air conditioning on, watching Lisbeth get into her own car and drive off. Mark seemed to have got over his sulkiness from before. In this respect he was different to Lisbeth, who could hold a grudge for days. 'He must know something. This can't just have been a coincidence,' he said.

'I'm sure it wasn't,' said Henrik. However, the chances were now extremely slim that anything useful would turn up in the investigation before Monsen's press conference, which was the only thing that mattered now.

'It's a mess, boss.'

'Yep.'

'What are we going to do?'

They sat for a while, each with their own thoughts.

'Look,' said Mark. 'If you want me to cancel my leave and stay here and work, I can. I'm sure my wife would understand.'

'No,' said Henrik. 'Absolutely not. You're a good father and husband, Mark. It was wrong of me to suggest you should drop your family holiday.'

'But that's what *you're* doing, isn't it?'

Yeah, because I want to stay in Copenhagen and keep an eye on Jensen, thought Henrik. 'Ah, you know me,' he said. 'I'd do anything to get out of spending time with my wife and kids.'

'Really?'

'No, not really,' Henrik lied. It was too horrific a truth to admit to, even to himself. 'It's just a delay. I'll be on the road to Italy soon enough. I was only concerned to think who'll replace you on the case meanwhile. Wiese says he has someone in mind, which rather scares me.'

Mark laughed. 'I'm sure that whoever it is, they can't be that bad.'

36

Sunday 10:49

The brunch crowd was out in force at the Christianshavn café that Jensen and Gustav had come to regard as their personal living room. Couples, groups of friends, families with prams and toddlers were crowding inside the three small red-painted rooms, talking, laughing and eating from plates laden with avocado toast and poached eggs. Through the open windows came the smell of warm canal water and cigarette smoke.

Life went on.

As if nothing had happened.

Gustav went immediately to the back of the café where Jensen found him scowling angrily at a couple who had dared occupy their regular table, a cool and dingy booth that was perfect for private conversations. 'How long are you going to be?' he asked them.

'It's OK, Gustav, we'll find somewhere else,' Jensen said, pulling at his arm, before the couple at the table got the chance to tell them to get lost. 'Other people have a right to come here too.'

'That table's ours,' said Gustav. 'I scratched my initials on the seat.'

Jensen laughed. 'Don't let the owner hear you say that.'

She had offered to buy him brunch as a means of making up for Kristoffer's frosty reception at the penthouse. He had left without even saying hello to Gustav, mumbling something about a meeting.

'Man, he was rude,' Gustav said. 'Always seems so nice on TV.'

'Not rude. Preoccupied. He has a demanding job and a lot on his mind.'

'He was annoyed about me turning up.'

'Surprised. How did you ever manage to find it?'

'You are kidding, aren't you?' said Gustav. 'That place has been in all the glossy magazines. Everyone in Copenhagen knows where Kristoffer Bro lives.'

'But how did you know I'd be there?'

'If you think your new boyfriend is a secret, I've got news for you. The word's gone all round *Dagbladet*.'

Jensen remembered that Markus, the newspaper receptionist, had seen her with Kristoffer. Markus who couldn't keep a secret if he was paid to.

They found two seats outside on a bench, balancing their smoothies on their knees while they waited for their food to arrive. Gustav kept getting up every five minutes to see if the couple were making a move to leave.

'Any news about Aziz?' he asked, sucking noisily on his straw, as he kept his eyes fixed on the entrance.

'None whatsoever.'

'Do you think he's dead?'

'No.'

'Me neither,' said Gustav. 'It's like, someone that big and strong can't just die. So, what shall we do?'

'I don't know,' she said, her eye caught by someone leaning against a doorway across the street. 'Do you see that man over there? Do you think he's watching us?'

'Who?' said Gustav, looking up just as a couple of buses passed. By the time they had gone, the doorway was empty.

'Never mind,' she said, shaking her head. 'I must be imagining things.'

Gustav took a long drag on his vape. 'What about the body in the harbour?'

'Still nothing, but given they've found the head, there has got to be news soon.'

'There's a press conference tomorrow morning, according to Twitter.'

Jensen nodded, wondering idly if Henrik would be there, or one of his colleagues. She didn't want to see him. It had been wrong of him to blurt out the stuff about Kristoffer's father like that, just because he was desperate to have her all to himself.

What did Henrik have against Kristoffer? If it was some police matter, then it was unethical for him to share it with her, surely. Whatever had happened to his family, Kristoffer would tell her in his own good time, in his own words.

He had been right about Google. The first search item that came up when you typed Kristoffer Bro was 'wife'. She imagined thousands of women, checking him out, wanting a bit of him.

Kristoffer was striking rather than good-looking: tall with a broad chest, the kind of guy who looked good in a suit. His appeal was in his eyes, the gaze that told of his sparkling intelligence, that he played to win. Though some women would need little persuading, knowing how rich and powerful he was.

She told herself that none of that mattered to her. As she

had got to know him, she had seen other sides to him: a certain vulnerability, as if he was worried his success might be snatched away from him at any moment. Perhaps that stemmed from the loss of his father, the thing in his past he was so reluctant to tell her about.

She had read everything she could find about Kristoffer online. There was nothing going back further than about fourteen years ago, when Kristoffer had started his company in his bedroom as a twenty-two-year-old, and no reference to his earlier life in any of the many articles written about him.

He had been interviewed repeatedly by the media, collecting gongs and showing up at red-carpet events. The women on his arm had changed frequently. In one year, she counted ten, all of them tall and beautiful.

He had never invited her along to anything. There had never been an article about the two of them in the magazines: 'Billionaire Kristoffer Bro spotted with mystery brunette'. Not that she wanted any of that, but she was undeniably the odd one out.

'Empty heads, the lot of them,' Kristoffer had told her. 'Not smart like you, Jensen.'

There were no social media accounts apart from a sanitised and inactive profile on LinkedIn. No embarrassing articles or spats on Twitter, no photos of him smiling with friends. Over and above those taken by the media, there was just one other photo of Kristoffer, leaning against a doorframe, eyes fiery, arms folded across his chest. Leaning forward slightly as if he was about to have a dig at the photographer.

She kept a low profile herself and never shared anything personal. With one of Denmark's most common surnames, and having ditched her embarrassing first name, no one could find her, except for her articles in *Dagbladet*, and that had always felt good to her.

But, unlike Kristoffer, she wasn't a famous entrepreneur rumoured to be one of Denmark's richest citizens under the age of forty. 'Gustav, can I ask you a question?' she said, finishing her drink.

He was on his feet again, stretching his neck to see inside the café.

'Is it possible to delete certain stuff about yourself from search engines, to make yourself appear in a certain way?' she said.

'I suppose so. Anything is possible if you know how. But I can't see why Aziz—'

'Oh, I don't mean him. I was just wondering.'

'Fie would know,' said Gustav.

Jensen nodded, thinking of the schoolgirl hacker who had helped them before. 'Let's go and see her today,' she said. 'I need to get her to take a look at Esben's laptop anyway.'

Gustav composed a message. 'Told her we'd be there at two.' Then he jumped up like his seat was on fire and ran inside the café. 'Quick,' he shouted. 'They're leaving.'

He was seated almost before the couple had got up, ignoring the dirty looks they sent him.

God love you, Gustav.

Their food arrived, big plates stacked with pancakes, banana and bacon soaked in maple syrup.

Jensen ordered another round of smoothies. They had lots to discuss, but it would have to be later when Gustav had filled his stomach.

Food to Gustav was like coffee to Henning. She knew that getting any sense out of him before he had eaten would be impossible.

37

Sunday 13:26

Skovhøj, a home for vulnerable young adults in Roskilde, looked the same as always, except for the windows in the low red-brick buildings, which had been thrown open wide to make the heat more bearable.

Gustav had beaten Jensen by several minutes on his e-scooter from Roskilde station. By the time she turned into the drive on her bicycle, sweaty and breathless, he was already sitting on the kerb vaping.

Fie greeted them at the front door, flanked by Tobias, the centre manager, with his beard and topknot. She was dressed in a sleeveless pink top and jogging pants, with black-and-white sliders on her feet. The skin on her arms was mottled and puffy, her smiling eyes buried deep in her face.

A hacker since before she knew what the word meant, with an extraordinary talent for mining online data, Fie could have worked anywhere and made a fortune, but the world outside the institutional walls of Skovhøj frightened her.

'Can I have a word?' said Tobias to Jensen, as Fie dragged Gustav off to her room.

The Magstræde case back at the start of the year had taken its toll on Fie, and Tobias remained fiercely protective of her. She had lost her best friend.

Her only friend.

'I'm glad to see you've finally taken down the Christmas decorations,' Jensen laughed, nodding at the windows, which had been decorated with gold stars the last time she had visited. The common area was unchanged, with its big sofas arranged around a communal TV. Thumping music could be heard from down the hall.

Tobias's eyes were smiling, but she could tell that he was about to get serious with her. 'I'm glad that you and Gustav have come to visit Fie. As you know, she doesn't really have any friends.'

'We're her friends.'

'Not really, Jensen.'

He was right, real friends didn't just show up when they wanted something. 'We like her,' she said.

'And that's good, but I ask you to remember that she's vulnerable. It has taken us ages to get her to stop self-harming.'

'I'm sorry to hear that.'

'I'd like at some stage to see her in her own flat, a paid job, but any little thing could set her back.'

'I'd never do anything to harm Fie,' said Jensen.

'What I'm saying is don't use her. Don't get her to do stuff for you and then disappear again. Like last time.'

Jensen realised he was right. She knew Gustav had been to see Fie a couple of times, but she hadn't been to Roskilde once, or as much as sent a message.

'I'm sorry,' said Jensen. 'I promise I'll do better.'

'I know you'll try. Now go,' said Tobias, smiling again.

Jensen found Gustav and Fie sitting side by side at the desk in her living room, staring at an enormous screen. 'It's good to see you, Fie,' she said. 'How've you been?'

'Look what she found,' said Gustav excitedly, not taking his eyes off the screen.

Jensen did a doubletake. 'Wait a minute, is that—?'

'Carsten Vangede's USB,' said Gustav. 'The one I made a copy of before it was stolen from your flat.'

Fie was typing rapidly. 'Gustav brought it here a while back.'

'You didn't mention that,' said Jensen.

'I forgot.' Gustav avoided meeting her eye.

Forgot or wasn't sure I'd approve, thought Jensen.

'Don't worry,' said Fie. 'I hadn't done anything with it. Nothing seemed to make sense. Until I looked at it again earlier, when you told me you were coming today.'

Jensen's heart began to beat a little faster. 'And?'

'First, I went through all the paperwork and organised the information. It's all invoices from suppliers to a couple of restaurants and a place called Zoom Bar.'

Jensen nodded. 'That was Carsten Vangede's Nørrebro place.'

'Well, every third invoice has been double-booked in the system.'

'By the accountant,' said Gustav.

'Yes,' said Jensen. 'And then the accountant pocketed the difference. It's how the scam works. We know that much.'

'Right,' said Fie. 'I then went through all the other documents. Seems Carsten Vangede had tried to find out where the accountant deposited the money he siphoned off. The statements from the bank showed that they went to a company rather than straight to the accountant's personal account, and this is where things get complicated.'

Fie pointed to a diagram on the screen, loads of boxes and lines and arrows.

'Vangede found that the recipient was a company called DanFinans Holdings,' said Fie, pointing to the bottom of the screen. 'You won't find anything about it online. It's new. Registered at a solicitor's office, no accounts filed yet. The money trail ends with DanFinans.'

'So, that's it?' said Jensen.

'No,' said Gustav. 'Listen to this.'

'I couldn't see at first what it was that he had tried to do,' said Fie. 'Lots of different registered companies, accounts, lists of directors. But then I ran them through this software and found that they're all linked. It's like a chain. Location, registration, time of filing accounts, directors, names. All of these companies have something in common with the next in the chain.'

Jensen couldn't see where this was going. She sat down on Fie's couch, pushing aside an assortment of stuffed toys.

'It all ends in one place. This company, registered in the Cayman Islands.'

Fie pointed to the screen. Jensen leaned close to read the name. 'What the hell?'

'Yep. Amaliekilde Holdings,' said Gustav triumphantly, slapping Fie on her back. 'Told you, there's nothing Fie can't do.'

Jensen recalled whispering the name Amaliekilde to her source, solicitor Ernst Brøgger, on Amalienborg Castle square, while the soldiers in their bearskin hats and sky-blue trousers marched up and down in front of their red-pencil guard shelters. Brøgger had recoiled as though she had shouted into his ear through a megaphone. She could still see him, marching off with a deep frown on his face, hands swinging by his side.

'So DanFinans Holdings is linked to Amaliekilde Holdings?' said Jensen. 'But surely that's only tangentially. A bit like saying I'm related to Queen Margrethe if we go back far enough?'

'No, there are links all the way through the chain. To establish this pattern, Carsten Vangede would have had to follow hundreds of dead ends.'

'It all fits,' said Gustav. 'Vangede must have looked up Amaliekilde and, somehow, found the property in Vedbæk. Perhaps he hadn't managed to establish a connection yet.'

'Perhaps there isn't one,' said Jensen. 'In any case some-one found out what he was doing, and he ended up dead.'

All three of them fell silent for a moment. Jensen thought of what Tobias had said. 'Fie, listen to me carefully. I want you to make a copy of Vangede's files and what you have discovered and put it in a place where no one will ever find it. Then delete it completely from your computer so there's no trace left. You've done amazingly well, but someone out there doesn't want us to know these things. The original USB was stolen from my flat in Christianshavn. We're only here now because Gustav thought to copy it.'

'But it's got to mean something,' said Gustav. 'We can't just—'

'I don't want Fie to get into any danger, Gustav,' said Jensen. She turned to Fie. 'Please do as I ask.'

Fie nodded solemnly.

'There's something else.' Jensen opened her bag and took out Esben's laptop, which she passed to Fie with a folded sheet of paper. 'Take a look at this.'

'Whose is it?' said Fie.

'A member of parliament who happens to be a friend of mine. I've noted the log-in details for the Gmail account and the date and time of some anonymous, threatening emails sent to it. I want you to find out who sent them – and Fie?'

'Yes?'

A chill ran through Jensen as she echoed Carsten Vangede's words. 'Be careful.'

38

Sunday 14:16

Henrik's phone buzzed. Wiese.

> Any news?

Henrik typed angrily.

> No. Like there wasn't 5 mins ago when you
> last asked me, you pain in the neck.

He deleted everything but the first word. Things were bad enough already between him and his boss.

Mark had left with somewhat less of a spring in his step after Henrik had suggested that going on holiday in the middle of an investigation meant he wasn't a real detective. The incident room had the usual atmosphere of defeat tinged with despair. Only a handful of investigators were in. He knew all of them, but they weren't his people.

Not like Mark and Lisbeth.

He got out his phone, wondering if Lisbeth was back from her trip to the beach by now. He wouldn't put it past her. She had picked up a habit or two of his from working in his team.

You in the office?

The answer came immediately, with a sad-face emoji.

Yes. Shoot me now.

Fancy a walk?

They met outside and strolled through the dusty streets around the new flats and building sites. The area felt abandoned, as if everyone in Copenhagen had taken off on holiday at the same time. Lisbeth looked tired.

'How was the beach?' Henrik asked.

She laughed drily. 'Hell. Screaming kids everywhere and Josefine and I had an argument.'

Henrik nodded his understanding. The office had been a place of refuge to him for years. 'That was rough back there in Monsen's office yesterday,' he said. 'I hope you're not taking it personally. Shit happens, and the accusing finger has to point somewhere.'

'I'm OK.'

'Want to share?'

'No,' said Lisbeth. 'What are you after?'

'Can't I just want to see a colleague for a nice chat?'

'That would be a first.'

'Ouch,' said Henrik, pretending to be hurt.

'Henrik, you're not my boss any more.'

'Don't remind me,' he said. 'Anyway, it was Aziz I wanted to talk to you about.'

'The missing Syrian? His wife's getting anxious.'

'She OK otherwise?'

'For now,' said Lisbeth. She turned to him. 'You know what I think?'

'That I should open a formal investigation? Do things properly? Yes, you told me. But I'm not going to. For now.'

Was he wrong? His instinct was telling him to do as Jensen had asked and keep things on the quiet. A friend of his in forensics was going to check Esben Nørregaard's property later tonight, as a personal favour to him.

'Then keep me out of it,' Lisbeth said. 'I don't want any more trouble.'

Henrik fished a USB stick with Nørregaard's CCTV recordings from his pocket and handed it to her. 'Just take a look at this.'

'What is it?'

'From the security cameras at Esben Nørregaard's house. Aziz was there the morning he disappeared. He can be seen clearly fighting with three men, before collapsing on the ground. See if you recognise anyone?'

'Fuck's sake,' said Lisbeth. She looked around before pocketing the USB.

As Henrik knew she would.

'Esben Nørregaard thinks it's to do with someone trying to blackmail him for influence with the prime minister. He's been receiving threatening emails.'

'Not unheard of for a person in his position.'

'He thinks it's Leif Kofoed.'

Now he had Lisbeth's attention. She stared at him. 'Leif Kofoed? Is he even still alive?'

'I didn't think so either.'

'Wasn't he the one who killed those two security guards in Aarhus?'

'After torturing them for forty-eight hours? Yeah. Never proven, but that's what they say. Man's a total psycho.'

'I heard he married his kids' babysitter.'

'Who drowned in mysterious circumstances two years later, eight months pregnant with his child. Yep. Well, apparently, he looked up Esben Nørregaard in person a little while ago. He wants to build a golf course in North Jutland and thought Nørregaard could help oil the wheels for him.'

Lisbeth stopped abruptly. 'Wait. You're telling me Leif Kofoed is in Denmark?'

'No one knows where he is exactly. If you're able to find out, I'd be extremely grateful, but be discreet. Kofoed is a nasty piece of work. You never know where his spies might be lurking.'

'Please tell me you don't mean on the force.'

'I wouldn't rule it out.'

A woman approached them on the pavement, pushing a pram with shopping bags hanging off the handle. She was talking on the phone to someone, laughing, not sparing the two of them a single glance.

'Don't you wish you could be like that?' said Lisbeth.

'Like what?'

'Blissfully ignorant of all the bad things people do to each other for money?'

'Often. But I'm sad to say that train left the platform some time ago, for both of us.'

'Josefine's talking about having kids,' said Lisbeth, biting a nail.

'You want to?'

'I don't know.'

'Shouldn't you talk about that before you get married?' said Henrik.

('Shouldn't you be sorting out your own shit before doling out advice to others?' said his wife in his head.)

'We have. Josefine's a wonderful person. I don't deserve her really.' Lisbeth looked at her engagement ring. She rubbed her bare arms despite the heat, her face painted with the same sort of guilty misery that Henrik felt whenever he thought of his wife.

Nearly everyone had left when he got back to the incident room. What was he going to say at tomorrow's press conference? The journalists would want answers and he didn't have any.

In front of him were the files noting everything they knew already, which seemed like very little. He thumbed through the photos that forensics had taken of the corpse. What had happened to the man's head? And where was the body of the smaller man whose head they had found in a bin?

He held the photo up to the light and looked at the long gash on the torso. The edges were ragged and leathery. David Goldschmidt at the Forensic Institute had said that perhaps the corpse had collided with something when it was floating in the harbour.

If they were right, and the body had been dumped from the back of the now burned-out car at Refshaleøen, it would have sunk somewhere below the boats that were moored there.

Henrik stopped in his tracks.

What if?

He picked up his phone and dialled the mobile number that David had once been careless enough to give him. Goldschmidt's kid, a little boy, was screaming his head off in the background. 'Henrik, sorry, now is not the best time as you can probably hear. I'm actually on holiday. As of yesterday. We're off to Bornholm in the morning. Is it urgent?'

'Yes,' said Henrik.

He waited while David handed the screaming toddler to his husband. 'Shoot,' he said when he returned.

'Do you remember the gash we found on the torso of the victim in the harbour?'

'I told you it wasn't the cause of death.'

'You did, but I wonder, could the damage have been inflicted by chains? I mean, the body might have been wedged fast at first, but ripped free and floated to the surface when it began to bloat? We know that the victim was an exceptionally big man.'

'Could be. It would take about twenty-four hours or so for the gases to develop sufficiently to make the body buoyant, but with the heat wave, it could have happened faster. Why are you asking?'

'I'll tell you as soon as I work out if I'm right,' said Henrik and hung up.

He made one more call to set things up for the morning, before starting to read the case files all over again from the beginning. There had to be something they had missed. Besides, he didn't want to go home before he was sure everyone was in bed and the suitcases packed for the family holiday he wouldn't be going on.

39

Kristoffer was out when Jensen got back, having spent the rest of her Sunday afternoon at the newspaper.

The teenager who had stabbed a boy to death at Ørestaden had walked into a police station with his parents and confessed to the murder. She had taken ages to file the story, her words seeming empty and inadequate. Two young lives were ruined. Boys younger than Gustav. Whatever she wrote could never undo senselessness on that scale.

As she had cycled to the flat in Nordhavn through the shadowy streets still holding the day's heat, Copenhagen had felt like a city she didn't recognise, brooding with menace.

And out there somewhere was Aziz. Lying dead. Or hiding out, hurt and desperate. How were they ever going to find him?

She sent a text to Kristoffer.

Just got back. Where are you?

She kicked off her sandals and headed for the bathroom, the floor tiles deliciously cool under her burning hot feet. In the shower, she stood for ages, hanging her head and letting the cool water stream down her back.

Gustav had kept on at her on the journey back from Roskilde, wanting them to discuss what Fie's discoveries meant, wanting them to go to the house in Vedbæk straightaway. 'We must find out who owns it. Ask them about Vangede.'

'No, Gustav. That's the last thing we should do. There are cameras everywhere on that property. Whoever lives there isn't going to roll out the red carpet,' Jensen had reminded him.

'But we're so close.'

'Sometimes as a journalist you have to sit on information until you get more, no matter how counterintuitive it feels,' she had said.

She wrapped her hair in a towel and put on a clean dress. Then she opened Kristoffer's white wine fridge and picked the least expensive-looking bottle she could find. Not that this meant a lot; everything Kristoffer owned was the best of the best.

He freely admitted that he hadn't bought any of it himself. 'Wouldn't know my arse from my elbow when it comes to that sort of thing,' he had told her.

Jensen thought of the art dealers and wine merchants and interior designers who would be rubbing their hands with glee whenever he crossed their path.

She poured herself a large glass of wine, watching the condensation cloud the glass, and walked into the living room, checking her phone for messages and breaking-news alerts.

None.

She had teased Kristoffer about the flat. The white sofas that could have seated a football team. The grand piano he couldn't play. The huge paintings that looked like the disturbed black marks of someone mentally ill. The fact that he had to open a hundred cupboards to find everyday items: toilet paper, towels, salt.

The flat was bigger than the sports hall at her primary school. Bigger than *Dagbladet*'s canteen, and mostly empty. There were no personal items anywhere, no photographs of friends and family, no old notebooks, no letters about rubbish collections and yoga classes stuck to the fridge.

She ran her finger along the top of a white lacquer sideboard. It came away clean. There were three large art books untouched by human hand. She opened the doors and drawers in the sideboard. All empty aside from a Bang & Olufsen remote control.

Where did Kristoffer keep his stuff? The spare batteries and Sellotape and old bills that everyone else had lying around? There was no need to look in the bedroom. She already knew there was nothing in there but his clothes and some bottles of cologne.

He had cleared a wardrobe for her, and she had filled the shelves with bundles of clothes and underwear, phone chargers, pens, make-up, an old bicycle helmet and a pair of sandals. Kristoffer hated her leaving stuff around the flat, even as little as a bunch of keys on the kitchen counter.

She tiptoed down the hall to his office, which was next to the spare bedroom where no one ever stayed and where the cushions on the bed still had their shop tags attached.

The air in the office was stale, unused, the view from the window facing away from the water. It didn't look like a room Kristoffer spent much time in.

She set down her wine glass on the large walnut desk,

taking care to keep it away from the wood where it might leave a ring. She began opening the desk drawers and looking inside, hesitantly at first. She found two old mobile phones without sim cards in the top drawer, otherwise nothing.

Like his social media profile, Kristoffer's home was squeaky clean.

There was only one place left to look.

Going through the pockets of the jackets in his wardrobe made her feel like a cheated wife looking for evidence of a mistress. In the inside pocket of a navy blue linen blazer that he had worn for their first date, her probing fingers finally found something.

A key.

Just a normal brass key with a jagged edge.

She went to the front door and tried it. She tried it in the locks on the balcony doors, the guest bathroom and the expensive bicycle Kristoffer kept on a rack in the hallway, but it fitted nowhere.

She was lost in her own thoughts and didn't hear the front door. Then Kristoffer was beside her, looking flustered, as if he had been running. 'What are you doing, Jensen?'

She turned around, hiding the key behind her back. 'Why didn't you answer my text?' she said.

'I asked first,' he said, glaring at her coldly.

'Nothing,' she said. 'Just restless and curious. You know what I'm like.'

The look on Kristoffer's face said that he didn't believe a word of it. He headed for his office with his laptop bag under one arm. Too late, Jensen remembered the glass of wine she had left on a copy of the *Economist* on his desk.

Shit.

40

Monday 07:31

Henrik peered over the edge of the quay at Refshaleøen and watched the divers searching the muddy water below. Thankfully, it was too early for the usual crowd of blood-thirsty voyeurs to have gathered. It was still cool, but the early sunlight held the promise of heat that would all too soon be unbearable.

A moment later, he sensed a presence in the corner of his vision. A man in dark clothing had appeared a few metres further along the quay and was looking into the water with open curiosity.

Here we go again.

'Police,' said Henrik, holding up his warrant card. 'I need you to step back, please.'

He recognised the tramp he had last seen when he had visited the site to look at the burned-out car, which had now been removed and forensically examined. The technicians had found nothing of use. Of course.

The tramp had a long white beard. His rusty bicycle was

parked a short distance away, the handlebars laden with plastic bags. Henrik caught a whiff of urine in the air.

'What's going on?' said the man, mouth full of bad teeth.

He held a notebook in his trembling hands. It was falling apart. Something was written in it, in tiny block capitals, surprisingly delicate.

'Just an exercise,' said Henrik. 'Now move along, or I'm going to have to get some officers to come and shift you.'

The man stayed put. 'So, it has nothing to do with the car that was here a few days ago?' he said. 'They've removed it now, but it was completely burned out, you know.'

'What car?' Henrik looked around, feigning ignorance.

They stared at each other in silence for a bit, the tramp looking offended that Henrik wasn't up for a conversation. Henrik felt sorry for the man. 'Where do you live?' he asked, his voice softening.

'What business is it of yours?' said the man, looking at him as if he had asked a ridiculous question. Then he went on his way, shaking his head and pushing his bicycle noisily over the uneven ground.

Lunatic, thought Henrik, turning his gaze back to the water while making a mental note that the tramp would have to be interviewed formally.

One of the divers had surfaced and was shaking his head at Henrik. He motioned at the man to go back under and continue the search, all the while trying to ignore the sense of failure that was building in him. His theory, forged out of desperation, was turning out to be too good to be true. What was he going to do now? The press conference was less than three hours away.

'DI Jungersen?' said a female voice with a slow Jutland accent.

Henrik turned to find a stout-looking woman of about

fifty, with short grey hair, dressed in black trousers and a light blue shirt with a warrant card dangling from her neck. She was approaching him at speed.

Henrik lifted his shades. 'Who's asking?'

'Detective Sergeant Ravnsbæk. Tone,' said the woman, shaking his hand with the strength of a wrestler. 'Wiese sent me. I thought you'd been informed.'

'He mentioned something. I didn't think—'

'So, I was rather surprised when I arrived to find you'd already left without me.'

'What?'

'I don't think I need to repeat myself. We're meant to work as a team.'

Henrik felt himself grow hot. Who did this jumped-up Jutlander think she was? 'One, I didn't know you were coming. Two, I do whatever I damn well please,' he snapped.

'So I've heard,' said Tone Ravnsbæk, standing right in front of him, arms at her waist. 'You don't scare me, Jungersen.'

'Excuse me?'

'You must know what everyone's saying about you.'

'I don't, as it happens. Do tell.'

'Let me see. Unorthodox methods? Bad temper? Loose cannon? Womaniser?'

Not something you need to worry about, honey, thought Henrik. 'Did they also tell you that I have the best detection record on the force?'

'They did, which is the reason I'm here. I wanted to see what all the fuss was about, so when Wiese asked me, I jumped at the chance.'

'Well, in that case you might want to keep in mind that I'm the one who's boss,' he said. Tone Ravnsbæk, his new buddy, had to be Wiese's sick joke. Except the man had no sense of humour, which meant it was another deliberate dig to undermine him. 'Right now, I could kill for a coffee,' he said.

'There's a café 500 metres in that direction,' said Tone, pointing. 'Don't worry, I'll hold the fort while you're away.'

Henrik stared at her, and she stared back.

'What?' she said. 'You're not saying I'm here just to fetch coffees, are you? I don't think the good people in HR would make much of that.'

'I wasn't asking you to,' said Henrik, feeling himself blush.

'Oh, I think you were. You might have that Mark Søndergreen running after you like a puppy dog, but that's not going to happen with me, so don't bother trying,' said Tone.

Henrik turned away from her and made an angry face at the air. 'What kind of a name is Tone anyway?' he said.

'My Dad is Norwegian. It was his mother's name. Now, if you're not going to get your caffeine fix, perhaps you could bring me up to speed on the case? I read all the files so far and have a couple of ideas of my own. Why don't—'

'Stop,' said Henrik, raising one hand to silence her. 'When I want your opinion, I'll ask for it. If you've read the files, you know as much as I do.'

'But you're pursuing a theory, aren't you? I mean that's why we're here now, isn't it? I'd like to know what you're thinking.'

'I'm not thinking anything. Just turning every stone. Like we do. Only this particular one doesn't appear to have anything under it,' he sighed and turned to head for the coffee shop. 'I'll be five minutes. Don't move or speak or do anything until I get back.'

But Tone wasn't listening. She was craning her neck to see what the crew in the water were up to. He would have to talk to Wiese. This woman was not someone he could work with.

He had moved no more than twenty metres when she began to shout. 'Wait, Jungersen, they have something.'

He ran back to where she was standing, once more looking over the edge into the water. One of the divers was manoeuvring something heavy to the surface.

'I'll call forensics,' said Tone and sprinted away.

The thing in the water looked like a bundle of clothes, but it wasn't.

Henrik felt his pulse rise.

It was a body.

A badly decomposed, headless corpse of a short, thin man wrapped in chains.

41

Monday 10:27

There were no spare seats when Jensen and Gustav arrived at the press conference in a baking hot room rigged with TV lighting and cables. Gustav pushed through the crowd to find them two standing places along the wall near the podium, where a row of microphones announced the presence of the major TV networks and a couple of *Dagbladet*'s rivals.

After several days without updates, the room was humming with anticipation that something big was going to be announced.

The whole country was talking about the macabre discovery of a decapitated body in the harbour, followed by a head being found in a bin several kilometres away. The journalists were hoping the police would finally tell them who the man was.

Jensen kept checking her phone for messages from Kristoffer but, so far, he was maintaining radio silence. Their conversation last night had been tense.

'What were you doing in my office?' he had asked her,

eyes flashing, as he emerged with the tell-tale glass of wine she had left on his desk.

'I was just ... looking for a pen. Do you know, you're seriously short on office supplies in there?'

'Bullshit. Tell me the real reason.' He had been looking at her in the way that made it impossible to lie to him, as if he could see into her and read her mind. 'OK, I was curious. You tell me so little about yourself, I was desperate to find a scrap of something personal. A photo, perhaps, of your parents, or an old book you're fond of.'

Kristoffer had stormed off then, forcing her to follow him into the kitchen when he had yanked open the fridge door and snatched a bottle of expensive French mineral water that he had proceeded to point at her. 'I told you I don't like dwelling on the past. I thought you and I were similar in that regard. I was obviously mistaken.'

'But it matters where we come from, doesn't it? It might help me understand certain things about you. Like why I can't find anything that truly belongs to you in this place,' she said.

'You're no different, Jensen. Where's your stuff? Didn't you buy everything new in IKEA when you rented my flat in Christianshavn?'

Touché, Kristoffer.

'I told you already my stuff's in England. I wasn't sure I'd be staying in Denmark, so it seemed easier to buy new things,' she said.

Would she ever bring her container here? Unpack the old posters and rugs and knick-knacks from London? She hadn't missed any of it once, surprised at how easy it had been to leave everything behind and start again. Kristoffer was right, she too had wanted a clean break with the past. 'But I've got no secrets. You can ask me anything,' she said.

Kristoffer tore at his hair, his eyes fiery. 'Do I really have to repeat myself? I don't want to know who or what you were before. We're here now, that's all that matters.'

'Not to me,' said Jensen.

'I'm starting to understand that. I'm no longer sure that you and I are well matched. Honesty, integrity and trust between people is an absolute must for me.'

'And for me, but come on, Kristoffer, you've got to give me a little to work with.'

'It's all out there in the media. Nothing stopping you reading the many articles about me.'

'I have, and it's like your life only began when you founded your company. Why, Kristoffer?'

That was as far as they had got. He had looked at her with a sad, almost disappointed expression and walked out of the flat. Where had he spent the night? Was he going to tell her that it was over?

She didn't want it to be. If Henrik hadn't said those things he said, if he hadn't tried to spoil everything, none if it would have happened.

Gustav pushed his phone under her nose. 'Look,' he said. 'You have over two thousand new Twitter followers since last Monday, including the prime minister's press secretary.'

Jensen gave him an affectionate shove. The Twitter account had been his idea and she had no hand in running it, but Margrethe would be delighted. Something to sweeten the Swedish wunderkinds who were crawling all over the newspaper with their charts and spreadsheets.

The noise in the room dropped to a low mumble as a line of grim-faced men and women entered and took their seats on the podium. One of them fiddled nervously with some printed sheets, drinking water and spilling it on his white shirt.

Henrik.

His eyes darted here and there before settling on his hands. He hadn't seen her.

She knew that once, during her fifteen years as a foreign correspondent in London, there had been some sort of scandal where Henrik had been caught on TV losing his patience with a female reporter.

He hated press conferences.

A big man with a gruff voice and a solemn face who introduced himself as Chief Superintendent Mogens Hansen said a few words before handing over to Henrik, who spoke fast and robotically. 'Early this morning at around seven a.m. we recovered a second headless body from Copenhagen harbour by Refshaleøen.'

A murmur of shock reverberated around the room. The photographers began to snap away frantically in a frenzy of flashes.

'Forensics have determined that, in all likelihood, the body belongs to the same victim as the severed head recovered from a bin in Sydhavnen on Friday. The victim appears to have died from a gunshot to the chest. Our two victims are as yet unidentified, but we have grounds to believe they may be foreign citizens. Our theory is that the killings are linked to organised crime, but we don't know how. We're pursuing a number of leads, ruling nothing out or in at this stage. I'd like to appeal to any member of the public who may have information relevant to this case to come forward.'

Henrik paused, shuffling in his seat. 'Any questions?'

The room turned into a sea of waving hands. 'Here,' shouted Jensen. 'I have a question.'

Henrik's gaze widened briefly when he spotted her. Then he resolutely picked someone else.

He fielded about fifteen questions, most on the identity of the victims (unknown as he had previously pointed out), suspects (none) and motive (unknown).

In the end there was just Jensen who remained unanswered, after a reporter from a TV crime-stopper programme asked what the police were doing to keep the public safe. 'There is no indication of danger posed to the public,' Henrik said. 'And if there are no more questions, we'll get back to work. You'll be told as soon as we have material developments to share.'

The journalists began to pack up their things, making calls, turning to each other to discuss the case, their excited faces betraying their lack of thought for the victims. Until Chief Superintendent Mogens Hansen cleared his throat loudly and the room fell silent again. He pointed at Jensen. 'I think that young lady over there has been trying to get your attention for a while,' he said to Henrik.

'*Dagbladet*,' she said, sensing Gustav raising his phone behind her to begin filming. 'I was beginning to think I was invisible,' she said, to a couple of laughs from her assembled colleagues.

Henrik looked like he wished he had never been born.
Good.

'So, the head of the first victim is still missing. What's your theory?'

'We don't have one,' said Henrik.

'How hard can it be to find a severed head?'

'It could be anywhere. Like I said earlier, we're pursuing a number of leads,' said Henrik, grabbing the pile of papers in front of him and starting to rise from his seat.

Jensen continued, louder this time, 'Isn't this an example of the extraordinary inability of Copenhagen Police to get results, even in simple investigations? Almost a week after the first body was found, how can it be that you still don't have a clue as to who it is? Shouldn't we expect more of our police force?'

The room had fallen completely silent. The broadcasters had been dismantling their cameras, but now they began to film again.

'This investigation is far from simple, and we're working as fast as we can,' Henrik said.

'That's not what it will look like to most people watching this. As far as they're concerned, you just told them that you have no answers to even the most basic questions. Yet, you are certain there is no danger to the public. How can we trust you on that?'

Henrik had turned bright red, the lighting reflecting off his shiny scalp.

'Let me,' Mogens Hansen intervened. 'As we said earlier, the manner of the . . . disposal of their bodies, suggests these men weren't picked at random. We maintain that the public are safe. As for the record of the force, may I remind you that our success rate is over ninety percent.'

'Three major unsolved murder cases in as many years. Will this be the fourth?'

'As Detective Inspector Jungersen just said, we are working as hard as we can to solve these heinous crimes and bring the people responsible to prosecution. Now, if there are no more questions, I thank you all for coming.'

As Henrik left the room, his elbow steered forcefully by Mogens Hansen, he sent Jensen a long, hard stare.

42

Monday 11:18

'What on earth was that all about?' said Tone as they were making their way back to the incident room.

'You know *Dagbladet*, always on the look-out for someone to blame, preferably in the establishment.'

'I read that journalist's coverage of the Magstræde and Ordrup cases earlier this year. She's good. Seems she even had a hand in solving them?'

'Allegedly,' said Henrik.

'She doesn't appear to like you very much.'

You can say that again.

There was everything wrong with what had just happened at the press conference, and the fact that his wife might be watching the news later was just the start of it. It would be the first time she would have seen him and Jensen together. Henrik suspected she had always known that something had happened between them but lacked hard evidence. Would his indiscretions be apparent to anyone watching the video clip, including his eagle-eyed wife? His spat with Jensen in front of the cameras had been aggressive, but this almost made things worse. Love and anger were similar emotions, both fuelled by passion. After many years of being married to him, his wife would know this better than anyone.

He had been about to lose his temper again, something that hadn't gone unnoticed by Wiese, who had been shaking his head demonstrably as Henrik left the podium. Monsen, on the other hand, had patted him on the back as soon as they were outside in the corridor. 'Good man, Jungersen, good man.'

Just what was wrong with Jensen? There had been zero trace of affection or empathy in her voice when she questioned him. When they had last met, she had demanded angrily to be free of him, to be allowed to build a relationship with another man, without him interfering and ruining everything. Was that how she saw him, like some kind of egotistical monster?

All he had wanted was to burst the bubble she had built around Kristoffer Bro, but maybe he ought to let Jensen discover for herself what the man was like. 'Let's focus on solving our case, shall we?' he said to Tone.

'Sure. While you were preparing for the press conference with Monsen, I took the liberty of organising things back here. To say they were chaotic is an understatement.'

Henrik stopped just inside the incident room, lost for words. The tables had been pushed together, with detectives working on their laptops all the way down one side and papers laid out in neat piles on the other. At the end of the room, the whiteboard had been rearranged with forensic photographs of both victims on the left and on the right a large map of the harbour showing where the body parts had been found. Alongside it was a larger map of North

Zealand, showing the location of the summerhouse by Roskilde Fjord, the shop where someone had spotted an English-speaking tourist out of season, and the beach where Ida Kaurup had observed a couple of Danish men in leather jackets throwing a bundle into the water.

A knotted white sheet containing bloodied clothes and some personal possessions, weighed down with stones, had been recovered from the area by divers.

No murder weapon.

No mobile phones.

'All right, whose is this?' said Tone angrily pointing at a coffee mug that had been left on top of a neat pile of papers. 'No food or drink in here. You should all know this by now.'

A couple of the detectives looked up with pained expressions. One of them shook his head miserably at Henrik as if to say: 'Don't bother arguing with the mad woman.'

'I thought we could go to your office first. Review the whole case, what we know and what we still need to discover. I've read everything, of course, but I'd like to understand what you make of it,' said Tone.

'Sure,' said Henrik, staring at the whiteboard as if in a trance. Lisbeth and Mark were good detectives in their own ways, but he had never seen either of them operate remotely like Tone. Maybe it was too early to complain to Wiese. Give the woman another chance.

'Are you coming?' she said.

They went through the case from the beginning, Henrik seated behind his desk, Tone in the chair opposite. He had insisted on getting coffee from the canteen before starting, trying unsuccessfully to clear his brain of what had happened with Jensen that morning.

The press conference was showing on all the major news

channels by now, the clip of Jensen laying into him running on repeat and giving him a stomach-ache.

He began to reel off the facts. 'About two weeks ago now, two bodies were dumped in the water by Refshaleøen. They had been wrapped in chains and their heads and hands had been removed cleanly with an axe. One of the bodies tore free from its poorly secured chains and rose to the surface, drifting further into the harbour, where it was discovered by a local resident in a passing motorboat. The head of the second victim was found in a dustbin on the premises of Copenhagen Food Distribution on Friday, and we found the second body this morning, with signs of a gunshot to the chest. We should hear from the post-mortem soon,' said Henrik. He remembered to his regret that David Goldschmidt at the Forensic Institute would have left for his holidays on Bornholm by now, meaning he would have to deal with someone new.

Tone continued where he left off. 'No database match on the first victim's DNA, nothing from Europol, and we're still waiting for the analysis to come back on the second victim. I chased again this morning. Forensics have had the head since Friday, so we should hear something today.'

'Right,' said Henrik. 'Good. Now we established a connection between the burned-out hire car found at Refshaleøen and an unidentified male travelling to Denmark on a fake British passport seventeen days ago. We believe this man went to the summerhouse by Roskilde Fjord along with the second victim. In order not to arouse suspicion, they pretended to be a family named Smith, requesting a cot and a highchair to be placed in the cabin. Our assumption is that the hire car was later used to transport their bodies to Refshaleøen.'

Tone nodded. 'Mark Søndergreen got some people

started on looking through the footage from the CCTV cameras out there. I just checked with them. There's nothing usable. The killers picked a blind spot to drop the bodies in the water, apparently.'

Henrik nodded. 'The summerhouse was scrubbed clean, aside from a small amount of blood on which we have no match so far. Before we have a match, we can't conclusively establish a link to the bodies recovered from the harbour.'

'I chased that one up this morning also,' said Tone. 'There's no match with the first victim, but they're checking against the second.'

She was wearing a thin gold wedding band. Henrik pitied the husband who had to live with that kind of industriousness.

'Where are you from?' he asked her, by way of catching his breath.

'Horsens. I got transferred to Copenhagen recently.'

'So, you moved your family here?'

'No, my husband still lives back home. I'm renting a room over here.'

'That must be tough.'

'Why? I asked to come. My husband and I can see each other on my days off.'

'Still.'

'It's called public service, Jungersen. It's not supposed to be easy, and we sure as hell don't do it for the money.'

True.

'So, what else have we got?' said Tone.

She was looking through her slim black notebook, her observations written out neatly in a way Henrik could only dream of. He had always told himself that he had a good memory and didn't need notes. Now he wondered if that were still the case.

The old man out at Refshaleøen had been holding

a similar black notebook in his hand. What were those scribbles of his? Some kind of obsessive record keeping? 'Wait,' he said, remembering that the man still needed to be interviewed. 'There was a tramp out there this morning.'

Tone nodded. 'I saw him.'

'He had a notebook, a bit like yours. Might be gibberish, but worth checking with him, just in case he has been noting down licence plates. I am pretty sure he lives out there. Maybe he saw something?'

'Got it,' said Tone. 'Anything else?'

'That's about it,' said Henrik, deciding that he couldn't tell her about Aziz. Someone as strait-laced as Tone would turn the missing Syrian into a thing, and he had promised Jensen discretion. Though she had just treated him like dirt in front of the TV-viewing public, he knew his life wouldn't be worth living if he went back on his word.

There was a knock on the door.

'Got a moment?' said Lisbeth, looking at Henrik.

'We're actually busy,' said Tone.

'It's OK,' Henrik said. 'Lisbeth used to work on my team. I think you and I were done anyway?'

Tone sighed, snapping her notebook shut. 'I'll take a team out to Refshaleøen, find your tramp,' she said, pushing past Lisbeth while glaring at her provocatively.

'Charming,' said Lisbeth as Tone's determined footsteps grew fainter down the hall. 'Who was that?'

'Oh, just Wiese's latest dig at me. Tone is the new Mark, for the next two weeks anyway. She's all right, though, once you get to know her.'

'You've changed,' said Lisbeth, laughing. 'Anyway. I did some more research into Leif Kofoed or whatever name he uses now. No one knows anything, or is willing to talk at any rate. Last spotted in Lima two years ago.'

'Lima. Isn't that in—'

'Peru, yes. Though the sighting was never verified. Nor do we have any evidence that he's in Denmark. Sorry.'

Henrik wasn't surprised. Kofoed wasn't the type to leave a trail. 'Recognise anyone from Nørregaard's CCTV?' he said.

'I've got someone looking at it but I'm not hopeful.'

'What do you think happened to the Syrian?'

'They struck him with something. A knife or some sort of injection. I don't know what. Though ... I don't think it killed him,' said Lisbeth.

'No?'

'No. If it had, why remove the body?'

'Precisely what I was thinking,' said Henrik. 'That's not to say they didn't kill him later, of course.'

'No,' said Lisbeth. 'If it was a straightforward kidnapping, they would surely have been in touch by now with some demand or other.'

They both pondered that for a moment.

'And there have definitely not been any sightings?' said Lisbeth.

'One, in Nørrebro last week, but unconfirmed, and frankly the witness could just as easily have been mistaken. Aside from that, not a peep. He hasn't used a bank card, looked up any friends or been spotted anywhere.'

'So he's either dead, being held against his will some-where, or really excellent at lying low.'

'But where?' said Henrik.

Lisbeth shrugged.

'And more importantly, why?' Henrik continued. 'Why not walk into the nearest police station and report what happened to him at Nørregaard's place?'

'Same reason people normally keep stuff from us. Fear.'

'Of getting caught?'

'Or being labelled a snitch. Or because they think that whatever is going on, they can handle it better than we can.'

'You might be onto something, Lisbeth.'

'You can thank me later.'

43

'Twenty-seven thousand views on Twitter,' said Gustav.

'Shut up,' said Jensen. 'I need to get on with this article.'

Margrethe had been ecstatic that Jensen's spat with Henrik had made all the news bulletins. 'Fantastic work,' she had said, beaming. 'This is exactly the kind of thing we need more of.'

'Not really,' Jensen had replied. 'News about reporters making news isn't real news. Remember who once said so?'

'The number of times they've clicked on the video says our readers disagree with you.'

'I went in too hard,' said Jensen. 'I'm sure the police are doing everything they can.'

'On the contrary, your challenge was long overdue. I want you to write a feature on it, as well as the news about the second body. I'll get someone to interview the Commissioner, right to reply and all that,' Margrethe said.

Jensen had written and filed the news article as soon as she had returned from the press conference, but the feature wouldn't come. She had just been angry with Henrik and couldn't concentrate on turning it into the kind of attack on the police that Margrethe wanted.

Her and Henrik, on film, in a public space felt wrong. Their relationship had been lived out in the shadows until now: in his car, in dark corners of restaurants and on deserted beaches and woodland paths.

On the other hand, perhaps the episode had served as the clean break with the past that they both needed.

'By the way,' Gustav said from behind his desk. 'I've looked everywhere for Amaliekilde Holdings.'

'Yes?'

'Can't find a mention of any company by that name.'

'I didn't think you would. I already looked.'

'Amaliekilde is the name of a natural spring, apparently, on Bornholm.'

'I know that too,' said Jensen.

She tried to return to her article.

Impossible.

'Wait,' she said after a while. 'Deep Throat was born on Bornholm.'

'Ernst Brøgger?'

'Yes, Henning told me that.'

'Lots of people are from Bornholm.'

'But the way Brøgger reacted when I mentioned Amaliekilde to him. It was like he was shocked.'

Gustav sat up in his chair. 'What, you think it's his company? His house in Vedbæk? Yeah, you're right, it could be. He never told us where he lived.'

Jensen thought about it. Could this be the reason he had asked her to drop the case? Because the trail led back to him? But if that were true, why would Brøgger have asked her to investigate in the first place? It didn't make sense.

'Maybe,' she said. 'Brøgger is probably the only one who can tell us.'

'But he's not getting back to you, so he's obviously not keen to talk about it. And we don't know where he is,' said Gustav.

An idea came to her. Brøgger owned a traditional Danish lunch restaurant in a basement in the plush centre of the city. They had met him there once. He had told them he always sat at the same table for lunch.

'I'm popping out,' she said to Gustav.

'What? But the story . . . Margrethe said.'

'Tell her I'll finish it later. Just need to check something first.'

Brøgger's basement restaurant was cool and dark. The sun didn't make it down through the windows set high on the wall, through which you could see the feet of busy Copenhageners rushing past.

Only a few of the tables were occupied with people eating open sandwiches with herring, liver pate and roast beef, piled high with remoulade and crispy fried onions.

The place smelled like childhood, of beer and rye bread, with a hint of the tobacco absorbed by the walls before smoking had been banned. Decorated with wood panelling, brass lamps with green glass shades and paintings of rural Danish scenes, it looked as if it hadn't changed in more than half a century.

Brøgger's regular table was occupied. Jensen got her hopes up as she approached, but the person glaring at her from behind a newspaper when she cleared her throat to announce her presence was a woman with blonde hair and reading glasses on a chain around her neck.

Jensen went up to the bar where one of the waiters, a tall

man in a long white apron, was checking his phone. She thought she recognised him from last time she and Gustav had met Brøgger. 'Seen Ernst Brøgger lately?' she said to him, smiling.

'Who?' said the waiter. He turned his back to her, suddenly busy printing out a bill.

'I'm a friend of his. I need to get hold of him urgently,' she said.

'I don't know anyone by that name,' the bartender said.

'But he owns this place.'

'I wouldn't know anything about that. I just work here. Now, what can I get you?' he said.

Deflated, she slumped onto one of the bar stools and ordered a draught Carlsberg, which came ice cold in a tall glass. Perhaps she would get lucky. Perhaps Brøgger would show up if she waited a while. She could do with some time to collect her thoughts, think of new leads for her and Gustav to pursue.

She checked her phone again. Still nothing from Kristoffer. Was what she had asked so unreasonable? To know something, anything at all, about him?

She wondered if he was stressed about something at work. Since selling his data warehousing company he had stayed on as a special advisor to the Board which, as far as Jensen could tell, involved him doing as he pleased. Lately, however, he had seemed to have got busy again, working all hours.

Jensen pushed her Carlsberg away, most of it undrunk. It tasted off, bitter somehow. Her stomach was rumbling with hunger, but the smell of lunch was making her feel sick.

'Can I get you something else?' said a voice behind her. She turned to find a man of Esben's age, seated at a nearby table. He had finished eating and was having a brandy with his coffee. 'Or perhaps you're not thirsty?' he said, pointing to her abandoned lager.

'You a regular here?' she asked him.

'I come here now and again,' he said. 'How about that drink?'

'Know the guy who owns the place?'

'No, should I?'

'He's in his late sixties, maybe past seventy, horn-rimmed glasses, expensively dressed. Usually sits over there.' She pointed to Brøgger's table where the woman with the blonde hair and glasses was applying lipstick in the mirror of a powder compact.

'Doesn't ring a bell. What do you want *him* for? A bit too old for you, isn't he, seventy?'

Yeah, like you're not.

'It's nothing. Forget I asked,' said Jensen.

'So, what's it to be?'

'What?'

'The drink.'

'If I want a drink, I will buy one.'

'Suit yourself.' The man drained his coffee and frowned at her as he got up, straightening his belt over his considerable girth. 'Say, you look kind of familiar to me, but I can't place you. Put me out of my misery, where do I know you from?'

'You don't.'

'Got it,' he said, snapping his fingers. 'You're that *Dagbladet* journalist, aren't you? Jensen.' The man raised his phone at her. 'Saw you on the news earlier.'

'No,' said Jensen, leaving the money for her drink on the bar and heading for the exit with one hand across her face, before he could take a photo. 'That wasn't me.'

214

44

Henrik picked up the mail from the doormat as he stepped into the empty house. His wife and children had left at the crack of dawn for Italy. He told himself that he might still join them once the case was solved.

('And pigs might fly,' said his wife in his head.)

He was still trying to process what he had just learned from David Goldschmidt's colleague at the Forensic Institute, a woman with a blunt, black fringe who was almost as round as she was tall.

'Why couldn't you just have told me on the phone?' he had said to her as he donned his PPE gear, reluctant to enter the forensic cellar, lined with stainless steel and white tiles, without David's reassuring presence by his side.

The woman who had presented herself as 'Lola Steffensen, but you can call me Lola' had already been wearing hers. 'This has to be seen to be believed,' she said. 'I can't wait to tell David about it, such a shame he wasn't here to witness it himself.'

215

As they approached the stainless-steel table, he was about to remind her that they were dealing with murder, and to show some decorum, when a sharp smell of rusted iron, seawater and rotting flesh hit his nostrils. Lola had placed the chains in a pile to one side. The corpse was covered in a sheet of thin green paper which Lola removed without David's usual health warning.

The man on the table, whose severed head had been placed by his body, was slight and short, about half the size of the first victim. Was this the brains of the outfit, and the bigger man the brawn?

The chain had been secured around the man's body by a padlock. The divers had found another chain at the bottom of the harbour, along with an open padlock, which explained how the body they had found by the Opera House had risen to the surface and drifted further into the harbour.

'Anything characteristic about the chain that might help us find who did this?' said Henrik.

'No,' said Lola. 'It's the sort you can buy in any DIY store. The padlock too. People use them on gates and fences, so they're pretty common, but you might not need to worry about that. Have a look at this.'

Lola pointed into the dark crater in the man's chest. 'I wasn't sure at first what I was looking at. It seemed impossible. Like something you only read about in a pathologist's textbook.'

'Put me out of my misery, please,' said Henrik.

Lola pointed to a greyish looking item lodged in the wound. It was the size of a small carrot.

'Is that what I think it is?' said Henrik.

'Yep, it's a finger,' said Lola, smiling at him broadly and pointing. 'You can see the nail there,' she said.

Henrik looked at her, not comprehending. 'The victim's finger?'

'No. We're testing, but I'm almost certain it isn't.'

'Then whose?'

'I once read about a similar case in England,' said Lola, pointing to the corpse. 'The wound suggests a sawn-off shotgun was used. The shooter lifts the gun, takes aim, but leaves his finger over the end of the barrel. In this case, the finger has been shot off close to the knuckle. The force of the shot wedged it deep inside the wound. I believe you're looking at the killer's finger.'

Henrik considered this. The murders had looked like a professional job, but the shot-off finger and unfastened padlock suggested otherwise. 'Can we get a print?'

'I'll get one for you, but if your killer is as hapless as it would appear, then you might want to check with the local hospitals. It's not the sort of injury you can treat at home with a plaster and a couple of paracetamols. It's highly likely he would have sought medical attention.'

On his way back to the car, Henrik had phoned the team asking them to call round the hospitals immediately, with strict instructions to let him know the second they found anything. They might be close to discovering who murdered the two men, and, most importantly, why.

It was going to be a long night. He needed a shower and a few hours' kip. He traipsed guiltily through the silent rooms of his house; without his family there, it felt like a stranger's home.

A piece of jewellery twinkled on the floor in the kitchen. His daughter's bracelet. He had often yearned to have the house to himself, to be left in peace with his football and a few cans of beer, but there was no pleasure in it now.

He sent another text to Jensen.

> I know you hate me, but could you have found
> a less public place to vent your anger?

He had sometimes thought it would be easier if she found someone else, to put a stop to his never-ending feelings of guilt towards her, but now he wished to God that she had stayed single.

There had been no news from his wife. Not even a short message to let him know that she and the kids had arrived safely at their overnight stay in Austria. He grabbed a beer out of the fridge and turned on the TV, then switched it off again. He was restless, on edge, as he checked his phone for the hundredth time.

There was a missed call from Lynn Walker at the Metropolitan Police. He pressed her number, and she answered straight away. From the background noise, it sounded like she was still in the office. 'Hello Henrik.'

'Please tell me you have some good news for me.'

'I believe so. You know that DNA sample you shared? Well, there was no direct match, but there was a close one. Christos Karagiannis, repeat offender, human mountain. Serving time for violent robbery.'

'A close match? What does that mean?'

'Father, brother, cousin, uncle. It's not possible to determine exactly, but listen. I made some enquires. No one has seen his son Nick around for a few weeks. Apparently, he takes after his father, in physique and disposition to violence. I'll find out for sure, but I showed the photo in the fake passport you sent me to a few people, and they reckon it's him.'

'Nick Karagiannis?'

'Yes. I think he's your victim.'

'One of my victims, you mean.'

'What?'

'I have two.'

Lynn Walker whistled quietly. Henrik could hear that someone had entered her room and was talking to her. 'Got to go,' she said. 'Send me whatever you have on the second victim. Maybe they both flew in from London.'

'Will do. Call me as soon as you know anything more. We'll need to get someone flown over to identify the body as soon as possible – and thanks, Lynn, good work,' said Henrik and hung up.

He called the team to pass on the news, then headed upstairs, knowing that it would be impossible to sleep now. In his youngest son's bedroom, he lay down on the bed with his nose in the pillow, longing for the boy and his uncomplicated view on life.

The two of them had spent many happy hours here on the PlayStation, snuggled up to one another, Henrik secretly putting his nose on his boy's hair and inhaling his scent. Oliver had been excited to go to Italy. They had talked about playing volleyball in the pool. Henrik couldn't let him down, he just couldn't. He told himself that as soon as significant progress on the case had been made, he would get in his car and drive to Italy.

('Sure you will,' said his wife.)

Henrik closed his eyes, tried to concentrate on his breathing.

Just then his phone began to vibrate.

Tone Ravnsbæk.

'I found your tramp.'

'Did he say anything?'

'He's dead.'

45

Monday 20:01

'Kristoffer?'

The blinds were drawn in the penthouse, and the place was completely dark, except for a flickering light coming from the living room. Music was playing, a soft jazz piano, and there was an unfamiliar scent about the place.

Jensen finished a text message for Henrik and dropped her bag in the hallway. 'Anyone home?' she shouted, a sudden cold feeling running through her. Was there someone else in there with Kristoffer? She pushed open the door to the living room. 'What are you . . .?'

She stopped.

The white room sparkled with what looked like a hundred candles. The lights were reflected in the big mirror on the far wall, creating a sense of infinity. On every surface there were vases with flowers.

'Welcome home, darling,' said Kristoffer, naked, handing her a glass of champagne.

'What's all this?' said Jensen as he leaned over and kissed her on her neck.

'Just something to show you my affection,' he said. 'I know things have been a little tense lately. All my fault. Only, as you may have discovered, I'm rubbish at talking about my feelings.'

Jensen smiled. 'Not one of *my* strengths either.'

'Let's try and be good at it together,' said Kristoffer. He took her glass and set it down with his own. 'But first, let me show you what you mean to me.'

He unbuttoned her shirt dress and pulled it off her, along with her underwear, all the while keeping his eyes on her. Then he knelt and began to kiss her body all over, and the thought that had tried to force itself to the front of Jensen's mind dissolved into meaninglessness.

46

'Christ's sake,' said Henrik as he walked up to the low concrete building covered in graffiti. The team had rigged up lights and taped off the area, erecting a white tent over the tramp's body. The place was crawling with scene-of-crime officers in white body suits, reflecting the blinking blue lights of the emergency vehicles. Thankfully, someone had blocked the access road, or they would have had the full complement of rubberneckers by now.

Tone Ravnsbæk approached him with her military gait, falling in step beside him. 'The doctor is just having a look, though the cause of death is pretty obvious.'

She handed him his protective gear. A minute later, he pushed aside the tent opening and stepped in. He recognised the tramp's long white beard. Pretty much the rest of his face was gone, the tell-tale devastating work of a sawn-off shotgun.

'His notebook?'

'Nowhere to be seen. Not clear if anything else has been

taken. His bags have been upended. Nothing there but trash,' said Tone.

'I'm sure it wasn't trash to him,' said Henrik. 'What was his name?'

'Tommy Ewardsen. He was forty-eight.'

'What?'

Henrik felt guilty. He had assumed that the man was at least twenty years older, a loon not worth listening to. Someone must have seen the two of them talking on the quay that morning. Had the killers assumed that Tommy had passed vital information on to the police and wanted to make sure he wouldn't appear as a witness? Perhaps Tommy had noted down a number plate that could lead to the killers. Or perhaps there had been nothing but innocent scribbles in his notebook, but the killers hadn't wanted to take any chances. In any case, Henrik should have reacted, or he might not now be faced with a third body.

'What are you thinking?' asked Tone.

'I'm thinking that the media will be all over this. Another failing and yours truly will be in the firing line.'

'But you couldn't have known,' said Tone. 'It wasn't your fault.'

'I should have used my instincts.'

He thought of Jensen and her public lambasting of him, which now felt entirely justified. Though it seemed Jensen was feeling guilty about it. She had finally texted him back, not with an apology, but with the closest she got to contrition: a piece of useful information.

Somehow, she and Gustav had managed to track down the person who had been sending threatening mails to Nørregaard. There was even an address in Birkerød, but it would have to wait now.

The doctor had finished and was packing up. Henrik

nodded to thank him and indicate that he could leave. A photographer stepped in and began to take photos of the body.

'Anyway, we've got the print from the finger lodged in the second victim's chest,' he said. 'We should be able to find out pretty soon who did this, and that ought to shut up the media.'

His phone began to buzz.

'We've got him, boss,' said the woman at the other end, one of his team of detectives.

'Who?'

'The shooter. Jønne Olsen. Walked into accident and emergency at Hvidovre hospital the night between Monday and Tuesday last week. Was treated as an out-patient and sent home. Refused to provide a reason for his injury.'

'Is he known to us?'

'Oh yeah. Since he was sixteen. Two spells in prison. GBH. Robbery.'

'Good work. Check with forensics if there's a print match with the finger found in the chest of victim two.'

'Already did. The answer is yes. And Ida Kaurup, the dog walker, has identified Olsen from a photo as the man she saw throw a bundle in the fjord.'

'Get me his address.'

'Texting it to you now.'

Henrik ran for his car.

'Where are we going?' said Tone.

'To arrest a killer.'

47

Jensen woke to find Kristoffer standing over her and refilling their champagne glasses. Her head was pounding, her mouth dry.

'Did anyone ever tell you, Miss Jensen, that you are a delectable specimen?' he said.

'What time is it?' said Jensen, rolling over in bed in search of her mobile phone. 'I must have drifted off.'

There was a one-word message from Henrik.

Thanks.

Fie had once more come up trumps, somehow managing to track down the person who had threatened Esben and his family with an imaginative catalogue of horrors. She had given Henrik the man's address. If he wasn't going to do anything about it, then she and Gustav would.

'I tired you out,' said Kristoffer, handing her a glass. 'Who cares what time it is.' He lay down beside her, took her phone out of her hand and placed it on the bedside table. 'You know, Jensen,' he began. 'I have never told anyone what I'm about to tell you, but you wanted to know. It's . . . difficult for me to talk about, so bear with me.'

Jensen put her head against his chest. His heartbeat was steady, calm.

'A long time ago, when I was eighteen, something terrible happened. It was the week I graduated from high school and things were already hard, as Mum was in hospital, dying from stomach cancer.' He held his hand over his eyes and paused for a moment. When he resumed his story, he sounded almost breezy, as if determined not to show any emotion. 'So there were a lot of hospital visits, in between my exams. I think I told you that I'm an only child, so it was just me and Dad caring for Mum. Anyway, I managed to graduate along with my classmates, but didn't join in any of the parties that followed, except this one time. I wasn't in the mood for celebrating, but Dad was adamant that I should go out and enjoy myself, despite what was happening to Mum. He knew that school hadn't always been easy for me, because of my weight.'

'Your weight?'

'Yes. I was big back then and got bullied quite badly.'

'So did you go to the party?' said Jensen.

'Reluctantly, yes, with a lot of persuasion. It was only a couple of streets away from our house. I had a few beers, but remember feeling out of it, like I couldn't relate to the others. They were having fun, dancing, getting drunk, but Mum was in hospital being eaten up from the inside by this horrible disease. It felt wrong, you know?'

'I can imagine,' said Jensen, recalling the few school parties she had attended after her mother had decided to up sticks in Copenhagen and relocate them to the middle of nowhere in North Jutland. She had watched the others as if from behind a sheet of glass, feeling no kinship with them whatsoever. Shortly afterwards she had left school to become a reporter for the local newspaper. 'What did you do?' she said.

'I made my excuses and left, but when I got back to the house, I knew something had happened. The front door was open and all the lights were on, though it was late, and Dad would normally have been in bed asleep. A chest of drawers we kept in the hallway had been knocked over and the drawers emptied of hats, gloves and scarves. I shouted for my Dad, but there was no answer. It was the same in the other rooms: furniture knocked over, drawers emptied, everything a total mess.'

'And your Dad?'

'I found him lying on the floor in his bedroom, in his pyjamas, blood everywhere.'

Kristoffer stopped, pinched the bridge of his nose. Jensen stroked his arm gently and he swallowed a couple of times.

'He had been beaten to death,' he said, his voice choked. 'It was assumed he had woken up on hearing the people breaking in, perhaps remonstrated with them. I wish he hadn't. They beat him with the metal lamp from his bedside table so savagely that one of his eyes came out.'

Kristoffer began to cry. Jensen held him tight. 'Who did it?' she asked softly after a long while.

'Some drug addicts, probably,' said Kristoffer, his voice thick. 'They didn't take the TV or anything, so they were probably just looking for cash. The police never found them. But I'm not surprised to be honest. The investigators were completely useless. They even suspected me at one point.'

'Really?'

'They must have been desperate. Just because they couldn't find who did it.'

'What happened to your Mum?'

'She never found out what had happened. She was so ill by that point that she was sleeping most of the time. I couldn't bring myself to tell her. She and Dad had been together since they were sixteen. She died a few days later. Suddenly, completely unexpectedly, I was an orphan.'

'Kristoffer, I'm so sorry,' said Jensen.

'So, you see, I'm not very good with all that family stuff.'

'Me neither,' said Jensen. 'It's just been me and my mum for as long as I can remember and let's just say she's not going to win any parenting competitions.'

'I think that's what's made me so determined to succeed. After all that stuff happened, I kind of reinvented myself. Started again, sold the family home, used the money to buy my first flat in Christianshavn, founded my little empire. Lost the weight and got fit. I had to do it all by myself, and it was tough, but I made it. And then I got lucky, met some investors who believed in me. When I sold my company, they got rich too. One of the first things I did was to buy this place. I threw out all my old stuff. It was a new start for me, a final jettison of all the sadness and hurt of the past, and frankly I've never felt the need to go back there.'

Jensen knew what he meant. It was Margrethe who had made her what she was. Margrethe who had recognised something in her as a green reporter, eventually sending her to London as a foreign correspondent. 'You might say the same about me. I was never someone people reckoned with. It's all been about proving them wrong,' Jensen said.

'Look at us,' said Kristoffer, wiping away tears. 'A couple of misfits.'

'Not in all ways,' said Jensen, snuggling closer.

There were many questions on her mind about what had happened to his father, but they could wait. It was understandable that Kristoffer had tried to distance himself from the horror of it. Why had Henrik thought that this reflected badly on him?

'I'm glad we talked. It's good that there are no secrets between us,' Kristoffer said, blowing his nose loudly on a tissue. 'And now it's your turn to share. I want to know everything that's going on in your world. Has that missing Syrian turned up? Are the police any closer to solving the murders in the harbour? What does my brilliant lover know that no one else does?'

He kissed Jensen on the forehead.

Her phone rang before she could answer him.

Unknown number.

'Hello?'

'Ah, Miss Jensen, finally.' A male voice with an old-fashioned accent, like something out of a Danish movie from the 1950s.

Jensen walked into the hall. 'Who is this?'

'My name is Leif Kofoed. I believe we have mutual friends?'

Jensen didn't reply.

The man laughed quietly.

'I'd like to offer you an interview. An exclusive, as you journalists call it. I don't often speak to the media. In fact, you'd be hard pushed to find any articles about me anywhere. So come on, what do you say?'

'When?'

'I'll send a car for you. Would nine a.m. tomorrow morning outside *Dagbladet* suit you?'

48

Rottereden (the Rat's Nest) was a basement bodega, covering a floor area so small that it was not obliged to uphold the smoking ban. Red-and-white chequered tablecloths dotted with filled ashtrays and Carlsberg coasters could be seen though the dirty windows, like a glimpse into a distant past. A game of billiards was in progress and, judging by the raucous laughter, someone was making a night of it.

There had been no Jønne Olsen to arrest when Henrik had turned up at his address with Tone and half a dozen police officers. A woman wearing a dressing gown and smoking a cigarette had emerged from the flat next door just as they had begun hammering on the door and were preparing to force entry.

'Go back inside and stay there,' Henrik shouted at her.

'He's not in,' she said, making no move to leave. 'Believe me, you'd know if he was. Sometimes he has his music on so loud my ornaments are literally shaking off the shelf. I've told him a thous—'

'Where is he?' Henrik snapped.

'How should I know?' said the woman, dropping her cigarette butt on the floor and stepping on it. 'You could try Rottereden. I've seen him in there a few times,' she said, slamming the door in his face.

A sign stuck to the door of the bodega advised visitors to 'push hard'.

Henrik's heart sank. There was no way they could make a discreet entry, asking a few people if they had seen Olsen anywhere about. They might as well get the claxon out.

If Jønne was in there, a big *if*, he might still have his shotgun on him. In the cramped space, if he lashed out it was sure to end in disaster.

Henrik signalled to the others to wait. He would go in alone, check the lie of the land. With his black leather jacket and unshaven face, he could easily pass for a drinker.

The smell of his youth struck him as soon as he pushed the door open: cigarettes and beer. That and the swift realisation that he was fooling precisely no one.

The men and women assembled in the Rottereden might have been drinking solidly for hours, but they knew a cop when they saw one. He looked at their closed faces as the room fell silent around him, but for the soft thud of a struck cue ball and the piped music.

'OK,' he said. Holding up his hands. 'I get it. No welcome parade. But in case you were wondering, I'm not here for you. I need to speak to Jønne Olsen. Anyone seen him?'

No one gave him a reply.

He turned out not to need one.

It was just a quick glance, but it was enough. A thin lad with a bad ginger beard looking for a swift second into the back room where a big unit of a man had got up and was running for the fire exit.

231

Jønne Olsen.

Henrik ran, but suddenly there were chairs in his way, people with bottles that dropped on the floor and smashed. By the time he finally made it, cursing as he stumbled up a short flight of stairs to the back door and emerging into a courtyard with bicycles and wheelie bins, Jønne had scarpered. A gate was open at the back, leading to another street.

'*Pis*,' Henrik shouted, kicking a bin hard and hurting his foot in the process.

'Secure the area, now. And get the dogs out,' he snapped at Tone when he had rejoined the others. 'I want him found and arrested before daybreak.'

Before arriving at Olsen's flat, they had received news of the link they had been waiting for: they had a match between the spot of blood found at the Roskilde Fjord summerhouse and the second victim, whoever the man was.

Jønne Olsen would have bled profusely when he accidentally shot his own finger off. He and his accomplice must have decided to drive back to Hvidovre hospital to seek medical attention. Then later they returned, this time bringing plastic sheeting, to dismember the bodies and sweep the summerhouse, before wrapping the personal effects in a bedsheet and throwing them into the fjord.

They probably used the plastic sheeting to lift the now headless and fingerless corpses into the back of the hire car. Then one man drove the hire car to Refshaleøen, followed by the other in a separate vehicle. The two men wrapped the corpses in chains and dropped them into the harbour, then set the hire car and DNA evidence alight before fleeing, watched by the tramp who noted their number plate in his little black book.

It all fitted into place, except for the motive. Why had

the murdered men been in Denmark, and why had they been taken out?

While Tone got on her phone to orchestrate the manhunt for Jønne Olsen, Henrik took big gulps of night air and told himself to calm down. They would get Olsen sooner or later and, when they did, they'd have no trouble nailing him to the crime, given that his finger had been found in the dead man's chest.

Henrik was very much looking forward to hearing Jønne Olsen explain that one away.

49

Tuesday 11:59

Leif Kofoed was as far from looking like a psychopathic criminal as it was possible to get, decided Jensen, as she ducked under the rotor blades that were whipping up the sand along the beach and blowing it into her eyes.

She walked away from the sea towards the man waiting for her in the dunes. He appeared to be alone, though she suspected there would be some hired muscle watching them, if what Henrik and Esben had said about Kofoed was true.

She had debated long and hard whether to accept his invitation. An invitation from an elusive expat billionaire with an alleged hardcore criminal past who wanted to return to Denmark to build a major golf resort in North Jutland, like some would-be Donald Trump.

That's how she had explained it to Margrethe, for whom there had been no question that she must go. 'It's a good story. A true eccentric. Never going to happen, of course, but find out what drives him.'

According to Esben, Kofoed was a man who was used to

getting his own way. Henrik had called him a nasty piece of work who had served time in prison.

All the more reason for interviewing him, in Jensen's book. Not wanting them to dissuade her, she hadn't told Henrik and Esben where she was going, something she had fretted about on her way across Denmark. Only Gustav and Margrethe knew what she was doing, and neither had her exact location.

The very thought that Leif Kofoed was capable of inflicting harm on anyone now seemed laughable. The man shaking her hand under the baking hot sun was seventy if he was a day, bald under his hat, wearing metal-framed glasses and carrying a walking stick.

The driver he had sent to pick her up had told her nothing, so it had been a surprise when she had found herself boarding a helicopter, then traversing Denmark, watching the islands glide past in the sunshine far below.

When she had at last met Ernst Brøgger in front of Amalienborg Castle, he had called it a tiny kingdom that he would do anything to defend. She wondered now what he had really meant by that. Had he been talking about defending his patch against those who would take it from him? Was Brøgger the mystery owner of Amaliekilde and the holding company by the same name? Was this the real reason he had asked her to investigate what had happened to Carsten Vangede, to find out how much Vangede knew?

The fact that Brøgger still hadn't contacted her suggested she was right.

She supposed Leif Kofoed had intended to impress her with the helicopter ride and couldn't deny that it had worked to some extent. 'Welcome,' he said, leaning on his walking stick. 'Or should I say welcome back?'

'What do you mean?' said Jensen.

'It was here in North Jutland that you first became a journalist, was it not?'

'Yes, but how—'

'And then from there to *Dagbladet* thanks to that debonair whistle-blower Esben Nørregaard, and the scoop he gave you. I believe your mother still lives along the coast. A landscape painter, is that right?'

Jensen was astonished. She had always thought of herself as anonymous, unknown and unfindable. 'How do you know all this?'

'Information is what I built my business on. I always do my research. I believe in this aspect, we're alike? You'll be surprised what you can find, Miss Jensen, or should I be using your first name?'

Jensen stared at him. 'You know my first name?' she said quietly.

'I'll admit it was hard to find. Such a shame, a lovely name and yet you haven't used it since you were a little girl.'

'It's a stupid name.'

'And, of course, there's another Aalborg connection. That apprentice of yours, Gustav Skov, isn't it? The nephew of your esteemed editor-in-chief Margrethe Skov?'

'Sounds like you know already.'

'True. And I know about his little, shall we say, act of defiance. This is still much talked about at the high school and among those cruel boys who bullied him. I understand that they don't regard the matter as closed.'

Gustav had begged to come along when she had told him about the interview. Now she was glad she had turned him down. 'Why me?' she said. 'You give your first interview in many years, and I'm the one you pick.'

'Because I hear that you're the best and I never settle for less.'

236

Jensen ignored the flattery and decided to go straight in. 'Esben told me that you looked him up recently, in Dyrehaven, asking him to introduce you to the prime minister and others.'

Leif Kofoed seemed unperturbed. 'That's correct. Esben Nørregaard and I go way back. I wanted him to support my project, put in a good word for me.'

'But he refused.'

'That's also correct. Sadly, Esben does not agree that my scheme has any chance of succeeding and he told me so.'

'Did that make you angry? Did you put pressure on Esben afterwards? His driver, Aziz Almasi, is missing after being assaulted at Esben's property. Do you have anything to do with that?'

Leif Kofoed laughed. 'So many questions, I like it, but I must disappoint you. It did not, no I didn't, and no I haven't. It's typical Nørregaard, to think that he's that important, to see green-eyed monsters where there are none. Comes from being a politician, I suppose, always needing to watch one's back.'

'Something I gather you're not so bad at yourself,' said Jensen. 'So you had a conversation with Esben, he refused your request, and then you walked away and left it there?'

'Again, you're correct. I since discovered that Esben has lost influence somewhat with the prime minister for being too outspoken. I believe that's the real reason he turned me down. Now, if there is nothing else, let me show you—'

'Wait,' said Jensen. 'You were right, I *have* done my research. Not that there's much to find. You've done a good job of keeping a low profile for all the years you've spent outside of Denmark.'

'Thank you, I take that as a compliment.'

'But I know you once served time in prison for murder.'

'I did,' Leif said. 'It taught me a valuable lesson.'

'Not to get caught?'

'That nothing was worth as much to me as my freedom. I have lived by that since,' said Kofoed.

'Who was the boy and why did you kill him?'

'It's a sad story, almost sixty years ago. I will tell you one day, but for the moment, let's call it a crime of passion,' said Kofoed. 'Now, it's rather hot here. If you have satisfied your curiosity as to my person, I should like to show you my plans.'

'I've more questions, but they will keep,' said Jensen. 'So where is this land you're planning to build on?'

Kofoed's hand swept over the dunes and the marshland behind it, the heather and grass as dry as tinder. 'You're looking at it.'

50

'Sit up straight when you're being talked to,' Tone barked at the man opposite them in the interview room.

Lars Bjerre did as he was told, lazily, after an encouraging nod from his lawyer who looked like the ink was not yet dry on her graduation papers.

Bjerre's request for legal representation had held things up, as had his three requests to use the bathroom and his insistence on getting a latte with three sugars before he would say anything at all.

They had found him in his bedroom at his mother's house, using the address in Birkerød that Jensen had managed to track down.

Henrik didn't want to know how she had done it, certain there was nothing legal about it. Ignorance was bliss as far as Jensen's methods were concerned.

Bjerre was in his thirties, currently unemployed, and sponging off his disabled mother, who claimed that he spent his days looking for work. In between allegedly writing job applications and smartening up his CV, Bjerre hung out on Twitter under a multitude of aliases, making life a misery for people by spouting hatred and threats.

'Now, I'm going to ask you one more time,' Henrik said. 'Why did you send those offensive emails to Esben Nørregaard?'

Tone's hands paused over the keyboard. She typed twice as fast as Mark. Except for ordering Bjerre to show some respect, she had thankfully stuck to Henrik's strict instructions to stay quiet during the interview.

Lars Bjerre shrugged. 'I don't like his face. He's always on TV, telling others what to do, the rich bastard.'

'You wrote that you wished his wife and children would get cancer and die. That they ought to be raped. That Esben should watch his step.'

'I never did anything.'

Bjerre's mother had said the same thing, crying as they led her son from the house to the waiting police car. 'What do you want him for? He never goes out, never leaves the house. I swear to you, he hasn't done anything.'

'Oh, but you did. Sending emails threatening violence carries a possible jail sentence,' Henrik said.

Bjerre looked as if he couldn't care less.

'Did someone ask you to it?'

'No,' said Bjerre, studying his nails.

'Are you familiar with the name Leif Kofoed?' said Henrik.

Bjerre looked up sharply. 'Who the hell is that?'

'Did Leif Kofoed put you up to it?'

'I've never even heard the name, so how could he have done?'

Henrik was inclined to believe him. Esben Nørregaard's theory that the old gangster was somehow threatening him and his family to get his own way with a Jutland golf resort seemed ridiculous. Most likely, Bjerre was a red herring, a lone troll who got off on verbal abuse.

They had seized his hard drive, and Henrik was willing to bet his police pension that Esben Nørregaard wasn't the man's only victim.

The interview had been a waste of time. Henrik began to pack his papers away. 'Interview ends,' he said.

'What happens now?' said Bjerre, with a sideways glance at his lawyer.

'Ravnsbæk here will get you to sign a statement and then you can leave.'

'That's it?'

'Oh sure,' said Tone. 'In your dreams.'

Henrik looked at her sharply and received an obstinate glare in return.

'We'll deal with your online offences later,' he said to Bjerre. 'But right now, I think it's fair to say you're less important to us than the ant I squashed under my shoe when I stepped into this room.'

241

51

Jensen had already written the headline in her head when she left Leif Kofoed waving goodbye with one hand on his hat, a tiny spot on the vast, empty landscape. By the time the helicopter landed in Copenhagen she had written half the article on her laptop.

The pictures she had taken had come out well. Though Kofoed had refused to allow her to bring a professional photographer, he had turned out to be a willing subject, posing in the dunes, an old man with his walking stick, casting a long shadow in the white sand.

He was obviously a shrewd businessman, and made no bones about his criminal past, but his desire to return to Denmark where he had been born seemed genuine. Jensen understood that desire, the curious pull of home after many years abroad.

'How did you make your money?' she had asked him.

'By investing in the right things at the right time.'

'Can you be more specific?'

'Take your boyfriend.'

'My boyfriend?'

'I told you Jensen, I always do my research very thoroughly,' Kofoed had smiled. 'Kristoffer Bro was a young lad with a good idea. No one was talking about data warehousing the way he was at that time. People's eyes would glaze over whenever he talked about it, but I saw something in him, something determined and resilient. A bit like you, young Jensen.'

She was speechless. Kristoffer had never mentioned anything about knowing Leif Kofoed. She raced back through their conversations, certain that she had mentioned Kofoed once or twice without him batting an eyelid in recognition.

'Kristoffer was virtually penniless. Had put everything he owned into starting the company and was running it from his bedroom, so I decided to fund him, against a stake in the company. Then, when he sold the company, we both got rich.' Kofoed paused and looked at Jensen. 'I can tell from your face that he never told you that, but I ask you to forgive him. He knows that I abhor publicity. In this aspect, he and I are very different, I suppose. In any case, over the years there have been many other Kristoffers. A few have failed, naturally, but those that have won out have rewarded me handsomely.'

'All sounds legit, so why the big secrecy, not telling me where I was going today, insisting on me coming alone, refusing to say where you live? It strikes me there must be more to it,' said Jensen.

'Oh, but I didn't say there wasn't,' replied Kofoed distractedly. He had stopped in the middle of the path. Only a large sand dune plantation and the sea were in sight. Nothing else. 'This is where I'm going to put the clubhouse,' he said, pulling a map from his inside breast pocket and carefully unfolding it.

The architect's drawings showed a huge development of houses set around a golf course. 'Mine will be over there. The biggest one,' he said, pointing. 'This resort will put the north of Denmark on the map, create employment for hundreds of people for years to come. It will be equal to some of the great Scottish links courses.'

'But you don't even own the land. It's all public.'

'I've made some substantial offers.'

'And you don't have planning permission and you're unlikely to get it, so in actual fact, it's nothing but a pipe dream.'

'But greatness comes from such dreams, Jensen. Once people understand what I'm going to do, they will come around to my way of thinking.'

Was Kofoed mad? Deluded? Potentially, but at the heart of things, he wanted what everyone wants. To be home. To be accepted and respected by his own people, perhaps on occasion loved and admired.

Jensen was keeping her article light, and her stance objective, but right here, right now, it was hard to see what was so bad about the man.

She hadn't been able to go back to sleep after he had called her last night and was desperate for a nap. It would have to be a quick ten minutes by her desk with her head on her forearm as soon as her article was finished.

She had to check on Esben.

And then she needed to ask Kristoffer just what the hell was going on.

52

Tuesday 18:07

Jensen knocked for the third time, after double-checking the number on the door.

'Go away,' came a voice from inside.

'Esben, for Christ's sake, it's me, Jensen.'

The door was quickly unlocked, the safety chain clinking against the wood as it was released. Esben grabbed Jensen's arm and pulled her inside, immediately locking the door behind her. He smelled of sweat and coffee. She counted three pizza boxes and an assortment of takeaway paper bags and empty water bottles. The bed was unmade. Esben must have refused to have his room serviced, but at least there was air conditioning, cranked up to the max.

'What the hell are you playing at?' said Esben.

'Me?'

'Your interview with Leif Kofoed,' said Esben, pointing angrily to his phone screen, on which was displayed the pictures from the dunes.

The article was online already.

245

CASTLES IN THE SAND:
THE BILLIONAIRE WHO WOULD BE KING.

'What about it? He offered me an interview.'

'Of course he bloody did. How did he even contact you?'

'He rang my mobile.'

'How did he get the number?'

Jensen shrugged. She hadn't thought about that. 'He seems to know everything about everybody. He must have seen my by-line in *Dagbladet* and got hold of it somehow. He knows that you and I know each other.'

'So I turn him down and next he comes to you, wanting free publicity for his little plan. And what do you do? Invite him to help himself to column inches.'

'What's that supposed to mean? If you had bothered reading my article, you'd know that I didn't exactly treat him with kid gloves.'

She wasn't going to tell him that Leif Kofoed was also acquainted with Kristoffer, a more likely reason why he had called her and not some other reporter. Maybe the whole thing had been Kristoffer's idea in the first place. She felt her indignation rise at the thought.

She hadn't told him that the call last night had been from Kofoed, and Kristoffer hadn't asked, the boyfriend who normally wanted to know every little detail of what she was up to.

Because he knew already. Think about it, Jensen.

Why hadn't he told her about his relationship with Kofoed?

Esben laughed sarcastically. 'He used you, Jensen. Now everyone knows that he's in Denmark and means business, friend as well as foe.'

'He's a sentimental old man with a stupid dream that's

never going to come true,' said Jensen, shivering in the icy room.

'That's precisely what he wants you to think. Why won't you listen to me? Leif Kofoed is evil, a convicted killer, blackmailer, manipulator and God knows what else. As unscrupulous a human being as you will ever encounter.'

'He says the police have nothing on him, which must be true, or he would have been arrested by now,' she said, feeling her cheeks grow hot.

'Just because that cop of yours and his pals aren't smart enough to catch him, doesn't mean he isn't guilty as hell.'

'We found the guy who sent you those threatening emails. Name of Lars Bjerre. No known links to Kofoed.'

'Of course not. That's how he operates. Doesn't mean it's not him. Come on, Jensen, what's the matter with you?'

'Well, I don't see how me refusing the interview with Kofoed would have helped us get any closer to the truth,' she said.

Esben didn't reply but sank onto the unmade bed and buried his face in his palms.

'What's the matter, Esben? Has something happened?'

'Someone's following me.'

'What?'

'I popped out earlier to 7-Eleven and felt their eyes on my back. Not actually seen anyone, they're far too professional for that. I just know they're there, so I'm not leaving the room now.'

Jensen had felt this herself several times lately. Were she and Esben being followed by the same people? 'I'll call Henrik,' she said.

'No, not him again. Tell me, what has he done to find Aziz? Nothing.'

'You don't know that,' said Jensen. 'When did you last

eat? I'll get you something from downstairs. And while I'm gone, get this place cleaned up, have a shower and a shave. Then we'll talk about what to do.'

She stayed until Esben had locked himself in the bathroom and she could hear the water running. Then she got up to leave.

And stopped.

A piece of paper had been pushed under the door onto the carpet.

Get out of here. You are in danger.

Aziz?

She opened the door, looked left and right and spotted a cleaner in uniform, pushing a trolley away towards the goods lift at the end of the corridor. 'Stop!' she shouted, but the woman merely increased her speed.

Jensen ran, finally catching up with the woman and putting her hand on her shoulder. 'I said, stop.'

The woman looked frightened. 'It's got nothing to do with me,' she shouted in English with an Eastern European accent. 'I only put the note there.'

'Who gave it to you? Come on, it's important.'

'I was smoking outside. In the street, because they don't like us smoking in the back yard. This man came up to me, offered me 200 kroner to push the note under the door.'

'Big guy, very tall?' Jensen stretched her hand up far over her head. 'Black hair, maybe a baseball cap, spoke with an accent?'

'Please don't say anything. I could get fired for this.'

'Don't worry, I won't, if you'd please just tell me what the man looked like.'

The woman glanced up and down the corridor before

speaking. 'He was . . . not like you described. Not tall. And he was wearing a hood over his face so I couldn't see it. Said to me in English that if I did this for him, I'd be helping his friend.'

Jensen let the woman go and got out her phone.

53

'I'll speak to the hotel security team at once,' said Henrik, as soon as he walked through the door.

'You'll do no such thing,' said Esben. He was wearing a white flannel robe reaching to his mid-thighs. His hair was still wet from the shower. 'We don't want any more people to know I'm here.'

Henrik sighed. 'I'll see if I can rustle up some CCTV, but if the guy was covering his face with a hood like that woman said, then we probably won't be able to identify him.'

'Perhaps Aziz asked a friend of his to take the note to me?' said Esben.

'Or someone who wants you to think so,' said Henrik. He turned to Jensen. 'Send a picture of the note to Amira. Find out if it's Aziz's handwriting.'

Jensen quickly composed a text. The three of them listened to the swoosh as it sent.

'Now what?' said Esben.

'Now we get you out of here. Someone knows where you are, which means others can find out,' said Henrik.

Esben shuddered. 'But where?'

'There's your summer cabin in Hornbæk,' said Jensen.

Henrik shook his head. 'Too obvious. We'll have to put you in a safe house. I'll call Lisbeth.'

'No,' said Esben. 'Nothing official. No one must know of this. If anyone in parliament finds out, all hell will break loose.'

'How about my flat in Christianshavn?' suggested Jensen. 'It'll be hot, but you'd be quite safe. There's a video alarm.'

'I'll put someone on watch outside,' said Henrik.

Esben's jaw tightened. 'No.'

'That's agreed then,' said Jensen. 'Pack your things, Esben, you're coming with us and no arguing.'

Her phone pinged. Amira. Jensen's heart sank as she read.

Not Aziz's writing. What does it mean?

'Dear Lord, Jensen, could you have found anywhere smaller to live?'

Esben and Henrik were both panting after climbing the kitchen stairs to the Christianshavn flat. It was late, but not dark. A pale blue light came through the dirty windows.

They had cycled from the loading bay at D'Angleterre, Jensen alongside Henrik who had been riding a cargo bike with Esben in front under a plastic rain cover. Just another Danish family on their way somewhere.

This had been Gustav's idea. He had brought up the rear on his e-scooter, wearing his teenage boy cloak of invisibility as he scanned the streets for anyone who might be following them. His price had been pizza, which he had gone off to collect, with an extra order for Esben.

251

'It's cosy, I'll admit,' said Jensen. 'But you'll find everything you need here.' It felt strange to be back. She had been happy here, for once feeling like she really did belong in Copenhagen.

Until someone had broken in.

Twice.

The flat smelled stale and dusty. She looked out of the kitchen window for a sighting of the young double bass-ist who lived across the courtyard, but his curtains were drawn. The flowers and plants surrounding the picnic table far below looked almost dead from the heat.

'Why keep the flat when you've moved in with your boyfriend?' Henrik asked.

Jensen sensed Esben pricking up his ears. 'What boyfriend?'

'No rush to get rid of it,' she said. 'Kristoffer owns this place. It was his first flat in Copenhagen. Since then, he's bought loads of others, of course.'

'Of course,' said Henrik.

Jensen ignored the sarcasm.

'Will someone please tell me who we're talking about?' said Esben.

'Oh,' said Henrik, before Jensen could intercept. 'You don't know? Jensen is dating the IT entrepreneur Kristoffer Bro.'

'Well, well, well,' said Esben, looking around the flat. 'So, this is where it all began.'

'According to Bro, yes. If you believe him,' said Henrik.

'Kristoffer had a great idea. And he worked hard. It *is* possible for a man to make his own fortune,' said Jensen.

'Ouch,' said Esben.

'Jensen thinks she knows her new boyfriend, but she's sadly mistaken,' said Henrik.

'What do you mean?' said Esben, his interest piqued.

Henrik and Esben. The two of them couldn't be more different if they tried, but in Kristoffer, they had finally found a common enemy. She hadn't yet found the right moment to tell them that Leif Kofoed was Kristoffer's financial backer. 'Stop it both of you,' she said resolutely. 'Can we try and focus on what we're doing here? Someone made contact, telling Esben to get out of D'Angleterre. We know it wasn't Aziz, so who was it?'

'Search me,' said Esben.

Henrik was moving around the flat, squinting up at the cameras Kristoffer had installed after her first suspected break-in where nothing had been taken. The system had failed days later when the burglars had made off with the USB sent to her by the bar owner Carsten Vangede before he died, but Kristoffer had since repaired it.

'Show me the webcam on your phone,' Henrik said.

Together they looked at the grainy video images of the flat with them in it. 'It's working,' Henrik said. 'Good. That means we'll know if someone tries to force entry.'

'So, what am I meant to do? Just sit here and twiddle my thumbs?' said Esben.

'When's your wife returning from holiday?'

'On Saturday. I'm meant to be picking her up from Kastrup.'

'Encourage her to stay away an extra week. Say a pipe has burst in your house or something like that,' said Henrik. 'I've got to get back to work.'

'Me too,' said Jensen. 'Get some sleep, Esben.'

She checked her phone. There was a message from Fie.

I found something. Call me.

54

'Wake up.' Jensen grabbed Kristoffer's shoulder, shaking him. She had cycled back to Nordhavn in record time. The fact that Leif Kofoed was his benefactor was not the only thing Kristoffer had been keeping from her, as she had just learned from her brief phone call with Fie.

'Jensen? What is it? Has something happened?' he said, blinking into the bedroom lights.

She had switched them all on as high as they would go. 'Remember I told you Esben Nørregaard had received threatening emails just before his driver disappeared?'

'Maybe ... yes,' said Kristoffer, holding up his hand to shield his eyes. 'But what's that—'

'The turd who did it is called Lars Bjerre and lives in Birkerød. Ring any bells?'

'None whatsoever.' Kristoffer was sitting up in bed now, naked, yawning and scratching his chest. 'What's this about?'

'Lars Bjerre worked for your company until about eighteen months ago. Does that help jog your memory?'

'Jensen, I've employed hundreds of people over the years. You can't expect me to recall all their names.'

'So you don't know Lars Bjerre at all.'

'I don't, really I don't.'

'And you had nothing to do with him wishing a horrible death on Esben Nørregaard and his family?'

'I swear to God. Jensen, you've got to believe me.'

He reached for her, but she evaded his grasp. 'That's the thing, Kristoffer, I don't think I can. There are too many things that worry me now.'

'What do you mean?'

'You didn't tell me that your first investor, the one who gave you your lucky break, was Leif Kofoed.'

'You didn't ask,' said Kristoffer, leaning back on his elbows. There was a sullen expression on his face.

'He invited me to interview him. The article's online now. You must have seen it. Was it you who encouraged him?'

'What?'

'Did you tell him I would be easy prey?'

Kristoffer looked away. 'It wasn't my idea, I swear. He asked for your phone number, and I gave it to him, that's all. Couldn't see the harm.'

'You expect me to believe that?'

'Look, Leif Kofoed has invested in countless companies over the years. It doesn't mean I'm in his pocket or anything. Jensen, don't be absurd.'

'He's a convicted murderer.'

'When he was eighteen.'

'I'm told he has no conscience whatsoever, that he's a complete psychopath.'

'He's an old man.'

Jensen bit her lip. There was nothing for it, she had to betray Esben's trust.

'Esben Nørregaard believes he's dangerous. He thinks Kofoed is trying to blackmail him into supporting his crazy golf-resort project. He also thinks that Kofoed is behind his driver's disappearance.'

'Blackmail?' Kristoffer laughed. 'You've got to be kidding me.'

'I ... don't know what to think any more. Why did you keep all those things from me?'

'I have no idea who the troll is who threatened Nørregaard. As for Kofoed, he hates any form of publicity, made me sign all sorts of paperwork before he invested, to make me sure I wouldn't tell anyone.'

Kofoed had said the same thing in the North Jutland sand dunes. He had asked her to forgive Kristoffer.

He reached out and stroked her hair. This time she didn't move away. 'But I'm not *anyone*,' she said. 'We live together. I thought we'd agreed we were going to be honest with each other from now on.'

'We are, I promise you,' said Kristoffer, pulling her close. 'I guess I'm just not used to it yet. Sorry, Jensen. Can you forgive me?'

She shrugged, kicking off her shoes, her anger all but gone. Had she overreacted, jumped to conclusions? It wouldn't be the first time.

'Now get undressed and come into bed,' Kristoffer mumbled.

By the time she returned from the bathroom, he was fast asleep again. There was a message on her phone from Gustav saying he had left Esben with pizza and headed home.

For what seemed like ages, she lay staring wide-eyed into the darkness, listening to Kristoffer's steady, untroubled breathing.

Then she patted barefoot into the spare bedroom, lay down on the cushions with their tags on and fell asleep.

Week Two

55

Yawning, Jensen parked her bike in the newspaper's courtyard and climbed the back stairs. It was still early and the office was quiet. Kristoffer had already left when she had emerged from the spare bedroom at 7 a.m., her mind churning with unanswered questions. She had woken up thinking about what Henning Würtzen had been about to tell her last time they had talked. Perhaps he knew where Ernst Brøgger was.

Kristoffer had left a note for her in the kitchen.

Spare bedroom now? We need to talk. Tonight.

She hadn't reflected on it at the time. It had been instinctive, a deep certainty that she couldn't stay in Kristoffer's bed a moment longer, not while things were unresolved between them. He was right: they badly needed to talk.

The top floor at *Dagbladet* was deserted, shafts of dusty light falling across the corridor from the open doors to the abandoned offices.

Henning's door was closed. She stood still outside for a few seconds, listening with her ear to the door. There was no sound. No tap-tap of two-fingered typing, no radio playing jazz.

She knocked before entering. 'Henning?'

The office was empty, the Velux window open with a half-smoked cigar balancing in an ashtray on the sill. The cigar was cold to the touch.

On Henning's desk were stacks of newspapers, next to his trusted silver scissors and fountain pen. A leaning tower of paper coffee cups rested against the Anglepoise lamp.

Jensen looked at the filing cabinets lined up against the back wall, packed with clippings. Henning had shown her the only article in the folder marked 'Ernst Brøgger', but he had to know more than was in the public domain. The only way to get the information out of him was to bribe him with coffee.

She decided to wait in her office until he came back but then changed her mind. It wouldn't take long to find 'Bro, Kristoffer' in the drawer marked A–B, though she doubted there was anything in it she hadn't read.

She was riffling through the folders when she heard a noise from the corridor. Quickly, she slammed the drawer shut and leaped back to the other side of Henning's desk.

The door opened wide, complaining on its hinges.

Frank Buhl, carrying a cardboard box under one arm.

She could see a frame with a faded picture of Frank shaking hands with a former Danish prime minister. A Beatles mug on top of old notebooks and printouts. 'What are you doing?' he said, frowning at her.

'Looking for Henning. Have you seen him?'

Frank laughed sarcastically. 'Little Miss Jensen with her head in the clouds.'

'What is it? Has something happened?'

'Henning had a stroke. Margrethe found him here, slumped over his desk, last night. He's at Riget.'

Jensen's hands flew to her mouth. 'My God, is he all right?'

'Pushing ninety with a bad cigar habit and a blood clot in his lungs? No, Jensen, I'd say he is not all right, but then you don't seem the type to care about such things.' He turned to go.

'Wait,' she said.

'What?'

'That box . . . is that . . . is it your last day?'

'What does it look like?'

'I thought there would be, I don't know, some sort of farewell reception.'

'Funnily enough, I didn't feel like one.'

Jensen looked at her hands, embarrassed at her thoughtlessness. 'What are you going to do now? For a job, I mean?'

'What's it to you?'

'Frank, I'm sorry. I know you and I haven't always seen eye to eye, but—'

'I was a crime reporter when you were still in nappies. I've seen it all, covered more cases than you've had hot dinners, sat in court for thousands of hours, stood outside the police yard in the driving rain waiting for news that never came.'

'I know,' said Jensen.

'And then, bam, you're out. The end.'

'Believe me, it wasn't me who . . . I never wanted this.'

'You sure about that? I'd have said the opposite was true. Congratulations, Jensen, you made it. Good luck to you.'

He began to walk down the corridor with his cardboard box, the sound of his clogs echoing in the empty space.

'Frank,' she shouted after him, but this time he kept walking.

56

Tone was already in the incident room when Henrik arrived, clutching his single-shot latte and whistling a tune to himself.

He was in a good mood after receiving confirmation from Lynn Walker in London that Nick Karagiannis had indeed flown to Denmark almost three weeks ago, and his family had not heard a peep from him since. A formal identification was taking place, but Henrik was satisfied that Karagiannis was their man.

'Ah, there you are,' said Tone before he had even sat down. 'We've got a match on our head. Sedat Osman. German citizen. Multiple convictions. Wanted in connection with a violent robbery in Cologne six months ago in which a security guard was shot.'

Two men, one from Britain, one from Germany, had travelled to Denmark and ended up decapitated and dumped in Copenhagen harbour. 'What was he doing here? And how did he know Karagiannis?'

'We don't know yet.'

'Hired killers?'

'Could be.'

Who had Karagiannis and Osman been sent to kill? By whom?

'Nice work, Ravnsbæk,' said Henrik, walking up to the whiteboard where Tone had already stuck a photo of Sedat Osman underneath that of Nick Karagiannis. 'Need to alert organised crime.'

'Done it already. By the way, Lisbeth Quist says hello,' said Tone. 'But—'

'And ask our German colleagues to send everything they've got.'

'Ditto. Should be with us soon, but there is something else I need to tell you.'

Jesus. Had the woman even slept? Henrik was relieved when his phone rang. He kept his eyes on the whiteboard as he answered, the cogs in his head slowly whirring.

'Jungersen.'

'Madsen.' It was the guard he had posted outside Jensen's flat in Christianshavn to keep an eye on Nørregaard. He sounded breathless.

'What do you want? I'm rather busy here,' said Henrik.

'I swear to you, I was only gone a few minutes, fifteen tops,' said Madsen.

'What are you talking about?'

'My stomach ... it's ... I needed to go. Well, you know what it's like.'

'Tell me, for the love of God.'

'It's Esben Nørregaard. He's gone. Flat's empty, door's open, no sign of the guy, a couple of chairs knocked over, that's all. It must have happened while I went to the toilet in that café down the street.'

'Fuck's sake, Madsen, couldn't you have used a tree or a lamp-post like everyone else?'

'It was a number two. Must have been all that coffee I drank to stay awake that got my system going. It's always—'

'Spare me the details,' said Henrik. 'Don't move an inch, I'm coming over. Get reinforcements, and a forensics crew. Now.'

He hung up.

'Fuck,' he shouted. 'Fuck, fuck, fuck.'

Losing Nørregaard was the last thing they needed. And it was all his fault. Because he had listened to Jensen and that idiot Nørregaard and kept everything quiet.

'What's happened?' said Tone, alarm in her voice. 'Is it to do with the case?'

Henrik looked at her, deciding the moment had come to bring her in. 'I don't have time to explain twice. Come with me and you'll find out,' he said, heading for the corridor at a trot while texting Wiese.

We have a problem.

Monsen was in his office looking through papers with his staff officer Hanne, who had joined the force around the same time as him. It was well known that Hanne did most of the big man's work behind the scenes. Henrik had challenged her on it a few times, but each time Hanne had shut him down, swearing undying loyalty to Monsen. There was a story there, some secret between them that he hadn't managed to get out of her.

Henrik knew first-hand how Monsen stood up for people and hoped to God things weren't about to change.

Monsen was drinking coffee from a large mug with the words 'The Boss' marked in block capital letters. 'Not now,

Jungersen, I'm busy,' he said, waving him and Tone away. He turned to Hanne. 'You've had how many RSVPs, did you say?'

'I'm afraid it can't wait,' said Henrik.

Wiese entered the room, in full Lycra and cycling helmet. 'What's going on?'

Monsen slammed his palms hard on his table and sat back in his chair with a deep sigh. 'Make it quick.'

Hanne wasted no time in making herself scarce. Smelling trouble, she knew, like any good police officer, that she was better off out of it.

Henrik rubbed his face hard with both hands, before he began. Tone, Wiese and Monsen were all staring at him. 'It's Esben Nørregaard,' he said.

'The MP?' said Wiese.

'That's the one. I'm afraid he's been kidnapped.'

Monsen sat up. 'Say that again?'

'Kidnap. I believe someone has taken him against his—'

'I know what bloody kidnap is, son,' thundered Monsen.

'Right, yes, well that is the situation.'

'Where did this happen?' said Wiese. 'When?'

'He was staying in a flat in Christianshavn and now he's gone.'

'What on earth was he doing there?' said Monsen. 'Doesn't he live in some mansion in Klampenborg?'

'He suspected someone was after him. There were emails, death threats. Though he didn't think anything of it at first. Not until his driver disappeared.'

Monsen buried his face in his hands. 'Wait a minute, his driver disappeared?'

'Yes. He's Syrian.'

Wiese frowned. 'Why are we only hearing about this now?'

'Nørregaard didn't want a fuss. We don't know what happened to his driver. It could be something completely unrelated. The man's wife didn't want it reported. They're refugees.'

'Wait a minute,' said Wiese. 'Let me get this right. Esben Nørregaard, a prominent member of parliament, receives death threats and his Syrian driver disappears. We could be talking about terrorism, right-wing extremists.'

'The threats against Nørregaard were personal, no obvious agenda other than wishing him a slow and painful death.'

'So, you just ... did nothing?'

'No. I arranged for his removal to a safe house yesterday.'

'You mean the safe house he has now been taken from?' said Wiese.

'Yes, thank you, Wiese,' said Monsen angrily.

'Anyway,' said Henrik. 'I'm heading out there now. Only I wanted you to know first.'

'Not so fast,' said Monsen. 'Who else knows about this?'

Henrik thought of Jensen but decided he could deal with her himself, and that she could deal with Gustav. 'No one,' he said.

'So how did you get to hear? I mean why did Nørregaard tell *you* about the death threats?' said Wiese.

'Look,' said Henrik. 'Can we take that later? I really need to go now.'

Monsen got up and walked over to the window, complaining loudly to himself. 'This is bloody inconvenient to say the least. It's my reception on Friday. We're already up to our necks in one embarrassing investigation and now we've managed to lose an MP. We'll have to get Police Intelligence involved.'

Police Intelligence. That old oxymoron.

'Of course, but let me go first,' said Henrik. 'I really need to find out what's happened.'

'Give me one good reason why I should trust you not to make more of a mess of this than you already have?' said Monsen.

'You can't afford not to,' said Henrik. 'Nørregaard's life may be in danger, and right now I'm the only one who knows the ins and outs. There's no time to brief anyone else. Tone, you're coming with me.'

'Yes, yes,' said Monsen irritably.

Wiese looked from Monsen to Henrik and back again. 'You're not seriously letting him go,' he said. 'Jungersen is already waist deep in shit and you're giving him a shovel?'

'Go, I'll do the necessary,' said Monsen to Henrik, picking up the phone, as if Wiese hadn't spoken. 'And get out of my sight, all of you.'

57

'Oh Henning, what am I going to do with you?' said Jensen.

The old *Dagbladet* editor-in-chief looked scrawny and rough-skinned, like a featherless bird, in his hospital bed at Riget. Someone had removed his dentures, shrinking his face. His beige suit had been folded neatly and placed in the bedside cabinet on top of his worn, brown leather shoes. On the table next to him was a glass of water with a straw, untouched, and yesterday's copy of *Dagbladet* opened on a completed crossword.

If Henning was able to do a crossword, perhaps he wasn't as ill as he looked?

A nurse with short grey hair and glasses entered the room. 'Ah. You must be ... let me guess ... Henning's granddaughter?' she said, her voice gentle and warm.

'No, I'm just ... a colleague. Henning and I work together.'

The nurse looked at her and nodded. 'There was another one of you here last night. She left just a few minutes ago, in fact. Tall woman, long hair, glasses? I thought I recognised her from somewhere.'

Of course.

Jensen glanced again at the boldly pencilled letters in the crossword: all Margrethe's work. She felt moved. Never mind that Henning was out of it; Margrethe hadn't wanted him to spend the night alone.

'Will he be OK?' Jensen asked.

'We'll see,' the nurse said, with the gift for non-committal responses that she shared with many of her profession. 'He's sedated for now, but you can talk to him, if you like. It might comfort him.'

The nurse rested her hand briefly, almost lovingly, on Henning's forehead, then left the room.

Henning didn't move. 'You can't die,' Jensen said to him. 'I forbid it.' She stroked his hand. It felt cool and dry, like lizard skin, the nails yellow and overdue a trim.

The windows were open. Somewhere outside a child was crying and being soothed by its mother. A man shouted something, eliciting raucous laughter from a young woman. A plane crossed the sky over Copenhagen.

Would anyone but her and Margrethe miss Henning when he was gone? The friendly nurse might think of him for a few days, but in time his face would blur into one with the thousands of dying people she must have seen in her time.

'Come back, Henning. You are not ready to go. *I* am not ready,' said Jensen, sobbing into the pale blue duvet.

Her phone pinged, startling her.

Gustav.

> The police are at your flat in Christianshavn.
> No one will tell me anything. What the hell is
> going on?

She rang him back immediately.

'Where are you?' said Gustav.

She kept her voice low, turned away from Henning. 'I'm at . . . never mind. What do you mean the police are at my flat?'

'Loads of police cars. They've blocked the road. I can't even get close. Something must have happened to Esben.'

'I'll call Henrik.'

'Way ahead of you. Not answering his phone.'

'OK, I'll head there now. Meet you outside. It's *my* flat, they've got to tell *me* what's happening,' she said. 'And Gustav?'

'Huh?'

'Stay where you are. Promise me.'

'Yeah, yeah.'

She grabbed her bag and ran for the door, stopping mid-floor. She glanced back at Henning, feeling a pang of guilt at leaving him. But, if anyone would understand, it was Henning. He, Margrethe, Jensen, they were all the same: newshounds for whom the world outside work barely existed.

'Same goes for you,' she said to Henning, jabbing her finger at him. 'Don't you dare go anywhere.'

As she waited for the lift, she called Henrik's number, but got no reply. Esben's number was going straight to voice-mail. 'Come on, come on, come on!' she said.

The lift doors opened and Jensen joined a young doctor with a stethoscope around her neck who looked like she would have slid to the floor with exhaustion, had she not been holding onto the handrail with one white-knuckled hand. Her face split in a jaw-dislocating yawn as Jensen tapped the close-door button repeatedly. 'Come on,' she shouted.

The doctor didn't even look at her. When the rattling lift finally reached the lobby, Jensen began to run, dodging in and out of the unbearably slow-moving crowds of patients and visitors.

Had something happened to Esben? Was he hurt, or worse? She would never be able to forgive herself. Aziz, if he was still alive, would never forgive her.

Henrik had said that he would put someone on watch. What had he been playing at? And what had happened to the alarm system in her flat? There had been no notification on her phone.

She jerked her bicycle from the rack and jumped on it. Pedalling as hard as she could, she headed for the main road and the heavy morning traffic flowing like a dirty river towards the centre of the city.

The van was no more than a shadow in the corner of her left eye. There was a loud crashing noise as it hit her bicycle, followed by silence. She had a brief look at the summer sky, pale, hot and empty, as she flew through the air.

Then nothing.

58

'Jensen. It's me. Something has happened. It's Esben, he ...
shit, will you just call me?'

Henrik felt his voice grow shrill as he left the message.
He looked at his phone, ignoring the flurry of text messages
from Gustav. It was Jensen he wanted to speak to. She was
going to tear his eyes out. Possibly never speak to him again.
He needed to explain, to get in there first.

Why wasn't she picking up?

Jensen's tiny flat was crawling with white-suited
scene-of-crime officers. Henrik was suffocating inside his
protective gear, desperate to tear the mask off his face so he
could breathe again.

It felt strange to be here, in Jensen's home. Though most
of her clothes were gone, her kitchen cabinets still had stuff
in them, glasses and plates from IKEA, some still in their
original packaging. Upstairs, next to her bed, was Esben's
holdall with his clothes and toiletries. Expensive brands that
were no good to the man now, wherever he was.

Henrik walked up to the forensics team leader. 'Give me something to go on, please.'

'It's an odd scenario,' the woman said. 'As you can see, there's been a significant struggle, which suggests Nørregaard did not leave voluntarily.' She gestured at the overturned dining chair, the mug of coffee that lay broken in a brown lake on the floor. 'On the other hand, there's no sign that the door has been forced.'

'So, Esben Nørregaard let his assailant in himself?'

'Looks that way.'

Henrik nodded. What he wanted to know was why the alarm on Jensen's phone hadn't gone off. Or if it had, why she hadn't called him.

Despite the knocked-over furniture, he had considered that Nørregaard had simply wandered out of the flat to get a coffee, or some equally brainless errand, until a witness had said that he had seen the MP being forcibly bundled into a car. The witness, a music student carrying an instrument case as tall as himself, lived across the courtyard from Jensen's flat and had been on his way home when he saw the incident. He had been about to call the police when the idiot constable on guard duty had appeared flush-faced and zipping up his trousers.

The witness only remembered that the car was silver-coloured and had tinted windows.

Great.

'Get someone to go through the street CCTV,' Henrik shouted at Tone, who was down on her haunches examining the broken coffee mug.

'Done that,' she said. 'They'll let me know as soon as.'

'Put a search out for the car.'

'Ditto.'

The suspected kidnapping of an MP was not something

273

they could keep under wraps for long. Monsen would be calling for a press conference, the prime minister would want to step in.

They might as well lob a hand grenade into Henrik's lap.

There was no more they could do at Jensen's flat. They would have to go back to the office and face the music.

He watched as Tone took a call. She rose from the floor and approached him, phone pressed to her ear. 'Jungersen,' she said. 'Good news.'

'They found Nørregaard?'

'No.'

'Then make it quick,' he barked.

'The second head has turned up.'

'What did you say?'

'I tried to tell you before, back at the office, before all this happened. You know how the other head turned up in the wheelie bin at the food distribution company?'

'Go on?'

'I read in the file that it had been found in a special bin reserved for food waste that hadn't been collected for a while. I thought maybe there was another bin, one for general rubbish, which had been collected on a different day. I was right. The refuse is all tracked so I soon found the dump it had been taken to. I've had a couple of officers going through the rubbish for the past twenty-four hours.'

Henrik remembered once searching a tip for a sim card under similar circumstances. It had taken over three weeks, but, in the end, it had led to a conviction.

'They've just called me,' said Tone, waving the phone at him. 'Jackpot.'

For one of the very few times in his life, Henrik was speechless.

274

59

Even for a man stupid enough to shoot his own finger off, Jønne Olsen's hiding place seemed extraordinarily dim-witted. Travelling less than a kilometre from the bodega he had fled in haste, he had sought refuge in the flat of his partner in crime, Bjarne Sommer, a man equally well known to the police.

Jønne's hand was still bandaged. For the rest of his life, he would be reminded constantly of his own idiocy. *At least there is some poetic justice in that*, Henrik thought, as he watched the two men being led from the flat into separate squad cars, wearing nothing but underpants and tattoos. Both were kicking and cursing.

Henrik and Lisbeth exchanged a sarcastic smile. 'Shall we?' she said, leading the way inside.

'Looking forward to it,' said Henrik, snapping on his latex gloves.

The flat was about one hundred degrees and stank of rotten garbage and weed. A joint was still smouldering in an ashtray, the TV blaring with a computer game stalled on a bloodied figure lying dead in a derelict building.

Henrik thought of Esben Nørregaard and shivered. Was that what had happened to the kidnapped politician? All hell had broken loose when he and Tone had got back to the office. The security service had turned up, grim-faced men and women thronging the corridors.

Henrik had been summoned by Monsen, who looked as though he would rather have stuck pins into his eyes throughout the emergency briefing during which the intelligence officers had tapped Henrik for every last drop of information he had in him.

Wiese had skulked off to his own office, as was his habit whenever things got difficult.

'You should have informed us the minute you found out that Aziz Almasi had gone missing,' the intelligence officers had said to Henrik. 'Your silence was a gross dereliction of duty.'

'I told you a million times. Nørregaard did not want to report it and I had no reason to think—'

'A Syrian refugee? Desperate? With a history?' they said.

'What history?' Henrik had looked at the intelligence officers, perplexed.

That was the thing with intelligence. You gave them everything you knew, and they shared nothing in return. It was a one-way street.

Bastards.

What did they have on Almasi? Whatever it was, they couldn't seriously believe that the Syrian had something to do with Nørregaard's disappearance, could they?

'No, no, you've got it all wrong. Almasi worshipped Nørregaard. He wouldn't . . .'

'It's not up to you decide what would and wouldn't happen.'

276

'Get back to work,' Monsen had said, when the intelligence officers had finally left them alone. 'We've got a murder investigation to wrap up. And stay off the Nørregaard case, you hear me? We'll deal with all that later.'

Was Jensen aware that there was something to know about the Syrian? If he could get hold of her, he would ask her.

CALL ME BACK, he had texted her as he and Lisbeth had driven to arrest Jønne and his mate.

He walked through the rooms in the flat, such as they were, lifting stuff, opening drawers and looking under the bed, until he heard Lisbeth cry out from the kitchen. He found her extracting a sawn-off shotgun from the back of a cupboard. 'Ah,' she said. 'They've removed the mechanism.'

Without the firing pin, it would be impossible for the technicians to match the cartridge rim they had found in the car at Refshaleøen to the gun. They spent another forty minutes searching for the missing parts, finally meeting up in the narrow hallway.

'Nothing,' said Lisbeth.

'Me neither,' said Henrik, shaking his head. He opened the door to the bathroom again. It stank. He'd already been through the cabinet under the sink, taken the back off it and dismantled the cistern, holding his nose. He lifted the toilet lid, taking an involuntary step back when the smell hit him.

Lisbeth followed him in and looked over his shoulder. The contents of the toilet bowl were grim. 'Ah,' she said. 'I see. That old chestnut.'

'You or me?' said Henrik.

They did rock, paper, scissors.

Henrik lost.

Lisbeth remembered that she had an urgent phone call to make.

Police officers weren't paid enough for the responsibility

277

they had to keep society safe, let alone sticking their arms into toilets in which criminals had defecated to discourage anyone from taking a closer look.

Henrik remembered seeing a plastic bag full of rubbish in the kitchen. He emptied it onto the floor, removed his white shirt, and stuck his right arm into the bag. Then he held in his belly and grimaced at the ceiling as he knelt by bowl and reached into the warm, stinking liquid as far as the U-bend. Sure enough, there was something there. Soon he was pulling out the pieces of a dismantled shotgun mechanism, rammed in as far as they would go.

Bingo.

There was nothing more the prosecutor could possibly want. They had two almost complete bodies with known identities. They had the murder weapon. They had prints from a finger found in the chest of one of the victims. And they had a witness who had seen the killers throw the victims' personal belongings into the sea.

Why had Jønne and his mate killed Sedat Osman and Nick Karagiannis? And, more importantly, what had the two men been doing in Denmark?

As Henrik washed his hands in Bjarne Sommer's dirt-encrusted sink, scrubbing them vigorously with a thin lozenge of leftover soap that he had scraped off the side of the bathtub, he knew there had to be more to the case.

He dried his arm on his shirt and put it back on before going to find Lisbeth.

'I have news,' she said. 'I've had a team going through all the staff lists from the food distribution company, going back to when it started trading twelve years ago.'

'And?'

'They just called me. Turns out Jønne worked there for a few months when he was eighteen.'

'What happened?'

'Sacked for poor attendance.'

'But he remembered where the bins were.'

'Obviously didn't think we'd be smart enough to put the body parts back together.'

'Like I said, not the sharpest tool in the box,' said Henrik.

Which made it even more puzzling what Jønne and his mate had been playing at. Whatever it was, he very much doubted it was something they had thought of all by themselves.

60

The first thing Jensen became aware of was a stabbing pain behind her forehead. The second was an overwhelming urge to throw up. She opened her eyes and tried for a moment to make sense of the dark, hot room, before leaning over the side of the bed. A paper basin appeared under her chin to catch the bile as she retched. She felt a dry, smooth hand on her forehead.

'That's it. Let it all out,' said a male voice.

A voice she knew.

She tried to sit up but felt a hand on her shoulder pushing her back into the bed and it was like falling into a void.

'There, there.'

When she woke up again, there was a bluish light at the window. Her throat was dry. There was someone sitting next to her bed. She reached for the glass of water beside the jug on the bedside table, feeling something pull on her hand. Tubes. Connected to a drip. A sharp pain in her left ankle. She lay back in the pale blue sheets and looked at her guest.

A man of a certain age, well dressed, in the sort of trousers people used to refer to as slacks, with a crisp, pink, short-sleeved shirt, tucked in. Horn-rimmed spectacles framing warm eyes. A summer tan but looking as though he had just risen from a cool bath. The type of leather shoes that yacht owners wear.

'Brøgger? What are you ...'

'Shush,' said Brøgger, AKA Deep Throat. He held the glass of water to her mouth and placed the straw between her lips. The water was lukewarm. 'You've had a bad fall. Has no one ever told you to wear a helmet when you cycle?'

'How did—?'

'Strictly speaking, it wasn't your fault. I mean you weren't looking where you were going, but against people like that you don't stand a chance.'

'What people? What do you mean?'

'I'm told they ran you down quite deliberately. A black van, fake plates, privacy glazing. Now, I know what you're dying to ask me. How do I know what happened?'

'No. Yes.'

'I've had someone looking out for you. They followed you here, to the hospital. Waited while you visited that old man from your newspaper, ran after you when you left. Say, where were you going in such a hurry? Good job you hadn't got far from the hospital. It could have been so much worse. My employee scooped you up and carried you back in.'

Jensen raised herself up on her elbows and waited for the room to stop spinning. She didn't remember any of it.

'You hurt your ankle. Got yourself concussed. A few scrapes on your legs. Lucky I'd say, Jensen, very lucky.'

'I've been trying to get hold of you for ages,' she said.

'I know,' said Brøgger. 'I sincerely apologise for that. I wanted to . . . sort things out myself. I guess I failed, which is why we're here now.'

Jensen looked at him. Was this Brøgger's confession she was about to hear? 'What are you talking about?'

'Lie back, Jensen, and close your eyes. The sedatives they gave you will be doing their work. While you relax, let me tell you a story.'

She did as he asked. Too exhausted to argue.

His voice was measured and soft. 'Once upon a time there was a family, with a mother and a father and two boys. The oldest boy was a handful, always getting into trouble. The teachers at school, the local police officer, the vicar, even his parents couldn't control him; only when his little brother spoke was he placid. He loved his little brother as much as it was possible to love someone, and the little brother loved him back. Time passed, and the boys grew up. The older brother went from bad to worse and the school threw him out, but the younger brother was clever and studious. When he was sixteen, he fell in love with a girl, so badly that he couldn't eat or sleep, but lived only for the stolen moments when he might see her, in lessons or at the bus stop going home from school. The girl had no idea of this. The boy wrote her letters he never sent, dialled her number but hung up before anyone in her house could answer, followed her home but did not declare himself. The boy lost weight and fell behind on his schoolwork, and no one could understand what was happening to him. No one, except his older brother. One summer, at the end of the school term, there was a party, and the younger brother went along in his finest clothes and a flutter in his heart, determined to finally tell the girl how he was feeling. Only to watch as another boy kissed the girl in the corner of the school dance hall. He cried for a month. When the month was up, his older brother left the house one morning with his father's hammer. They said not even the schoolboy's own mother recognised him when his body was found in a rocky crevasse. The older brother had blood on his hands when he came home. He was smiling, thinking his little brother would be pleased with what he'd done.'

'And was he?'

'He was horrified. He told the police, and his brother went to prison. His big brother never forgave him. Whatever little nugget of good he had carried inside of him up until that point, died.'

'Where did this happen?' Jensen mumbled. 'There are no rocky crevasses in Denmark.'

'There are.'

'Where?'

'On the island of Bornholm.'

Something stirred in Jensen's memory.

Amaliekilde.

The name of the mysterious house in Vedbæk that Brøgger had reacted so violently to when she had whispered it into his ear in the mist in front of the Queen's castle in Copenhagen. He had told her to stay away.

Amaliekilde was also the name of a natural spring on Bornholm.

'Your big brother . . .' Jensen said. 'What's his name?'

'Leif. He took my mother's maiden name after he left prison.'

'Kofoed.'

'He's a bad man, Jensen, always was. Something in Leif is broken, so he can't feel what you and I feel. You need to stay away from him. I tried to warn you. When you told me about the address you had found, I knew he was back in

Denmark. Where Leif turns up, chaos ensues, and people end up dead.'

So, Leif Kofoed had bought the property in Vedbæk and called it Amaliekilde.

Defrauded by his accountant Carsten Vangede, a Nørrebro bar owner, had tracked his money back to a company by the same name and somehow established a connection to the house in Vedbæk.

'So, it was Leif who stole from you and Vangede? Hardly world domination.'

'You still don't understand,' said Brøgger.

'Was it your brother who killed Vangede and made it look like suicide?'

Jensen had a thousand other questions. But a sudden sleepiness had taken hold of her that there was no escaping from, and she sank into the darkness once again.

The third time she woke up, there was sharp sunlight at the window and the chair next to her bed was empty.

'Good morning, sunshine,' said a female voice. Jensen turned to find a nurse fitting a blood-pressure cuff onto her arm.

'Where did he go?' said Jensen.

'Who?'

'The man who was here earlier?'

The nurse frowned at her. 'There hasn't been anyone here. You hit your head. It's not uncommon to hallucinate when—'

'No, he was definitely here. He must have left before you arrived,' said Jensen, sitting up. She was feeling better.

'Sure,' said the nurse under her breath. 'Whatever you say.'

'When can I leave?'

284

'You should be able to go home today,' said the nurse. 'Is there someone I can call to come and get you?'

Jensen set her feet on the floor and winced at the pain in her ankle. Everything hurt.

'But you need to rest. No going back to work.'

'Where's my phone?'

'In the cupboard, but there'll be plenty of time for—'

'Would you get it for me, please?'

There were twenty missed calls from Henrik. Increasingly panicked text messages.

CALL ME. NOW

'Call DI Henrik Jungersen at Copenhagen Police. He'll come for me,' she said. 'Where are my clothes?'

'In the cupboard. But you might want to ask your friend to bring you some clean stuff.'

Yeah, like that's going to happen.

'And the doctor said she needs to see you before you can leave.'

'Can't it wait?'

61

Thursday 09:20

Henrik was practically running down the corridor towards the lifts. Red-faced and swearing. 'Don't ever do that to me again, Jensen.'

'It's not like I got myself run into by a van on purpose,' said Jensen. 'Slow down, will you? I can't move so fast on these bloody crutches.'

'They said you're fine.'

'And I am, but . . .'

'I thought you were dead when that nurse called me,' said Henrik.

'I might have been, had it not been for . . .' Jensen paused. It was too complicated to explain. 'It was good of you to come. Don't know anyone else with a car who I could ask, and they wouldn't let me go unaccompanied.'

'So, I'm just a chauffeur. Nice. You should have called your boyfriend.'

'I would if he would answer his phone.'

Henrik stopped abruptly. 'Jensen, you and me and

hospitals. It ends here, you got that? I've had it with nasty shocks from you.'

'It wasn't my fault. Someone drove into me, and it wasn't an accident.'

'Who?'

'Esben told us he was certain he had been followed. Maybe it's the same people who tried to get me yesterday?'

Brøgger had asked someone to keep an eye on her. Perhaps he wasn't the only one.

'You didn't say anything about being followed before.'

'I wasn't sure. It was just a feeling.'

'Well, if you're intent on getting yourself killed, keep me out of it,' said Henrik and set off again.

'Wait,' said Jensen. 'What's happened to Esben? Gustav told me there were loads of police at my flat.'

'It appears someone has taken him,' said Henrik, pummelling the lift button like she had done herself only … how long ago was it? It seemed time had disappeared.

She thought of Henning, alone in his bed in the concrete castle of a hospital, wondering if he was OK. 'Taken?'

Henrik was blushing. 'He's gone. My guess would be that he was taken by whoever took Aziz. That's why I was trying to get hold of you.'

'I thought you'd put him under armed guard. You were supposed to look after him.'

'And I would have done. Properly, called in the reinforcements, if Nørregaard hadn't been so bloody stubborn about wanting to keep the whole thing under wraps. I'll get in big trouble for this.'

'Never mind all that. We need to find Esben. Urgently. And I need to speak to you. About Leif Kofoed.'

'Yes, I saw your little interview. Nice publicity for his madcap golf scheme.'

'It's not up to me to make moral judgements. I write what's in the public interest.'

'If there's anyone who isn't in the public interest, it's Leif Kofoed.'

'I know who he is.'

'You and me both.'

'I know his brother. That is, I didn't find out until a few hours ago that they were related. Anyway, the brother has been ... supplying me with information.'

'About Kofoed?' said Henrik.

'Not initially. But yes.'

'I'm aware the brother was hauled in by us on several occasions. Always maintained the two of them hadn't spoken since they were youngsters.'

'They haven't.'

'But it sounds like he knows stuff. Where is he?'

'I can't tell you that, but—'

'Don't give me that "can't reveal my source" bollocks, Jensen. We've been trying to get Kofoed for years. If his brother knows something, if you're withholding information ...'

'I can't tell you because I don't know,' said Jensen. 'I've been trying to locate him myself for ages. But I think I know where Kofoed lives.'

'Thanks, that's great.'

'So that means you can arrest him. He stole money from his own brother, and from Carsten Vangede, the bar owner who was found hanged. I told you about him. I think Kofoed, or someone who works for him, had Vangede killed and made it look like suicide. David Goldschmidt at the Forensic Institute told me it's possible to do that.'

Finally, the lift doors slid open. They waited in silence while an elderly couple holding hands shuffled out. The kind of couple the two of them would never be.

'Jensen, what you think is neither here nor there. We can't arrest someone without evidence,' said Henrik when they were alone again.

'Vangede left me a memory stick with Leif Kofoed's address in an encrypted file. That's evidence.'

'No, it's not,' said Henrik. 'Jensen, I don't have time to discuss this with you. I've got two dead bodies and a missing member of parliament on my hands. I can take you back to Nordhavn, or you can take a taxi. Your choice.'

'Wait,' said Jensen. 'Did you say that the people who hurt Aziz have probably taken Esben?'

'Yes.'

'So, if we find Aziz, we might find Esben?'

The thought came to her as she voiced it. 'I think there's someone we could ask. Someone who has been acting quite strangely lately.'

62

Thursday 10:11

Liron Vaknin did not seem surprised in the slightest when Henrik and Jensen approached his coffee van in Sankt Peders Stræde. He had a piece of chalk in one hand and was kneeling on the pavement, writing out his prices on a sandwich board. He took his time to get up. 'Jensen. I was wondering when you might be showing up.' He enveloped her in a bear hug.

Henrik noticed that she shut her eyes for a few seconds as she leaned into his chest. He coughed to break the spell.

Liron ignored him, holding Jensen at arm's length and frowning at her foot. 'What have you done to yourself, little girl?'

Jensen looked embarrassed. 'Got knocked off my bike. It's nothing,' she said. 'This is my friend Henrik. He's with Copenhagen Police.'

'Finally, we meet,' said Liron, shaking Henrik's hand while staring at him unblinkingly with his astonishing pearl-grey wolf's eyes. It felt like a warning. First Esben Nørregaard and now this man. What had Jensen been saying about him to her friends to make them greet him this frostily?

'Listen, Liron, we need to ask you something. It's important,' Jensen began.

'First things first,' said Liron, fetching a folding chair from the inside of his Tardis-like van and making her sit down despite her protests. He refused to speak before he had made them both a coffee. Jensen got an espresso, Henrik a single-shot latte, to his amazement. 'Nice and milky, just the way I like it,' he said. 'How did you know?'

'You look like the type,' Liron said, revealing gold teeth as he smiled and winked at Jensen. He looked like an old hippie in his leather apron, with dirty festival wristbands on one suntanned arm, a faded pink T-shirt and ripped jeans.

'Look,' Henrik said. 'If you know something, you need to tell us. It's a matter of life or death.'

'I'm all yours,' said Liron at long last when he had finished cleaning his equipment meticulously and putting everything away. 'Shoot.'

'Did Aziz come and see you?' said Jensen.

'Yes, he did.'

'What? Liron, why didn't you tell me?' Jensen shouted. 'You knew I was looking for him, that I was worried.'

'Because he made me swear that I wouldn't, and Uncle Liron always keeps his word.'

Henrik remembered Jensen telling him that she had once taken Aziz to meet Liron, who had brewed him a Syrian coffee. By all accounts, the two men had got on.

'Where is Aziz now?' said Henrik.

'I don't know.'

'You're sure about that?'

'It's the truth,' said Liron, looking him straight in the eye in the unnerving way he had.

'Well, did he tell you what happened to him? We have CCTV of him being assaulted by some men on his employer's private property,' said Henrik.

'He was. They took him.'

'Who?'

'He didn't know, but he managed to free himself very quickly and escape from where they were holding him.'

'Where was that?'

'Some flat, he didn't say where.'

'He was hurt,' said Jensen. 'You can clearly see him going down in the recording.'

'Yeah, they stabbed him in the side. A friend of mine fixed it. Used to be a nurse in Bosnia. Now he drives a bloody taxi. Anyway, I don't think they wanted to kill him. Maybe they thought he would be useful to them in some way.' He shook his head. 'Stupid people.'

'And what did he do once he got away?'

'He came to Uncle Liron and asked me to hide him.'

'Was it you who took that note to D'Angleterre?' said Jensen.

Liron frowned. 'What note?'

'The one telling Esben that he should leave immediately. Saying that he was in danger?'

'No. And it wasn't Aziz either. He couldn't understand why Esben moved out of the hotel. It worried him a great deal.'

So Aziz had been watching Esben and the people who kidnapped him. Why? Why not just come forward and explain what had happened? 'What's he up to?' Henrik said.

'He didn't say. Left my place this morning, thanked me for my hospitality, but assured me he'd be fine from here.'

'I don't believe you,' Henrik said, narrowing his eyes.

Liron stuck his hand in his jeans pocket and pulled out a key. 'Go see for yourself,' he said.

It took them less than ten minutes to get to Liron's flat. It was in a mansion block facing the Botanical Gardens.

Nice location for a man making his living selling coffee on the street, thought Henrik.

There was no sign of Aziz, except for a rolled-up blanket on the floor. A slightly damp towel had been folded neatly and placed on top. On the draining board next to the kitchen sink was a glass coffee cup.

'He's alive,' said Jensen.

'Hallelujah,' said Henrik. He had expected the flat to be a mess, cushions on the floor, incense sticks, clothes every-where, but in fact it was hard to tell that someone was living there. The bedroom, the combined kitchen and living room, even the tiny bathroom, were all swept clean. The few clothes were folded and squared away in the wardrobe. There was no TV and only an armchair and a small table in the living room. Naked lightbulbs. Nothing but a few tins in the kitchen cupboards.

It was the sort of flat that might belong to a soldier. Or someone who wanted to be sure of being able to leave quickly, should the need arise.

Henrik made a note to look into Liron Vaknin as soon as he got the chance.

'What do we do now?' said Jensen.

'*We* are not doing anything. I'm taking you back to your boyfriend's place for some rest.'

'But can't I just—'

'Trust me, we're doing everything we can to find Nørregaard and Aziz. There's nothing you can do, Jensen. Besides, I brought you something to read, in case you get bored.'

63

Thursday 11:48

The concierge at Kristoffer's block of flats, a short, bald man with whom Jensen had exchanged a few smiles, but never spoken to, rushed to the entrance when he saw her approach on her crutches. She was carrying the paper folder Henrik had given her under one arm and it was threatening to slip and fall onto the floor.

'What happened?' said the concierge as he escorted her to the lift, carrying the folder. A badge on the lapel of his jacket said his name was Søren.

'Just a fall,' said Jensen. 'I landed awkwardly.'

'You should be more careful,' he said. 'By the way, that teenage boy called round again.'

'Who?'

'The one who said his name was Gustav,' said Søren. 'He asked if I'd seen you. He seemed concerned about you.'

'It's all right, I'll call him,' said Jensen. 'Is Kristoffer home?'

'I haven't seen him today,' said the concierge. 'I assume he's travelling again?'

Well, if he is, he hasn't told me, thought Jensen.

'I'll be OK from here,' she said, stepping into the lift. Søren handed her the folder and she smiled at him, trying to transmit a sense of calm that she didn't feel.

'Hello?' she said to the empty flat.

There was no sign that Kristoffer had slept at home. Come to think of it, she had received no messages from him last night. No anxious voicemails asking her where she was.

She tried calling him. Still no reply.

There was more luck with Gustav. 'Where have you been?' he shouted. 'I waited for you for bloody ages at your flat. Margrethe's furious that you didn't turn up for work this morning.'

'I'm at Kristoffer's. Tell Margrethe I'm not feeling well. I'll explain everything. Come over and see me later?'

She stood by the sink and drank two large glasses of water, fishing in her bag for the strong painkillers they had given her at the hospital. Her head was throbbing, and she felt nauseous. Drinking Liron's espresso on an empty stomach had been a bad move.

There was a packet of granola in the cupboard, but no milk. She ate a small handful straight from the packet and washed it down with more water.

Her phone buzzed. A text message from an unknown number.

> Anne-Sophie Wagner here. I'm the doctor who just treated you at Riget. I need to talk to you. Call me back as soon as you can.

Jensen didn't have the energy for talking, least of all to a doctor. Her ankle would be fine with a bit of time to heal, and she knew concussion wasn't something that could be treated.

She slipped the phone into her pocket, picked up Henrik's folder and brought it out onto the balcony. It was a copy of an old typewritten police file. From the punch holes you could tell that it had been lifted from a ring binder. There was no note from Henrik, no introduction to what she was about to read.

She leafed through the file. There were dozens of pages of interview transcripts and black-and-white crime-scene pictures that hadn't come off well in the photocopier.

A few pages in, there was a post-mortem report with a handwritten note at the front.

Ole Bødker, male, 58.

His injuries had been marked on the outline of a human body: there were ticks on the forehead, eyes, mouth, both hands, torso, legs and feet. By the description of the trauma to his body, it wasn't the sort anyone had a chance of surviving. The report recorded that the victim had lost one eye and eight teeth, been stamped on and repeatedly kicked in the abdomen and head.

The victim asphyxiated on his own blood and vomit, Jensen read.

She leafed through the folder. There were pictures of a yellow-brick bungalow with a post box at the end of a garden path, an address in the town of Slagelse.

Why had Henrik given her this?

She thumbed back to page one and began to read.

64

'Where have you been?' said Tone as she and Henrik headed downstairs to interview Jønne Olsen.

'Just something I had to take care of.'

'The people from the intelligence service were looking for you.'

'Have they found Nørregaard yet?'

'Not to my knowledge. I asked them, but they told me to stay out of it. Monsen and Wiese advised us to be cooperative and hand over any information, which I did.'

'Good.'

'But I'd already got the guys to gather any CCTV in a radius of 500 metres from the flat, and I didn't see any reason to stop. So far, they've managed to trace the silver car for one kilometre.'

'Which direction?'

'The airport.'

'Did you tell the intelligence team?'

'Sure did.'

'And?'

'They told me to go and get coffees for everyone.'

'And did you?'

'What do *you* think?' said Tone.

Henrik laughed. 'You did well, Ravnsbæk, but let's leave Nørregaard to them now. We've still got three murders to solve.'

'Got it,' she said. 'Oh and by the way, before we go in, Ida Kaurup, your witness from Roskilde Fjord, has confirmed that Bjarne Sommer was the man she saw with Jønne Olsen that morning.'

Bless you, Ida, and the day you were born.

Jønne Olsen had asked for and been given a lawyer which meant he wasn't as stupid as he looked. He was seated next to the thin, bespectacled woman, arms folded across his chest and a paper cup of coffee untouched in front of him. Someone had given him a grey tracksuit to wear. He could not have looked less likely to confess if 'no comment' had been tattooed on his neanderthal forehead.

'How's your finger?' said Henrik with a big smile, receiving a silent scowl by way of reply.

'So we're not here to determine whether you shot Sedat Osman. The fact that the tip of your finger, with a complete print, was found in the victim's chest says you did.'

'Can we skip the sarcasm and get on to the questions?' said the lawyer. 'I take it you do have questions?'

'Oh yes, plenty,' said Henrik, pretending to consult his notebook in great detail. There was nothing in there but scribbles, shopping lists and random thoughts, but interviewees never liked to be kept waiting. It made them nervous.

Jønne's legs began to bob up and down.

Now they were getting somewhere.

'Why did you kill Sedat Osman?'

'No comment,' said Jønne.

'Who told you to kill Sedat Osman?'

'No comment.'

'The wound in Nick Karagiannis' head is consistent with the shotgun that we found in your mate Bjarne's flat. Where did you get the weapon from?'

'No comment.'

Henrik asked ten more questions to which Jønne gave the same answer.

When Henrik announced a break in the questioning, Jønne looked at him smugly.

Bjarne Sommer, seated with his own lawyer in the room next door, was more cooperative. 'What's he been saying?' he asked as soon as Henrik had kicked off the interview.

'Who? Your best friend Jønne?' Henrik smiled. 'Why? You worried about him dumping you in it?'

The lawyer shook his head at Sommer, who managed to hold his tongue.

'No need to worry,' said Henrik. 'You were spotted by a witness, throwing effects belonging to the victims into Roskilde Fjord, so you're already implicated.'

The lawyer looked up angrily. 'When was this? Why wasn't I told?'

'Oh, it just happened,' said Henrik. 'This is me telling you.' He turned to Sommer. 'I take it the killing was Jønne's idea?'

Sommer stared at Henrik in silence.

'I wonder how much money you were offered. Bet Jønne took the larger cut, seeing as he was the one wielding the shotgun. Still, it hardly matters now, given neither of you will see any of it.'

More staring.

Sommer cupped his hand to his lawyer's ear. The lawyer shook his head vigorously, and Sommer resumed his staring, but now there was a vein throbbing at his temple, and his face was gradually turning dark red.

'Must hurt taking the rap for something that wasn't even your idea and not getting as much as a single krone in return.'

The lawyer put a restraining hand on Sommer's arm.

'Who was it? Who told you to do it?' said Henrik.

Sommer looked as if he was about to explode.

'OK,' said Henrik, sitting back in his chair. He made a sign to Tone to stop typing. 'I wanted to give you a chance to tell me in your own words what happened, but never mind now. I'm sure Jønne will fill in the blanks.'

'We weren't supposed to kill them,' burst out Sommer. 'Just scare them off. That's what we were told.'

Henrik smiled. 'Dumb and dumber scaring off a couple of hired killers from overseas? Oh, I can see that happening.'

'They took it badly. The big guy was completely out of control.'

'Nick Karagiannis, you mean?'

'Yeah. Total monster, he was. Jønne meant to just scare him, but suddenly the gun went off in the guy's head. It was self-defence,' said Sommer.

'Tell that to the judge,' said Henrik. 'I'm sure he will believe you.'

'It's the truth. Anyway, when the big guy copped it, the little one went mental and started running at Jønne.'

'Sedat Osman?' said Henrik.

'Yeah. Jønne didn't have time to think before he fired the shot. That's how it happened, with the finger. In any case, we couldn't just let him go, could we? Not after he'd seen the whole thing.'

'Of course. And then you were forced to cut him and Nick Karagiannis into pieces?'

'That was Jønne's idea. After he'd had his hand seen to.'

'Big boy made you do it.'

'I panicked.'

'My client would like to have a break now,' said the lawyer.

'No, I wouldn't,' Sommer snapped.

'I bet whoever asked you to scare the fellas off, was delighted to hear what you'd done.'

'Jønne deals with him,' said Sommer and clammed up, finally heeding his lawyer's warning.

Too late.

Tone held her hands expectantly above the keyboard.

'Deals with who, Bjarne?' said Henrik warmly.

'Before you start talking again, let me put you straight,' said Henrik when he and Tone were back with Jønne and his lawyer and had restarted the interview. 'We know what happened. Bjarne told us. We also know it was you who dealt with your ... let's call him a customer.'

'Do I need to warn you about coercing my client?' said the lawyer.

'Not at all,' said Henrik, looking straight at Jønne. 'I'm not embellishing the truth here. Once he was given a chance to think, your friend was only too happy to talk to us. So really, we have all we need, and this is just an opportunity for you to give us your side of the story.'

Jønne raised his eyebrows at his lawyer who got busy looking at her papers. Henrik waited. He could hear Tone's level breathing. They both knew something was coming. Something good.

For once.

'We weren't told who they were,' said Jønne at long last. 'He just said to do what we had to do to get rid of them.'

'For the benefit of the transcript, please can you give us the full name of the individual you just referred to?' said Tone.

'You said you knew already,' Jønne protested, but both Henrik and Tone just stared back at him deadpan.

'Kristoffer Bro,' he said, finally.

'The billionaire?' said Henrik.

'Yes,' said Jønne.

Henrik felt his heart begin to beat fast. He couldn't wait to tell Jensen when he got the chance. Never mind her boyfriend battering his father with a bedside lamp. Olsen and Sommer had just implicated Bro in ordering a muscle job on two foreign assassins that had ended in a messy double murder, not to mention the shooting of an innocent homeless man.

Why had he done that? There was only one way to find out, thought Henrik, and it wouldn't require any help from the moron across the table from him. 'Interview ends,' he said, gathering his papers and scrambling to his feet.

Two minutes later, he and Tone were getting into his car outside the building. 'We'll start with Bro's flat. Send a squad car ahead, will you?' Henrik said. 'Or are you going to tell me that you did that already?'

Tone snapped on her seat belt and smiled.

65

Jensen closed the folder with the copies of the police files and got up from her chair, limping to the edge of the balcony for a view of Nordhavn. The water in the harbour was pale and still, mirroring the hot white sky. Beyond it lay the city with *Dagbladet*, her tiny apartment, Liron's coffee van and, somewhere, whether dead or alive, Esben and Aziz.

She closed her eyes against the sharp sunlight, which was bouncing off the shiny surfaces on the balcony. She had recognised the events described in Henrik's folder from Kristoffer's story of how his father had died.

This meant that Kristoffer had to be Lars Bødker, the son of the deceased who had been mentioned several times in the documents.

Why had he changed his name? Losing your father in an aggravated burglary was tragic, not something embarrassing that you wanted to distance yourself from, was it?

Unless it was his inauspicious background that Kristoffer had wanted to break with. The house in Slagelse looked

like any other house, comfortable, normal, not quite fitting the myth he had encouraged about himself: a tireless
entrepreneur who had worked himself up from a difficult
start in life.

Ole Bødker had been an electrical engineer, his wife a
stay-at-home mother. Perhaps that had seemed too ordinary
to Kristoffer and in need of embellishment. Hardly a reason
for Henrik to imply that he had done something terrible.

Kristoffer had been interviewed several times after his
father's death and, as far as Jensen could tell from the transcripts, he had never changed his story: he had arrived home
late from a party to find his father lying dead in a pool of
blood.

She had recoiled when reading the name of one of the
interviewers: *Henrik Jungersen*.

Must have been one of his first cases as a detective. For
each interview, he and his fellow officer had got tougher
on Kristoffer. The boy who had hosted the party had told
them Kristoffer hadn't even been invited. Why had he lied
about it?

'I'm overweight. No one likes me,' Kristoffer had said.
'I was embarrassed to tell my father the truth, that I hadn't
been invited to any of the graduation parties, so I gate-
crashed,' he had told them.

In that case, why did no one else who was at the party
remember seeing him there?

'Because they were all off their faces by the time I turned
up,' he said.

Why, if one or more intruders had forced their way into
the Bødker household, had the police not managed to find
as much as a single fingerprint that didn't belong to one of
the family?

'They must have been wearing gloves.'

Why, given the Bødker's house was surrounded by close neighbours, had the police not succeeded in finding a single person who had seen a stranger, or strangers, in the area that evening?

'I don't know. Isn't that your job to find that out?'

No signs of a break-in. Nothing taken.

'The old man must have let them in himself, and we've nothing to steal. Perhaps that's why they beat the crap out of him.'

It was obvious from the transcripts and notes that Henrik and his colleague had had serious doubts about Kristoffer's story and had tried in several ways to disprove it.

No suspect had been found and, over the years, the case had ended up in the growing pile of unsolved murders.

Two notes in the file gave Jensen an uneasy feeling: firstly, Kristoffer had not visited his mother in hospital after his father had died. And secondly, Kristoffer had been absent from his father's funeral in the local church, which only a few of Ole Bødker's work mates and neighbours had attended. Was this the same Kristoffer who had cried when he had told her about losing his parents?

Shortly after the murder, he had sold the family house and moved away from the area.

After a couple of years in which it seemed that Lars Bødker had ceased to exist, Kristoffer Bro had turned up, a blank slate, ready for his story as a self-made IT entrepreneur to be written.

Jensen had only managed to find a single interview in which Kristoffer had mentioned his parents. The journalist had reported they had died in a car crash when Kristoffer was eighteen.

Had he reinvented himself as a means of forgetting what had really happened? Or because he had something to hide?

Jensen's thoughts circled back to the present. Why didn't Kristoffer have any personal items in the flat? Why was his office so swept clean of stuff, as if it had never been used?

And what was the key for that she had found in his blazer pocket?

She shivered. Kristoffer didn't appear to have discovered that the key was missing, which must mean that it was a spare.

Could be anything. A key to a bike he no longer owned, or a flat he no longer lived in. But in a place otherwise swept of personal effects it felt significant.

She grabbed her crutches and limped back into the enormous, empty flat. She stood still for a moment and looked around, but there was no lock left that she hadn't tried.

A thought came to her.

A long shot perhaps, but worth a try.

She practised in the lift, putting on her most casual voice.

The concierge greeted her with a smile.

'Say, Søren, would you be able to tell me where Kristoffer's storage room is? He asked me to fetch something for him, but I just realised that he never told me where it was.'

Søren didn't seem to suspect anything. 'You mean his lock-up in the basement? Only the penthouse gets a lock-up; it's one of the perks. Step out of the lift and it's straight ahead of you, beyond the bicycle cages, on the other side of the car park. Though, I'm afraid I don't have the key.'

'Oh, but I have it right here,' she said, patting her pocket. 'Kristoffer gave it to me.'

'I'll come with you,' Søren said. 'You shouldn't be going down there on your own on those crutches.'

Bad idea. If the key didn't fit in the lock, Søren would become suspicious. He might even shop her to Kristoffer.

'That's kind, but it won't be necessary,' she said. 'Besides, you can't leave your desk unattended and it's probably going to take me ages to find what I'm looking for.'

She went to the lift before he could argue, smiling at his disappointed face as the doors slid closed.

There were half a dozen cars in the basement, covered in tarpaulin. The air smelled of diesel and damp concrete. At the far end of the room, a corridor led in between two rows of bike cages to an unmarked door. Jensen noticed the CCTV cameras in the ceiling as she made her way across the concrete floor on her crutches.

Søren would be up there watching her on his security screens. If the key didn't fit, she would tell him that she had brought the wrong one down. If he asked about it again, she would tell him that Kristoffer had changed his mind. Søren might mention something to him about it, but by then she would be long gone. She wanted to get away, to be on her own, to think about what she had read in the police files.

To her relief, the key fitted. She fumbled on the wall for the light switch and shut the door behind her.

Her crutches rattled to the floor as her hands flew up to her mouth.

What the hell?

66

Thursday 14:39

Whether he had got out of bed the wrong side or was genuinely protective of his residents was hard to tell, but Henrik had rarely met a less cooperative individual than the concierge at Kristoffer Bro's place.

The luxury block of flats, with their views of the harbour, was one of Copenhagen's most expensive addresses. Personally, Henrik couldn't see what all the fuss was about. The raw concrete walls and minimalist furniture made the high-ceilinged lobby look like a warehouse after a closing-down sale. He and Tone had arrived with uniformed back-up, but still the concierge refused to answer his questions.

'I *said*, we're from Copenhagen Police and we need to see Bro as a matter of urgency,' said Henrik. He reached for the name badge on the man's lapel and pretended to read. 'Søren!'

The concierge folded his arms across his chest and looked at Henrik obstinately. 'It's my job to protect this place,' he said. 'Unless you can tell me what you need Mr Bro for, I can't help you.'

'Call the lift,' Henrik said to Tone. 'Kristoffer Bro lives in the penthouse. We'll deal with this clown later.' He turned to the uniforms. 'Stay here, make sure he doesn't move an inch.'

The concierge watched them blankly from his desk as Tone pressed the lift button. Nothing happened. 'Seems you need a fob to make it work,' she said.

Henrik marched across to the concierge and pulled him to his feet by his green blazer. 'Bro is wanted for arrest,' he said. 'The reason is none of your bloody business. Now call the lift and get us to the penthouse pronto or I'll arrest you as well.'

The concierge scrambled to his feet. 'Arrest? But Mr Bro's not in,' he stuttered.

'Right,' said Henrik, taking his phone from his pocket. Even if Kristoffer wasn't in the flat, Jensen would be. He needed to see that she was safe. 'I'm calling for reinforcements.'

'No, wait,' said the receptionist, fumbling through a large key ring. 'I'll take you up there, so you can see for yourself.' He stopped. 'I take it you have a search warrant?'

'We don't need a fucking search warrant,' said Henrik. 'Bro is wanted on suspicion of murder. Now take us to his flat this second.'

That shut the man up.

Momentarily.

'You must be mistaken,' he said in the lift. 'Mr Bro is a well-known businessman. I don't think—'

'Thank you, but I don't want to hear it,' said Henrik, holding up a hand to stop him.

The lift opened on a cavernous hall. Henrik and Tone

quickly searched the place, running from room to room. In the bedroom, Henrik felt his gut wrench at seeing Jensen's stuff in the closet. There was a glass of water by the sink; she had tossed her bag aside on the marble counter. It was full of junk: broken pens, chewing gum wrapped in receipts, a wrinkled apple.

On the balcony, there were signs that she had been sitting in one of the chairs for a while, reading the folder he had given her. It was on the floor, the photocopied documents spilling out of it.

'Is that a police file?' said Tone. 'How did that get here?'

'No idea,' said Henrik, but he could tell that Tone didn't believe him. She wasn't the type to let anything go; he would have to come clean with her later and hope she wouldn't run to Wiese.

There was no sign of Jensen's crutches.

Had something happened to her? Had Kristoffer known what was coming and taken her somewhere? Had she confronted him with the contents of the folder?

No more people going missing now, please.

Least of all Jensen.

He turned to the reluctant concierge who looked like he was about to open his mouth to protest again. 'Bro's girlfriend. I dropped her off here myself earlier today. Have you seen her?'

The concierge narrowed his eyes. 'Why? Is she wanted for arrest too?'

67

Jensen couldn't believe what she was looking at. Instead of the old cardboard boxes, bicycle wheels and lampshades that she had expected to find in the lock-up, there were four clean, white, soundproofed walls and a desk with a bank of four giant screens.

The screens lit up when she touched the keyboard. A box appeared on the first screen, prompting her to enter a password.

She nearly had a heart attack when her phone buzzed. It was another text message from the doctor at Riget, asking her to call back.

Not now.

She sat down in the high-backed black-leather office chair and tried all the combinations she could think of, which wasn't many. Kristoffer's date of birth. The name of his company, the names of Lars and Ole Bødker and the street they had lived on in Slagelse, the school Lars had gone to.

311

None were right.

'Of course, he wouldn't be so stupid,' she said out loud. Her voice sounded strange and flat in the padded room.

'You're right, I wouldn't,' said a voice behind her.

Kristoffer.

His voice was void of emotion.

No *Where have you been?* or *What happened to your leg?* How had he managed to enter without her hearing?

She pointed to the screens. 'What is this, Kristoffer?'

'My mission control.'

'What?'

'Let me show you.' He leaned across her and typed something too rapidly for her to follow. The screens changed. She was looking at dozens of little squares with black-and-white images. He pointed to one of them. 'Recognise anything?'

'That's my flat,' she said, looking at her tiny vertical pied-a-terre in Christianshavn, with the spiral staircase leading up to the mezzanine floor and the Velux window with a view of the church tower of Our Saviour.

A couple of people in white coveralls were walking around the rooms.

'Not yours. Mine,' he said. 'You're my tenant, remember?'

'The alarm system you installed. When I thought someone had been in the flat. That was so you could, what ... spy on me?'

'Spying is a big word. I like to come and go as I please in the properties I own, but you'd got suspicious, so I installed the alarm to reassure you.'

'So, it was you all along? I told you I had come home to find my door open, and you made me feel like I was imagining it. Instead, you ...'

She paused as the implications of what she was saying

312

sank in. 'Wait a minute.' She pointed to the screens. 'So . . . when we brought Esben Nørregaard there you would have seen the whole thing. That means—'

'Yes,' said Kristoffer. 'It was me. Me who got that little shit Lars Bjerre to write those threatening emails to Esben Nørregaard. Me who sent some people to take a look around his rich wife's house in Klampenborg to see what we could find to blackmail him with. Me who told the guys to take the Syrian to use him as a bargaining tool.'

'But why? What's Esben ever done to you?'

'Oh, it's more a question of what he will do *for* me. Nørregaard owes me.'

Esben had been convinced that someone was after him, someone who had once done him a favour and expected him to return it. He had thought it was Leif Kofoed. Had he been wrong all along?

Jensen recalled how, when she had talked to Kristoffer in the King's Garden, he had referred to Aziz's flat as being in Nørrebro. At the time, she couldn't remember telling him the location; now she was certain she hadn't. 'But your plan backfired. We know that Aziz got away.'

'The Syrian is unimportant,' said Kristoffer. 'Esben Nørregaard himself is far more valuable.'

'He said someone was following him whenever he left the hotel.'

'I had the place staked out but getting Nørregaard out from there was too risky with all the people about and security there is hefty.'

'That was you in the hoodie? Getting that maid to push the note under Esben's door?'

'Did he think it was the Syrian? That's what he was meant to think. I couldn't believe my luck when you took him to my place in Christianshavn.'

'Where is he?' Jensen shouted. 'What have you done to him?'

'He's safe,' said Kristoffer. 'For now.'

'You lied to me,' said Jensen.

'I could say the same about you.' He reached across her again and pressed a few more buttons on the keyboard. All four screens were now showing a picture of herself moving around in Kristoffer's flat a few days ago. Opening his wine fridge and looking inside. 'That was a five-thousand-kroner bottle of wine,' he said. 'And look now at you, searching my office.'

'You were down here watching me all the time. That's how you turned up so quickly.'

She remembered that he had been panting with exertion as if he had been running.

'I knew you found the key. I was just waiting for you to find this place. Took you long enough.'

Kristoffer smiled.

Then he went and shut the door.

And locked it.

'When you turned up wanting to rent my flat, it was serendipity,' he said. 'Of all the gin joints in all the towns in all the world, she walks into mine.'

'What?'

'*Casablanca.*'

'You're mad.'

'Oh, you thought it was a coincidence that we met?' he said. 'When I came around to repair your washing machine? You're very sweet, if you think I do that for all my tenants.'

'You killed your father,' said Jensen. 'Your name isn't Kristoffer Bro. It's Lars Bødker.'

'Ah, I see. DI Jungersen told you. Shame he's married.

314

I can't see him leaving his wife, so I wouldn't hold out for anything, if I were you. Do you know that he's been keeping you under surveillance?'

Jensen said nothing.

'Follows you around, sitting in that black car of his, thinking he's invisible.'

'At least he's honest with me. He told me what you did and like a fool I didn't believe him.'

'Well, if he did, he must also have told you that there's no evidence whatsoever. Nada. Zilch,' he said, forming a zero with his thumb and forefinger.

'Why did you kill your father?'

'I told you a thousand times. I don't want to talk about the past,' said Kristoffer, holding his hands over his ears. 'Let's talk about you instead. What made you visit that drunk Carsten Vangede in that shitty bar of his in Nørrebro?'

'Vangede?'

'Don't pretend you don't know what I'm talking about. What did he tell you?'

'Nothing I'm going to share with you.'

'Did he give you the spectacle case his accountant left behind? That was his only pathetic little piece of evidence.'

The events of the past few months passed before Jensen's eyes. None of it had been what she thought. 'So, our dinner in that Italian restaurant, and me moving in with you, was ...'

'Convenient. Don't get me wrong, I enjoyed it, but you're hardly my type. That must have been obvious to you from the start, clever reporter like you? I prefer my women taller, blonder, prettier.'

She recalled the many times he had pressed her for information, pretending to be interested in her work, and felt sick.

'Vangede had discovered that his money had ended up in an offshore bank account of a company by the name of Amaliekilde Holdings. Amaliekilde is a place on Bornholm, near where Leif Kofoed grew up,' she said.

'Ah, the famous USB. Carsten Vangede thought he was being clever by sending it to you. But hiding it in your underwear drawer? Seriously Jensen, I was expecting more from you.'

'So, it was you who siphoned off Carsten's money? Why?'

'Why not? If people are stupid enough to let money drain from their outfits.'

'But a small-scale, struggling entrepreneur like Carsten? A restaurant and a couple of bars?'

'Oh, he isn't the only one.'

'He isn't?'

'God no. I have thousands of businesses rigged up all over the city.'

'But Vangede found out what you were doing and refused to take it lying down.'

'Vangede was an arsehole. Not even his own family liked him.'

'So, you had him killed and made it look like suicide?'

'I couldn't possibly comment.'

'And Kofoed. How does he come into it?'

Kristoffer frowned. 'He doesn't.' He took a step towards her. His eyes were narrow and cold.

'Let me out,' she said. 'Søren knows I'm down here.'

'I can handle Søren, the little brown-nose.'

Both Henrik and Gustav were at work, thinking she was convalescing upstairs in the penthouse.

This is not good.

'So, what happens now?' she said, trying to keep her voice under control.

'Now it ends. Or let me rephrase that, *you* end.' He took a step towards her. She fumbled to get her phone out of the pocket of her dress while resting on her crutches.

'It won't work down here,' he said.

The phone slipped from her grasp and clanged to the floor.

'Besides, I'll be gone by the time anyone arrives,' he said. 'Well, goodbye Jensen. It was fun.'

He reached for her throat.

68

Thursday 14:54

'I don't understand,' said the concierge. 'She definitely went down here. I watched her myself on the security cameras to make sure she went to the right place. She said Mr Bro had asked her to fetch something. I told her where it was. She had the key, see?'

Henrik put his ear to the door. Nothing.

The door was made of steel with a good lock. He wasn't going to be able to kick it in. He hammered on it with his fists, but no reply came. He would have called Jensen but there was no signal on his phone.

'Well, she's not here,' said Tone, returning from a torch-light search of the basement. 'She must have left again.'

'She would have had to come through the reception. I would have seen her. I see everyone who enters and leaves the building.'

'Must have happened while you were upstairs with us in Bro's flat,' said Tone.

'No, I . . . oh no.'

'Take us to your CCTV control room. Right now,' said Henrik.

The three of them sprinted for the lift.

In the back office, the concierge had set out his packed lunch next to his thermos of coffee and a copy of *Dagbladet*. It was open on the sport pages.

They searched through the recordings, watching as Jensen made it across to the storage room on her crutches and disappeared inside.

'What was she going to fetch down there?'

'She didn't say.'

Jensen had clearly been lying to the concierge. What was she up to? They fast-forwarded through more than thirty minutes of dead pictures of the dingy basement before, finally, something else happened.

Tone, pointing to the man who had appeared on the screen. 'That's Bro, isn't it?'

'Yes,' said the concierge, sounding surprised.

'He must have entered through the parking garage,' said Henrik. 'Does he have a car?'

'Several, but—'

'Shit,' said Henrik. 'He's down there with her.'

'Wait,' said Tone, pointing to the other screen, the one showing the live feed from the basement. 'Who is that?'

69

Thursday 14:55

She had seen them on the CCTV screen over Kristoffer's shoulder as they had talked: Henrik, a woman with short grey hair whom she assumed to be his colleague and Søren, the concierge.

Henrik had been hammering on the door, but no sound had been heard inside the room, which meant no sound could be heard outside. Henrik's colleague had said something to him. After a moment's pause, they had left with Søren in tow, running away towards the lift and vanishing from sight.

Along with Jensen's last hope that she would be getting out alive.

Now Kristoffer had his hands around her throat, increasing the painful pressure with each second. He had surprisingly strong hands. If she had been able to speak, she would have attempted to talk him out of it, to appeal to a conscience he obviously didn't have.

She tried to kick him, to twist free, but with each

movement, she felt her power weaken. She had once read that some people in life-threatening situations would zone out or play dead instead of trying to fight their assailant, as an instinctive pitch for survival.

The expression on Kristoffer's face was entirely placid. Darkness began to appear at the corners of Jensen's vision. She felt herself slide down the seat of the swivel chair towards the floor, like a rag doll, her eyes closing.

This is what dying feels like.

The crash that came next was so loud that Kristoffer lost his footing and fell backwards onto the desk in shock. The room filled with shouting. Uniformed police officers. Henrik.

Gustav?

He was holding his folded e-scooter like a battering ram, hitting Kristoffer repeatedly on the head with it and ignoring Henrik, who was shouting at him to step aside so he could get a clean aim at Kristoffer with his gun.

Jensen felt someone lean over her. A woman with a strong Jutland accent, asking her if she could stand.

She couldn't.

The woman grabbed her under the arms and pulled her from the room.

70

Thursday 19:23

'I'm still not sure about this,' said Tone outside the interview room. 'I mean, given you have an emotional stake in what happened. If Wiese finds out—'

'He's not going to, is he?' said Henrik.

'Or your wife.'

Henrik grabbed Tone by the arms and bent down to her face. 'Listen to me. There is nothing between me and Jensen. Nothing whatsoever.'

'There must have been at some stage,' said Tone, twisting free. 'I could tell how affected you were by what happened yesterday.'

'Hang on just one minute,' said Henrik. 'Jensen and I, we ... It was a long time ago. Good people do wrong things, Tone. That might not have been your experience of life, but it certainly has been mine. Lots of wrong things. Stick too rigidly to that rulebook of yours and either you or it will break, take my word for it.'

He saw that she was thinking about it and went in for the

322

kill. 'Right now, I'm the one who needs to be in that room. Kristoffer Bro is mine. You know there's no one better to make him talk than me.'

'I saw those photocopied police files on Kristoffer Bro's balcony. Was it you who gave those to her?'

'Kristoffer Bro beat his father to death when he was eighteen.'

Tone looked surprised. 'Did he serve time?'

'He was guilty as hell. I was there. I knew he was lying, but we couldn't prove it. It was one of my first big cases. I was inexperienced and Bro was cold as ice.'

'Why did he do it?'

'I don't know. My theory is that he had begun to see his family as an inconvenience. His mother was already as good as dead, and he'd just finished high school, so there was nothing holding him in Slagelse. I reckon he decided to rid himself of a problem.'

'But, like you said, you couldn't prove it.'

'No, but I do know that he tried to strangle Jensen and confessed to kidnapping both Aziz and Esben, not to mention asking Sommer and Olsen to get rid of a couple of assassins. Now, let's get the bastard,' said Henrik, as he pressed the door handle. 'For everything.'

Tone followed him in, reluctantly. He recognised the look on Bro's face from interviews with other doomed suspects. It was that of a man who no longer had anything to lose.

They had found his car packed with a bag of belongings, including his passport, ready for his escape to a new life in a country without an extradition agreement with Denmark. There was a good list of those. No need for escaped criminals to live in hardship.

Instead, Bro would now be facing a long residency

323

courtesy of the Danish state. He would be lucky to get out before he was a pensioner.

The doctors had patched him up well. It turned out Gustav had only inflicted superficial damage: a split lip, a cut to one eyebrow and a matching pair of black eyes.

If Henrik had been the one wielding the e-scooter, Bro would be dead. 'Let's see now,' he said after taking his time to settle down and begin the interview. 'Ordering two contract killings, four if we count Carsten Vangede and Tommy Ewardsen. Illegal surveillance on private property. Fraud. Two counts of kidnap and attempted murder by strangulation. It doesn't look good, does it?'

Bro stared straight at Henrik, a Mona Lisa smile on his lips.

'We all know why we're here,' said his lawyer, one of the expensive types that celebrities hired when they were in trouble. 'Why don't you just get on with it?'

'Oh, and I didn't even mention your father.'

'Can we stick to your actual charges against my client?' said the lawyer.

'Right you are,' said Henrik, keeping his eyes fixed on Bro. 'Only, what I'm thinking is that a lowlife like you couldn't possibly have thought all that up on your own. So, I ask myself, who's the puppet master?'

The lawyer cleared her throat and glanced pointedly at her watch.

'OK,' said Henrik. 'Where is Esben Nørregaard?'

'Depends.'

'On?'

Bro smiled. 'How much you want to know.'

'If you're after some sort of trade on your sentence, you can forget it.'

Bro kept smiling. 'The offer is there.'

'Generous of you,' said Henrik. 'Sedat Osman and Nick Karagiannis then. What can you tell us about them?'

'Assassins.'

'I mean what can you tell us that we don't already know? Let's start with why they came to Denmark in the first place.'

'To kill me,' said Kristoffer.

'Really?' said Henrik. 'And why would they want to do that?'

'You wouldn't know, but being rich wins you no popularity contests,' said Kristoffer. 'Not everyone is happy to see me succeed.'

'Who ordered them to kill you?'

Kristoffer shrugged. 'I picked up on the grapevine that they were coming, but not who sent them. Like I said, there are a lot of options.'

'Don't worry. Our colleagues in the Metropolitan Police will tell us soon enough. I'm just curious why someone would find you important enough to kill.'

'I heard you the first time,' said Kristoffer. 'And I answered.'

'Could it have anything to do with a certain Leif Kofoed?'

Bro looked at him sharply. 'Why are you asking that?'

'You seem tense all of a sudden. Does that mean I'm right?'

'I have no dealings with Kofoed.'

'Oh really? I heard that he helped you get your business empire off the ground by investing in it when no one else would.'

'That was more than ten years ago. And it doesn't mean—'

'I'll decide what it means,' said Henrik. 'You must have

been very grateful for all that he did for you. Grateful enough, perhaps, to want to pay him back? Or maybe Kofoed has some sort of hold on you. Would he know something you're desperate to keep out of the public domain? Like what happened in Slagelse?'

'Where is this going?' said the lawyer, looking up from her papers. 'As far as I know there is nothing in the charges faced by my client linking him to Kofoed. Charges which, by the way, he has owned up to, except for your insinuations about the tragic demise of his father, which I shall leave to one side. For now.'

'OK,' said Henrik. 'Say we accept that the hitmen were in Denmark to kill you, which I don't believe for a moment, then why did you decide to kill them rather than report them to us?'

'Number one, I gave up any illusion of the police protecting us, the citizens, around the same time that I stopped believing in Santa. If you'd arrested those guys, a new pair of killers would have been sent in their place, and next time I might have missed out on the advance warning.'

'And you thought that Jønne and his pal Bjarne would be just the men for the job?'

'They weren't meant to kill them, just scare them off.'

'Oh sure.'

'It was an accident.'

'Right.'

'Self-defence.'

'If you say so.'

'I never told them to shoot, you can't prove that I did.'

'Wasn't it rather your pal Leif Kofoed they came to kill? I can imagine there are quite a few people around the world by now who wouldn't be sorry if the old boy was dead.'

'No, it was me.'

'And didn't Kofoed ask you to take care of his little problem for him, make it go away?'

'I haven't seen or spoken to Kofoed in years. I've nothing to do with him,' said Kristoffer.

'You mean to tell me that since coming back to Denmark he hasn't looked you up once?'

'That's right.'

'And you had nothing to do with arranging Kofoed's interview with Jen ... with *Dagbladet*?'

Kristoffer Bro smiled broadly and leaned over the table, folding his hands. 'Ah, I see. Of course, that's why you're taking such an interest in me.'

Henrik felt the skin on his neck and chest flush but managed to say nothing. Better to let the man opposite him have his little moment.

'I almost forgot about her. Such a ... vigorous and strange little thing. But each to their own,' said Bro. 'Don't suppose your wife would be too pleased to hear about her. Would be embarrassing if it got out at her school, or if your kids found out.'

Henrik felt as if smoke was coming out of his ears. His knuckles had turned white on the edge of the table.

'Good-looking woman, your wife,' said Kristoffer, laughing while his lawyer shook her head. 'I don't personally see why you'd want to cheat on her. Perhaps it's time she had her own little fun.'

In his mind's eye, Henrik was reaching for Bro's neck, knocking his forehead repeatedly into the table, until the flesh yielded, the bone splintered and the eyes in their sockets turned to mush.

He became conscious of breathing heavily.

Looking down, he found a firm hand on his arm, nails cut practically short, a slim, gold wedding band. Tone.

Shaking her head, as Bro kept on laughing. 'Not worth it, Jungersen,' her eyes said.

Let me be the judge of that.

Just once.

To wipe the smile off his face.

Of course, this was what Bro wanted. The man was finished. His money, his penthouse palace, his face in the glossy magazines, all gone. He had admitted to the charges. All he had left was to drag Henrik down with him.

Henrik took a deep breath. 'Let's get back to my questions, shall we? So you maintain that killing Sedat Osman and Nick Karagiannis was all your own idea and that no one else was involved?'

Bro laughed again. 'I had you rattled there, Jungersen.'

'But I have you by the balls, my friend,' Henrik smiled. 'And I'm about to squeeze a whole lot harder.'

71

Friday 13:26

'Good morning, your majesty,' said Gustav, barging into the bedroom and yanking open the curtains.

Jensen raised herself onto her elbows, squinting in confusion at the hot, bright sunlight that had momentarily blinded her. Gustav was dressed in boxer shorts and a T-shirt with a picture of a wide-open mouth. He handed her a tray from Margrethe's kitchen and her nostrils wrinkled at the acrid smell of burned toast. He had managed to scrape off most of the burnt bits, before adding a thin layer of margarine. The coffee was made from granules that Liron would have labelled as the devil's work; they were still floating on the surface of the cooling water.

'We're out of milk, sorry,' said Gustav, wiping a stack of ancient copies of *Time* magazine off the chair next to the bed and sitting down.

Her throat was sore. It hurt to swallow. She bit into a piece of toast, finding to her surprise that she was hungry. 'Thanks, Gustav, this is ... unusually thoughtful of you.'

'I've been waiting for ages for you to wake up,' he said. 'We've got to talk.'

'It's the drugs they gave me at the hospital. They make me sleepy,' said Jensen, scratching her hair.

She barely remembered hitting the pillow after Henrik had driven her and Gustav back to Margrethe's flat in Østerbro. Each of them had given a statement about the events in Kristoffer's basement, and Jensen had been examined by a doctor. Her headache was almost gone by now, but her ankle still hurt. Gustav had left her crutches leaning against a stack of oil paintings in the corner of the room.

Through the open window came the sound of birdsong, a radio playing in a neighbour's flat, a car passing by in the street. Normal sounds.

But nothing was normal.

Kristoffer was a killer, arrested and locked up.

Jensen sat up in bed, with both hands on the mattress and her bare legs dangling over the side.

'What the hell happened?' Gustav said, elbows on his thighs, clutching his beloved vape in one hand. 'You made no sense last night.' He listened in silence, his eyes growing bigger as she told him about finding the key and the lock-up and how Kristoffer, a boy from Slagelse with narcissistic and psychopathic tendencies, had probably killed his own father, before reinventing himself as an entrepreneur.

Gustav had turned up just in time to see Kristoffer drive into the basement under his building. Being Gustav, he had decided to follow the car in, tiptoeing a few steps behind as Kristoffer let himself into the storage room at the back of the basement and shut the door behind him.

'I was trying to work out what he was up to when Henrik and those other police officers turned up,' he said.

While they had burst open the door, he had grabbed

the nearest weapon to hand. 'I knew the guy was a creep. I could tell when I came to see you the other day. Fuck, Jensen, how could you waste your time on a loser like him?'

It was a good question. Something had dulled her faculties in all the time she had been with Kristoffer. Vanity? A yearning to be chosen? To not be alone? She didn't know, but it was never going to happen again.

Henrik had tried to tell her, and she had pushed him away.

Henrik.

She was angry with him. For having turned out to be right. For not letting her go, no matter how hard she tried to get away.

For existing.

'Ordering the killings of two people. Assassins. Here in Denmark. It doesn't seem real,' said Gustav, shaking his head.

'Don't forget siphoning money from Carsten Vangede's bar. His and thousands of small businesses like it.'

'And keeping *you* under video surveillance.'

'That too.' Kristoffer's stalking explained why she had felt herself being watched on so many occasions.

'Still, it makes a good story,' said Gustav, looking at her sheepishly.

'What have you done?' she said, frowning as he got out his phone.

He held the screen to her eyes, a bright yellow-and-black breaking news banner on top of the page. 'Margrethe wrote it, and that's my photo of Bro's arrest right there,' said Gustav, pointing. 'We broke it online yesterday. Everyone else has the story now. But don't worry, I didn't mention that you lived with the guy. There *was* a rumour going round the paper, but Margrethe killed it dead.'

'The pupil becomes the master. Your first scoop. Congratulations.'

Gustav took a pretend bow.

Something stirred in the back of Jensen's mind, something trying to surface from the cloudy pond of her memory.

It was quickly replaced by another thought. 'Oh no,' she shouted, standing up so fast that she stumbled and had to be held upright by Gustav's hot and sticky hands. 'Esben. Has he turned up? And Aziz, any sign?'

Gustav sat her back down again. 'Whoa, take it easy. The answer is no. And no. The intelligence service has taken over the investigation, according to Henrik. There's nothing we can do.'

I don't believe that, thought Jensen.

'We've got to go. We can't just sit here,' she said. 'Where's my mobile? I must call Henrik, find out what's happening.'

'There's no rush,' said Gustav, handing her the phone. 'He swore he'd call us when there's news.'

'He might have forgotten.'

They both listened until his recorded message kicked in. She knew it well; it had not changed in fifteen years, but she was astonished at how much younger and brighter Henrik's voice had sounded back then. Not jaded like these days.

'Well, I can't just sit here,' she said, getting up. 'I've got to get some air.' She began to look for her clothes on the floor. The summer dress she'd been wearing yesterday was stained with Kristoffer's blood. 'Where's Margrethe's wardrobe?'

'She's like ten sizes bigger than you,' Gustav protested, following her through the flat to Margrethe's bedroom.

On a hanger on the back of the door, Jensen recognised the light blue shirt Margrethe had been wearing when she had announced the latest round of redundancies at

332

Dagbladet. This now seemed to be in another lifetime. Yasmine must have taken it to the dry cleaners; it was still covered in a plastic sheet. Perhaps Margrethe never wanted to wear it again.

Jensen found an old denim shirt that was big enough on her to work as a minidress and tied a silk scarf around her waist. She caught herself in the mirror and paused. There were bruises on her neck where Kristoffer had tried to strangle her. She could still feel his hands there, recall the calm, untroubled expression in his eyes. 'I'm going for a walk. Call me the minute something happens,' she said, sticking her feet into her worn sandals, grabbing her crutches and heading for the door. 'And don't follow me. I need to think.'

72

'They don't make men like Monsen any more,' said the Commissioner.

'Not since the factory call-back,' shouted some joker from the back of the room to low ripples of laughter.

The great and the good of Copenhagen had turned out for Monsen's sixtieth birthday reception. Henrik was watching the speeches from the back, cradling a glass of warm white wine that he had no intention of drinking. He recognised a few famous faces: politicians, a judge, a minor TV star.

His boss, Wiese, was standing next to him. The two of them had acknowledged each other's presence with a sideways nod. 'Nice move sending me Tone to stand in for Mark,' Henrik said in a low voice, keeping his eyes on the Commissioner.

Wiese's lips parted in a grin. 'About time someone put a bit of structure into your work methods.'

'No, I'm being serious. I like her. She's a class act,' Henrik said.

Wiese sent him an astonished glance.

Henrik smiled to himself.

The room smelled of flowers and perfume, as far as you could possibly get from the usual aroma in the office. Gifts were stacked high on a long table, mostly books, red wine or whisky. There was also a cake, decorated in the blue-and-yellow colours of Monsen's beloved Brøndby FC.

The football club was part of the glue that had kept Henrik and Monsen close over the years. They had even gone to a few matches together, shouting themselves hoarse for ninety minutes, before heading out somewhere for a beer. Though this was some time ago now, before Henrik's kids had got old enough for him to take them along instead.

It was typical of Monsen to have gone ahead with his reception as planned, while a major search was underway for Esben Nørregaard. The intelligence service had insisted on keeping things under wraps to avoid exposing the vulnerability of politicians to kidnap and encourage copycats. Monsen had seized on this as the reason that his celebration had to go ahead. Cancelling would alert the entire force, and possibly the public, to the fact that something was seriously wrong, he had argued.

Just as well Monsen had no trouble pretending that everything was fine. He was beaming centre stage, tickled by the Commissioner's flattering oratory, occasionally wiping tears from his eyes. His wife, Rigmor, a university lecturer, was looking at him with benign tolerance, the way one might indulge a small child.

The Commissioner's speech was over, and Monsen was laughing and pressing flesh. Henrik turned to head back to the incident room, setting his untouched wine glass on a tray. He would gladly have settled for a cold beer.

He and his colleagues had clubbed together to buy six

bottles of red and a birthday card for Monsen. The gift looked insignificant against the rest.

'Jungersen.' He heard Monsen's booming voice, just as he reached the door. 'You can't be leaving already. We haven't even cut the cake yet.'

'An MP has been kidnapped,' Henrik pointed out.

Monsen shushed him, bundling him into a quiet corner, as he smiled left and right. 'Any news?' he said in a low voice.

'None. Bro is refusing to tell us where he had him taken. The bastard is trying to use it as some sort of bargaining chip.'

'Intelligence have any leads?'

'Your guess is as good as mine. They're interviewing Bro as we speak. Not that I'm holding out much hope for them.'

Monsen nodded, keeping his eyes on the room. 'And the driver?'

'Whereabouts unknown. We know he was captured but managed to free himself. It's possible he's hiding somewhere, keeping his head down till it's all blown over.'

'At least those other ghastly murders have been cleared up,' said Monsen, waving and smiling at someone on the other side of the room.

'In principle, yes.'

'You did well at the press conference. You're getting the hang of it. Good job that pesky journalist from *Dagbladet* wasn't there this time.'

Jensen.

Almost dead.

Again.

'But there are still unanswered questions,' said Henrik.

'There always are. But you have your confessions and that's the main thing.'

'But seriously, Kristoffer Bro, the intended target of a contract killing?'

Monsen shrugged. 'Why would Bro make up a story like that? He's finished anyway.'

'That's what I'd like to know,' said Henrik.

They watched as Wiese tried to join a conversation between the Commissioner and someone Henrik didn't recognise. Both ignored him. 'How are things between you and Wiese?' said Monsen.

'The man is a bureaucrat, but as long as I get results, he needs me,' said Henrik.

'You know you could go far, way further than Wiese, if only you'd keep that gob of yours shut now and again. You've got to respect the game, Jungersen, to get on in this world.'

Easy for Monsen to say. He had taken the game to heart long ago, attaining his high office with minimal work effort.

'Nah,' said Henrik. 'You know me. I'm happy as I am. Never had any big ambitions.' He looked at Monsen. 'Don't you ever miss it?'

'What?'

'The chase? The interviews? The grind and labour of an investigation? I mean, when did you last visit a crime scene?'

Monsen laughed and slapped him on the shoulder. 'All that's long in the past for me. It's a young man's game. Which is why I'm wondering when you're going to look after your own career a little. Think of what's next.'

Monsen gave Henrik's shoulder a telling squeeze and rejoined the bustle in the room.

What was next? Henrik had never thought about it. He didn't want to be promoted, just wanted to do his thing, solve his cases and catch the bad guys. The rest of policing, the *game*, was for the likes of Wiese and Monsen. Not everyone had to go places, though in the police it sometimes felt like it. The bosses didn't know what to do with you unless you had that forward motion in you.

As for retiring, they would have to carry him out of the office feet first. The thought of a life without work, without the routine of it, terrified him.

He was on his way out of the room when Rigmor stopped him, fixing him with her beady stare. 'Off so soon?' she said.

'Time and tide.'

'Not your scene, this type of event, is it?'

'How could you tell?'

She laughed. 'Nor mine, but Mogens loves all this. I just wish he'd retire so we can do the travelling we're always talking about while we've still got our own teeth.'

'Any signs of him reaching for his pipe and slippers yet?' said Henrik.

'You know Mogens, never works too hard, but he does love his job, so I've given him two more years of it. The day he turns sixty-two will be his last on the force.'

It would be the end of an era, Henrik thought. The future belonged to Wiese and his ilk.

He had said goodbye to Rigmor and was headed for the door when he noticed Tone marching towards him with an expression on her face that made his pulse rise.

'You need to come immediately,' she said. 'I think I know where Bro's people took Nørregaard.'

73

Jensen called Henrik a second time from the stairs but got his voicemail again. Did that mean there was a development in the case? Had Esben finally been found?

Thankfully, there was still nothing on the news about his kidnapping. Much as Esben was fond of publicity, it was unlikely to help him now. On the contrary, the criminals who were holding him might panic and kill him. That the police had managed to keep a lid on the story for this long seemed almost a miracle, given the propensity for big news to leak from their HQ at Teglholmen.

Jensen felt her mood darken. What if Esben and Aziz were dead? Maybe that was why the police weren't saying anything?

She thought of this as she hobbled inelegantly down the steps and into the street, her bag slung over her shoulder. She had to do *something*, but what? The only way she could stand it was to keep on moving forward, however aimlessly. She had managed to make it as far as one block on her crutches when she felt a tap on her shoulder.

'Miss Jensen?' That almost familiar voice, sounding like his brother but with a Danish accent frozen in time.

Leif Kofoed. In his crumpled summer suit and hat. With a sleek black car pulled up to the kerb a few metres away, engine running. 'We meet again,' he said.

Jensen looked around her, her heart thumping, but the street was empty. 'What do you want?' she said.

'Walk with me.'

'No,' she replied. 'I regret interviewing you now. I didn't realise who you really were.'

'I see, my brother spoke to you. I thought he might. In that case, won't you give me a right to reply?'

'I don't see the point.'

'Miss Jensen, you're shaking. There's no danger to you here, I can assure you.'

He is lying, she thought, glancing at the black car with the menacing black windows. There would be a burly driver inside, ready to leap out and bundle her inside, if she didn't play along.

'I just want to talk,' he said, pointing to a small square between the blocks of flats. There was a playground with a bench in the shade of tall trees and flanked by a thick beech hedge. 'How about we sit over there, just for a few minutes?'

Reluctantly, she followed him through the gate.

A father was watching two little girls taking turns on a slide, in between stolen glances at his phone. If anything happened to her, surely, he would see it and call the police?

As she sat down on the edge of the bench, as far from Leif Kofoed as possible, she realised how exhausted she was.

'You look pale,' said Kofoed.

'That would be because your protégé just tried to strangle me.'

'I know. He should have left you alone. I told him as much after he tried to run you over outside the hospital.'

She turned to him, astonished. 'That was Kristoffer in the van?' she said.

'You didn't know?'

Jensen could have kicked herself that she had put her mobile back in her bag, out of reach for any furtive recording. Kofoed was bound to get suspicious if she pulled it out now.

He laughed. 'I'm surprised. You're normally so sharp, Jensen. Far sharper than Bro.'

She looked up and caught the eye of the father watching his girls play. He was tall with wild blond hair and a bushy beard, a Viking tattoo snaking down one arm. When she didn't return his friendly smile, his expression changed to one of concern.

Kofoed continued, oblivious. 'I wanted to give Bro a chance to prove himself by ridding me of a problem. In return I promised to keep his dirty little secret.'

'He killed his father,' said Jensen.

'Yes, brutally.'

'Then you have something in common. Both of you were killers by the time you hit adulthood.'

'One of us more honourable than the other, I would have said.'

'A killer is a killer.'

'I never liked Bro, but I thought him useful. Until he messed up,' said Kofoed.

'What was the problem you asked him for help with?'

'People, Miss Jensen, always the same. People who want me dead. They are like flies. You swat one, another comes buzzing.'

'Your brother seems to think you deserve everything coming to you.'

'Ernst. I love him, you know,' said Kofoed, turning to her.

'Enough to kill the boy who kissed the girl he loved?'

'I paid my dues for that.'

'So, these two assassins heard that you're back in Denmark and travelled here to kill you, and you asked Kristoffer to take them out?'

'No. I asked him to get rid of the problem. What he did is on him. Needless to say, it ended in disaster.'

'With your full knowledge.'

'There is very little I don't know. It was me who told Bro that you were looking into the Vangede case. That you and that boy of yours had found my house. Well, Bro took a slightly unorthodox course of action to keep an eye on you. As always, he went too far.'

'Kristoffer said that operation was his. Placing accountants into businesses and then draining the money out of them.'

'Oh, he said that did he?' Kofoed laughed. 'Bro has nothing that isn't mine.'

'Your brother calls you a parasite. It's hard not to agree with him.'

They sat for a bit and looked at the girls playing on the slide. Out of the blue, one of them pulled her sister off the ladder. They heard the thump as she landed on the ground, then a deafening wail as the father ran across to pick her up.

'You got Kristoffer to take Aziz. His men turned up at Esben's Nørregaard's house to put pressure on him, but Aziz was there, giving them a hard time, so they hurt him, and you got the idea of kidnapping him as a means of blackmailing Esben.'

Kofoed said nothing.

342

'Only it backfired. Esben didn't discover that Aziz had gone for over a week, and by then Aziz had escaped his captors. But, as luck would have it, Esben turned up at my flat which Kristoffer was keeping under surveillance. You reacted immediately, having Kristoffer kidnap Esben.'

'That's a lovely story. And true, except it was Kristoffer who did it all. I suppose there was that wish to redeem himself but, of course, even in that he failed.'

'What do you mean?'

Kofoed looked at her meaningfully. 'I see. You haven't spoken your . . . friend yet.'

'Who?'

'DI Jungersen.'

Jensen got up from the bench abruptly. 'Has something happened? Has Esben been found?'

'Not as such. Let's say your friend and his colleagues have discovered where Kristoffer's people have been keeping Nørregaard. Alas, they're about to learn that he's no longer there.'

'So where is he?'

'Just now, this is unclear, but it's only a matter of time until I find him.'

'And then what? Are you going to force him to bend to your will and support your stupid scheme, which would never happen in a million years anyway? And how do you intend to do that now that you've no longer got Kristoffer to do your bidding?'

Kofoed smiled. 'You're wrong about my project. You'll see.'

She jabbed a finger at him. 'You think I'm just going to let you get on with it? I'm going straight to the newspaper after this. I'll write down every word you've told me.'

'And I'll sue *Dagbladet* for the last kroner left at the

bottom of its coffers and from what I hear that's not very many. Margrethe Skov wouldn't dare print it.'

'I wouldn't bet on it. Besides, I'll tell the police.'

'By all means. Call your little friend, but he will find no evidence of my involvement. This conversation never happened. You have no proof.'

They sat for a while in silence.

'You could play it differently, of course,' said Kofoed. He looked at her meaningfully. 'I could help you with your stories. All your problems ... gone. I can open doors that will otherwise remain permanently locked.'

'I don't need help from someone like you.'

'As much as I can be a help, I can also be a hindrance. Make things difficult for you.'

'I'll take my chances, thank you.'

'You, yes, but your mother? Living all by herself out in the dunes?'

'Are you threatening to harm her?'

'Did I say I was going to?'

Jensen shook her head. She was developing an intense pain behind her eyes.

Leif Kofoed got up with some difficulty and doffed his hat at her. 'Well, it was nice not to talk to you, Miss Jensen, and now I must bid you so long. I hope you will think about what I've said, and perhaps our paths will cross again?'

'I sincerely hope not,' Jensen mumbled.

Kofoed walked to his car, got in and drove off.

Jensen looked at the street down which he had disappeared. The people walking by on the pavement would have had no idea of the evil that had just passed among them.

The man with the blond hair and beard approached her, a daughter on each arm. '*Hej*. Are you OK?'

She frowned at him. 'Why do you ask?'

'You looked unhappy just now.'

Too right, I'm unhappy.

'Was that man bothering you?' he said.

Jensen didn't get a chance to reply as there was an almighty crashing noise of breaking branches behind them, followed by loud teenage cursing.

'Gustav? What the hell?'

The good-looking blond man wandered off, glancing over his shoulder at the two of them and shaking his head.

'Did Kofoed see me?' said Gustav. 'I don't think he saw me.'

Months ago, he had tried and failed to get a picture of Ernst Brøgger, hiding in the bushes in a freezing cemetery. This time, he must have been determined not to repeat his mistake.

Smiling broadly, Gustav held up his phone, and Kofoed's strange voice rang out across the playground as he played back the recording. 'I got the whole thing.'

74

'Strange to think that this could be it. Esben Nørregaard is freed and no one out there in the streets will be any the wiser,' Tone sighed.

They were sitting in Henrik's car outside an unremarkable red-brick block of flats in Amager, watching the black-clad special squad with helmets and visors disappear inside the stairwell like cockroaches into a crack in a wall.

'You mean we won't be getting the credit?' said Henrik. 'Nothing new in that.'

'No, I mean that someone can succeed in kidnapping a Danish MP and no one gets to hear about it.'

'Well, intelligence might well try and keep things hushed, but I wouldn't put it past Nørregaard to make it public so he can feature in his own little vote-boosting tale of fighting the forces of evil,' said Henrik.

His phone pinged. A voice message from Jensen. He quickly switched it to silent mode and tucked it in his jacket pocket. Now wasn't the time to bring her up to speed on the case. Tone had already caught on to their relationship, and the woman was as straight as a rod: any more evidence and she might shop him to Wiese for improper conduct.

'What was that?' she said.

'Nothing.' He leaned forward and gazed up through the windscreen at the fourth-storey flat.

'What do you think is happening?' said Tone.

The radio had gone momentarily silent.

Intelligence had been quick to swallow any embarrassment at being outmanoeuvred by Tone, a lowly sergeant. She'd had a team of IT investigators working around the clock to plot the route taken by the silver car seen outside Jensen's flat in Christianshavn. They'd used CCTV, and at one point even a camera fixed to a cash machine, and she had finally tracked the car to the flat in Amager.

Tone's actions had gone some way to make amends for Henrik's foolish mistake in using Jensen's flat as a safe house for Nørregaard. He cringed at the thought that Kristoffer had watched Nørregaard arrive, using the alarm system that he had rigged up himself under the pretext of keeping Jensen safe.

Bro had refused to tell them where Esben had been taken and by whom, and no amount of provocation from Henrik had been enough to break him.

The radio scratched into life. There was a barrage of shouts and noise, followed swiftly by a succession of 'CLEAR' as each room in turn was declared safe. 'No sign of Nørregaard. One person dead,' said the commander after a few moments.

The rapid-entry squad had left and only a few people from the intelligence team remained on the scene when, finally, Tone and Henrik were permitted to enter. Lisbeth and her boss, Biggie, followed them in. The flat was empty aside from the lounge where the furniture consisted of a couple of dirty mattresses, a round table and four chairs. The dead man was lying on his back on the floor halfway between the kitchen and the corridor, shot in the chest, with evidence that someone had tried in vain to stop the bleeding.

'Who is he?' Henrik asked the intelligence team leader.

'We don't know. Potentially some other victim, or one of the kidnappers.'

'What happened here?' said Tone, looking around.

'Perhaps they caught wind we were coming and moved Nørregaard to another location,' said Biggie.

'If that's the case, who's the dead guy?' said Lisbeth.

'Jesus, what a mess,' said Henrik.

No one disagreed with the sentiment.

'Is the victim anyone we know?' said Tone, strolling into the corridor.

Seconds later there was a deafening shot and the sound of a body falling to the ground.

Henrik drew his pistol and glanced around the corner of the doorframe to the corridor.

And looked down the barrel of a gun.

75

Friday 14:43

'Can't this thing go any faster?' Jensen shouted into Gustav's ear. She had left her crutches on the playground in Østerbro and was leaning into his back, arms around his skinny midriff as he zoomed deftly in and out of the crowds of cyclists.

'We're almost there,' he said, consulting the map on his phone stuck to the handlebars.

'We should have taken a taxi.'

'Not as fast as this.' As if to prove his point, he darted into the road and overtook a car on the inside, the driver staring at them in wide-eyed bafflement.

It was Friday afternoon on the kind of stiflingly hot day everyone in Copenhagen was almost getting used to, and traffic in the city was as languid and sticky as blood. People hung lazily around the waterfront in various stages of undress, talking, smoking, drinking. Oblivious to the drama unfolding elsewhere in the city.

Jensen and Gustav had already sent the recording of Leif Kofoed to Henrik and subsequently called him a thousand times. Going directly to Amaliekilde, the gated property in Vedbæk that Kofoed had made his home in Denmark, would get them nowhere. They might even scare him off. Calling the police and explaining everything to a clueless duty officer would take too long. The only option was to find Henrik, and fast. He might not be at his office at Teglholmen, but neither of them knew where else to go, and sitting around in Margrethe's flat waiting for something to happen was out of the question.

Gustav dumped the scooter by the entrance to the police building and ran for the door. She hobbled after him.

'Call DI Jungersen, now,' Gustav shouted at the officer behind the desk as they entered the lobby.

'We need to speak to him immediately,' she said.

The man looked perplexed. 'What's this about?'

'We ... can't tell you, it's top secret,' said Jensen.

The officer sent them both a sceptical look. 'Are you here to report a crime?'

'No. Yes. It's complicated, we really need to see DI Jungersen. Urgently.'

'You can't. He's not here.'

'Well, where is he?'

'That's confidential,' he said. 'I'll find someone who can take a statement. You might have to wait for a bit. You can take a seat over there.'

'Argh,' Gustav shouted. 'Don't you get it? There isn't time. It's a matter of life and death.'

'What is?' A slim, self-important looking man with reading glasses pinched on the end of his nose had stopped in his tracks on his way across the lobby. He had a pile of papers under one arm.

'Who are *you*?' said Jensen. She thought she recognised him from somewhere.

'Superintendent Wiese. What's going on here?' he said, observing her haughtily. 'Wait, you're that journalist from *Dagbladet*. The one who—'

'Yep, that's me.'

'Well, in that case, if you want another go at us, call the press office,' he said and began to walk away.

'Stop,' Jensen shouted. 'I didn't mean any of those things I said. We want to help. We know who's really behind everything. The murders, the kidnappings. We have a recorded confession, and the location of the man who made it. You need to go and arrest him.'

'Please,' said Gustav.

76

Friday 14:47

Henrik managed to duck back inside the flat's living room before the man fired his gun a second time and took out part of the door frame. He had seen just enough to realise that the shooter was still on the floor, head back, one arm raised with a handgun.

Tone was down, not moving and not making a sound.

Shit, shit, shit.

Henrik, Lisbeth and Biggie looked at each other briefly, both women nodding their agreement to his unspoken suggestion. When he moved, he knew they had his back.

Henrik remembered his training. There was no opportunity to aim for the arm and spare the man's life. If you wanted to be sure to stop someone, you had to aim for the largest area of vital organs: the chest.

He fired three times.

The man discharged his weapon once, at the ceiling, before he lay still, a halo of blood spreading slowly from under him. Henrik kicked the weapon out of his hand.

'Fuck, I thought you said he was dead?' he shouted at the team as they rushed to Tone's side.

There was no injury to her head or chest, but she had taken a bullet in her thigh.

The thigh was bad enough.

The femoral artery.

She had lost a lot of blood already.

Too much.

'Tone, come on, stay with us,' Henrik shouted at her, slapping her face with one hand, while pressing the other into her wound as hard as he could.

He screamed his frustration into the narrow hall, screamed to make Tone leave the warm dark place that she had slipped into.

'Her pulse is weak,' Lisbeth said, crouching by Tone's head with two fingers on her neck.

'Where's the fucking ambulance?' shouted Biggie at the armed officers crowding the doorway.

One of them repeated her words verbatim into his radio.

A minute later, they heard the sound of sirens approaching.

Henrik felt all sounds die around him. As if he was watching with a glass helmet around his head as the corridor filled with people.

The paramedics pushed him aside, going to work on Tone, shouting commands, but Henrik heard nothing as slowly he got to his feet, looking down at his hands. They were red and shiny with Tone's blood.

It could have been hours later, or just seconds, when he felt someone shake his arm and looked up into Lisbeth's eyes.

She was talking, snapping her fingers in his face.

'Hey, hey.'

He looked at her. She was holding a phone in her hand, her hand over the mic.

'It's Wiese. That journalist from *Dagbladet*, Jensen, she turned up at the station. Says Leif Kofoed's behind all of this, she has proof, and she knows where he is. If we find Kofoed, perhaps we'll find Nørregaard?'

77

'Strike, strike, strike,' shouted the commander in Henrik's earpiece, and the peaceful silence that had descended on Vedbæk with the end of the rush hour was shattered by a cacophony of noise as a team of armed officers burst through the metal gates to Amaliekilde and ran up the driveway. This time, nothing had been left to chance. In a matter of minutes before the raid, officers had evacuated the properties next door and blocked off the coastal road. Yet more officers had arrived by dinghy and taken up position along the beach, lest Kofoed and his entourage thought of escaping in the motorboat that was moored at the end of the jetty. A helicopter hovered menacingly over the villa, a disembodied voice on a loudspeaker telling the people inside to come out with their hands up. The whole operation was being filmed and the images beamed back to HQ where the top brass were watching, ready to celebrate a spectacular catch.

Henrik was outside the main gates with Lisbeth, both

sweltering in their bulletproof vests and helmets. Henrik's white shirt was stained with Tone's blood. He had managed to wash most of it off his hands, but it was still under his nails and in the callouses on his knuckles. It made him want to scream.

He looked at his watch. It felt like hours, but it had only been three minutes. Kofoed was hardly going to come out of his own volition. Most likely he was hiding somewhere on the property.

It was a further two long minutes before the commander piped up again, this time in a sombre voice. His words were the last anyone wanted to hear. 'He's gone.'

'What do you mean, gone?' Henrik said into his mouthpiece.

'As in, the place is deserted. No furniture, no people. Kofoed must have cleared out and taken off.'

'Have you been through everything? The basement, pool house, garage, shed, loft?' he said.

'Yes.' The commander sounded as deflated as Henrik felt.

News had spread rapidly on the force that a colleague had been shot and was fighting for her life. Operation Amaliekilde, the storming of Kofoed's presumed residence in Denmark, had come together in record time, everyone pumped to finally nail the man who had escaped justice for years.

Perhaps Jensen had got her information wrong. More likely, Kofoed had figured out what was going to happen and decided to make himself scarce. Aside from his first murder, the brutal beating of a schoolboy who had dared to kiss the girl his brother loved, this had been a pattern in Kofoed's life: flee to evade justice, leaving behind a trail of destruction.

Henrik told himself they still had Kristoffer, and Olsen

and Sommer. Their murders were solved, but all hell would break loose if it became public knowledge that the police had managed to lose a prominent MP.

The government had held a crisis meeting and determined that the news of Esben Nørregaard's kidnapping would be made public later that evening unless there was a breakthrough in the case.

Not even Nørregaard's wife knew what had been happening, though she had been making enquiries at his parliamentary office when he had failed to call her as usual in the evenings.

Ulla Nørregaard wasn't stupid. They wouldn't be able to keep the shit from the fan a lot longer.

He heard a commotion behind him. It was Jensen and Gustav, trying to break through the police cordon, but being held back by an overzealous officer. 'What's happening?' shouted Jensen. 'Why has everyone gone quiet?'

Their presence had been her condition for handing over Gustav's recording of her conversation with Kofoed. They didn't know about Tone yet; everyone was under strict instructions to keep the shooting quiet.

'He's not here,' said Henrik.

'That's not true,' said Jensen. 'It can't be.'

He ignored her and began to walk up the drive towards the house, followed by Lisbeth.

'We're coming, too,' said Jensen.

'Yeah,' said Gustav.

Henrik didn't bother arguing. He watched as Jensen and Gustav went ahead. There were weeds all over the gravel drive. It looked very far from the estate-agent images they had studied online.

'Esben?' shouted Jensen as she opened the front door and entered the house.

Henrik watched her patiently as she went from room to room, up the stairs and down into the cellar.

'He isn't here,' she said when she had finished searching the place, as if outraged that Henrik had broken some promise to her.

'I told you.'

'Where has he gone?' she said.

'Most likely left by air,' said Henrik, nodding at the helicopter landing pad on a raised part of the lawn.

Kofoed could be anywhere by now. He had probably transferred to a private jet somewhere in Germany, and was headed back to South America, having left the remains of his luckless entourage to pick up the tab.

Kristoffer was unlikely to ever leave prison, as were the people who had taken Esben to the Amager flat. As soon as Henrik had tracked them down.

'So, what are you going to do about it?' said Jensen.

'What do you want me to tell you, Jensen?'

'How you're going to find Esben and Aziz, of course.'

'I don't know,' said Henrik.

He felt at sea in a way he seldom had. When was the last time everything had gone wrong this thoroughly? One old man with a psychotic bent and a bit of cash to throw around had created more chaos in a few weeks in Denmark than most criminals managed in a lifetime.

Jensen had been attacked and was lucky to be alive. Tone had been shot in the thigh and taken to Riget, with no news yet as to her condition. They had all been made fools of. And an MP and his Syrian driver had been missing for so long that there was now no question the Commissioner would be forced to make the matter public, which was guaranteed to trigger a media storm of epic proportions.

He walked over to the panoramic windows and looked

out over Øresund towards Sweden. There was a thick layer of dust on the windowsill, peppered with dead flies. The garden was dead, the lawn brown. Most of the planting had perished in the extreme heat. A deck chair lay knocked over on its side.

If Kofoed had ever lived here, he was either not the man of luxury everyone thought him to be, or it was a long time ago. It was even possible that he had gone elsewhere in January when Jensen had first started digging into the Carsten Vangede suicide. If only he had listened to her then, they might not have been in this mess. Now, they would have to start again. Go back, gather all the evidence, look over everything. It would take months, years, and there might be nothing at the end of it.

Jensen came up behind him. 'Are you just going to stand there?' she yelled at him.

He was about to tell her to take her pimpled apprentice and get lost when her phone began to ring. She looked at the screen with a frown.

'It's Amira,' she said, before answering the call. 'Amira, hi, listen, it's not a great time, can I call you back?'

Not great is an understatement, thought Henrik.

He tried to suppress his concern. With Aziz gone for almost three weeks, he had reluctantly agreed to Amira leaving the safe house and moving back into the Nørrebro flat. Was this going to turn out to be another giant mistake?

'What? Amira, I can't hear what you're saying, slow down.' Jensen pressed the screen, and a loud noise came from the speaker. The sound of multiple excited voices.

'They're back,' said Amira, her voice full of happy tears. 'Aziz and Esben, they just walked through the door a couple of minutes ago.'

359

78

Friday 21:12

'A bit closer together. Yeah, like that. Now smile,' said Gustav, pointing his phone at Esben and Aziz who had their arms around each other, Aziz with his face turned slightly so that you couldn't see the sprawling bruise on it. With the hiding over, he was letting his beard grow back and the stubble was already thick on his chin.

Liron had declined to be in the picture, protesting loudly that the real hero was Aziz. Jensen reckoned there would be plenty of time to get the truth about his own role in Esben's release.

Henrik was standing away from everyone else at the back of the room, next to his colleague Lisbeth with the short blonde hair. He looked perkier than he had done at Amaliekilde before they had received the good news, but the failed raid was clearly still troubling him. He and Lisbeth were waiting to take Esben, Aziz and Liron away for medical examinations and to interview them thoroughly about what had happened. Aziz and Liron were going to be formally arrested for taking the law into their own hands.

Aziz had explained how he had been keeping a watch on Esben non-stop, first at the hotel and later in Christianshavn, only allowing himself a break from his constant vigil to shower and change clothes. 'I was gone for less than an hour, but in that time, Kofoed's people had managed to take Esben to the flat in Amager,' said Aziz.

'They thought we wouldn't find them. Fucking imbeciles,' Liron had supplemented.

'I'm very grateful they were wrong,' said Esben.

'How *did* you find them?' said Jensen.

'Many people buy coffee from me. People who know people,' said Liron cryptically.

'You should have called us. We would have dealt with it, and perhaps no one would have got hurt,' Henrik said.

'Dealt with it? I don't bloody think so,' said Liron. 'I hear the man you put on watch was busy zipping up his trousers when it all kicked off.'

'Never mind that. You have no authority to exercise force,' said Henrik. 'There are consequences.'

Unbelievable, thought Jensen. Was Henrik jealous that it was Aziz and Liron, and not him, who had got to be heroes and free Esben?

'A police officer got shot today. She's in the ICU,' Henrik said.

Liron looked away. Aziz stepped forward. 'I am very sorry,' he said. 'Where did this happen?'

'In the Amager flat after you got Nørregaard out.'

Aziz and Liron had explained how they had been staking out the place first and knew that Nørregaard was being held by four men whom they assumed (correctly, as it turned out) to be armed. 'We knew we stood no chance against all four of them, so we waited till two of them came out,' said Aziz.

'They won't be eating solids for a while,' Liron chipped in.

'Then we went around the back and up the kitchen stairs. Our only hope was to surprise the two guys in the flat, and it worked, but it all got a bit crazy. One of them took a stray bullet and went down, at which point his mate took off. We tried our best to stop the injured guy from bleeding out, but it was obvious he wasn't going to make it, so we left,' said Aziz.

'Well, the three others got away. They must have assumed the fourth man was dead. Getting the body away from the property with no one noticing would have been very difficult, so they left him. Unfortunately for my colleague, he had a gun and enough life left in him to put a bullet in her thigh, so you'll forgive me if I don't join in your Rambo celebrations.'

'Oh God,' said Jensen. 'Henrik, that's terrible. How's she doing?'

'I know a few of the surgeons at Riget,' said Esben, taking out his phone. 'Let me call them. What's your colleague's name?'

'Thanks, but your influence isn't required here,' Henrik snapped. He rubbed his face. When he spoke again, his voice had softened. 'Look, all I'm saying is this vigilante rescue mission has come at a cost. A crucial witness is dead and a police officer critically injured. This might all have been avoided.'

Liron shook his head but didn't say anything.

Esben held up his hands. 'Let's not jump to conclusions. I'm the last person to want to make a big fuss about what happened, but the truth is that Aziz here saved me from those people, which possibly means he saved my life.' He reached up and placed a hand on Aziz's shoulder. Next to the Syrian he looked almost like a child.

'Then we are quits,' said Aziz and shook Esben's hand, while Gustav snapped away.

'You might all want to keep it under wraps, but this story is definitely going into *Dagbladet*,' he said.

That's my boy, thought Jensen. 'Talking of which, we'd better head back to the paper and get writing before someone else beats us to it,' she said.

'Keep me out of it,' said Liron, a serious note in his voice leaving them in no doubt that he meant it.

Kofoed leaving the country before he could be brought to justice felt like an anticlimax, but she knew that it was some kind of victory. Sought by the police, with his powers on the wane, he was unlikely to make another visit home soon, if ever.

Ernst Brøgger would be relieved. Now he could carry on living in anonymity, without fear of his brother dragging his name into the mud.

'OK,' said Henrik. 'Tearful reunion over. Let's get you three down to the police station.'

Lisbeth offered to stay behind with the kids, so Amira could follow and wouldn't have to be parted from Aziz.

They were walking down the stairs in the Nørrebro apartment block and had almost reached the door to the street when Henrik's phone began to ring. Jensen heard him stopping on the stairs behind her.

'What is it?' she said.

'Wiese,' he mumbled to himself. 'What does he want now?'

He picked up. 'Jungersen.'

She saw his face turn white as he listened, his eyes flicking left and right as they did when he was concentrating hard.

Then the phone fell out of his hand as he sat down heavily on the stairs.

'It's Tone,' he said, staring at Jensen in disbelief. 'She's dead.'

79

'Knock, knock,' said Margrethe, who had appeared in the doorway of Jensen's office.

Gustav was seated on the dormer sill, his legs dangling over the side, as he blew bubble-gum-flavoured vapour through the open window. Jensen told herself this was better than him swivelling restlessly on his office chair driving her mad. She had been trying to concentrate on reading the day's news coverage in preparation for participating in an evening programme on TV. Not easy, with thoughts of Henrik and his colleagues racing through her mind. The news of Tone Ravnsbæk's death had just broken on all the networks.

'Want a seat?' she said to Margrethe, pointing to the sagging armchair with the faded orange cover in the corner of the room.

'In that old louse-riddled lump? No thanks,' said Margrethe, looking around in disgust. She was seldom seen on the reporters' floor.

'To what do we owe the pleasure?' said Jensen.

'Henning has woken up and is talking and eating.'

'Really?'

'Yes. He's come back from the dead like some Lazarus.'

He's not the only one, thought Jensen.

Aziz and Liron were still in custody. Liron had managed to stay out of the public eye, but there was already public pressure for Aziz's release, pending the court hearing.

'Glad to hear it,' said Jensen.

'You walked all the way upstairs to tell us that?' said Gustav.

'I thought I'd come and see you for once, rather than picking up the phone.'

Jensen looked at her boss sceptically.

'OK,' said Margrethe. 'I wanted five minutes' peace from the Swedes. Just five minutes. Fucking jobsworth, that Hugo Persson. Lacking entirely in imagination.'

'Are you regretting their investment?'

'*Nej, nej,*' said Margrethe, brushing Jensen's question away. 'There's no alternative, but they know nothing whatsoever about good journalism, so I'd be grateful if Persson and his humourless posse would keep out of my way. Speaking of which,' she said and unfolded *Dagbladet*, the front page of which was plastered with Jensen's story about Esben and Aziz, with Gustav credited on the photos. 'Jensen, this is the best I have ever seen you write.'

'Thank you.'

'But now is not the time to take your foot off the accelerator,' said Margrethe. 'I want a story about that police officer who got killed.'

Jensen looked at the ceiling. Margrethe wasn't going to like what she had to say. 'Gustav and I were both there,' she said. 'Yesterday, when her colleagues found out she had died from her injuries.'

'Excuse me, what did you say?'

'We've known since yesterday.'

'You knew,' said Margrethe. 'And you didn't think to mention it?'

'No, because I knew you'd be reacting like this, and they made me promise to keep it under wraps until today, to allow her family in Jutland to be told and come to terms with what's happened.'

'A police officer dying on active duty is a major deal, Jensen. The public have a right to know.'

'Some things come before the public's right to know.'

'Yeah sure. Matters of national security, perhaps.'

'Decency. Respect. Kindness.'

'Pah,' said Margrethe. 'You should have told me.' She turned to Gustav. 'At the very least, I would have expected more of my own nephew.'

'Jensen's cool,' said Gustav, his head in a cloud of vapour. 'She did the right thing.'

Margrethe looked from Jensen to Gustav. 'I see. Closing ranks on me. You two are getting far too cosy up here. Good job high school starts in August.'

'What?' said Jensen, looking at Gustav. 'You've decided to go back after all?'

'Yeah, might as well,' he said, pointing at Margrethe. 'Gets her off my back. Not sure anything else will.'

'That's brilliant,' said Jensen, though she felt the opposite. She was going to miss Gustav terribly. His mess. His gobbi-ness. Even the sweet smell of vape that always hovered about him. Perhaps he could still help her after school?

'Enough of the mutual affection club,' said Margrethe. 'Back to work, you two. And Jensen, make sure you get an interview with the dead police officer's husband. Take the train to Jutland, film the whole thing. We need to keep the pressure on now, make sure someone pays for this. Why was she even in that flat? Where were her superiors?'

Jensen was about to open her mouth to protest that Tone Ravnsbæk's family had surely been through enough when her phone rang.

The doctor from Riget.

Time to find out what she wanted.

She waved at Margrethe and looked past Gustav at the rooftops of Copenhagen as she spoke. 'Jensen.'

'Did you not see any of my text messages?'

'Sorry, I've been busy.'

'You know I don't have to do this. I'm busy too. I'm not even on duty now.'

'So why are you calling me?' said Jensen. 'What is it?'

A sudden hesitation at the other end. 'I'm not sure if anyone told you, but your test results ... I got the impression when I spoke to you that you had no idea. And I thought it's not right, that you should just carry on with your life without anyone telling you.'

'Tell me what?'

August

August

80

The sunlight cast long shadows across the lawn and caught in the cobwebs stretching between the topiary hedges. There was a smell of advancing decay in the air. Soon, it would be the end of summer. Henrik, for one, was glad to see the back of it.

He looked on as Lisbeth and Josefine cut the wedding cake inside the ochre-coloured orangery with the wide-open French windows, surrounded by their laughing and cheering guests. He had been surprised that both were wearing bridal gowns, having always imagined Lisbeth as the man in the relationship.

('You just don't get lesbians, do you?' said his wife in his head.)

It was the first time he had seen Lisbeth in a dress. She was pretty, with curls and flowers in her blonde hair, looking happier than he had ever seen her.

He had taken his glass of champagne onto the lawn and found a bench away from the bustle of the party. His wife had

371

been understanding after Tone Ravnsbæk's death. Though allegedly determined to start divorce proceedings as soon as she got back from Italy with the kids, thankfully she hadn't.

On occasion, she had even been affectionate, putting her hand in his or gently rubbing his back when she had found him staring into mid-air at the dinner table, in his TV chair or in the middle of some mundane task.

Something that had happened rather often lately.

He was grateful that she had decided not to join him at the wedding, perhaps sensing that he would spoil the day with his low mood. The thought of the two most important women in his life being in the same room, even for a few hours, was abhorrent to him. He saw Jensen looking at him now, through one of the open windows. She was with Aziz and Amira. No sign of Liron Vaknin, though Henrik knew Lisbeth had invited him.

He hadn't managed to discover anything at all about the Israeli.

Which usually meant there was plenty to find.

All in good time.

Inside the orangery an ensemble of string players struck up a romantic tune.

Jensen was heading towards him through the garden.

She was wearing a dress in a slinky, silky blue material that showed off her slight frame and matched her intense eyes. Her feet were bare. He thought he could still see pale marks on her throat where Kristoffer Bro's hands had been.

'May I?' she said, pointing to the seat next to him on the bench.

'Sure, but I should warn you that I'm poor company.'

'Me too,' said Jensen.

They sat in silence for a while. Henrik tipped his glass of lukewarm bubbles onto the grass. He noticed that Jensen was shivering with cold and was glad that, for once, she didn't protest when he put his leather jacket around her shoulders.

'You're thinking about Tone, aren't you?' she said after a while.

Henrik nodded and looked down at the black brogues he referred to as his dancing shoes. They were the only concession he had made to the happy occasion, deciding that morning that his usual black jeans and white shirt would have to do. It hadn't felt right to don his formal dress so soon after he had worn it at Tone's funeral. It had been the worst day of his life. Hundreds of officers in uniforms and white gloves had turned up at the church in Horsens. Henrik hadn't been able to look Tone's grief-stricken husband in the eye. In his eulogy, the man had insisted tearfully that Tone had died doing what she loved.

'It wasn't your fault. The intelligence service should have secured the premises before they called you in,' Monsen had told him.

But even the intelligence service couldn't be blamed. Henrik knew from experience how hard it could be to find a pulse in a person close to death. The killer had been shot in the chest. He didn't look like somebody about to wake up and shoot a police officer. His gun had been hidden under his body. If there was a failure, it was that it hadn't been found and removed.

'But it *is* my fault,' Henrik had told Monsen. 'Not in a criminal sense, but because I was Tone's superior, and I should have protected her.'

Monsen hadn't said anything to that, just patted him affectionately on the back and sent him out of his office. They both knew Henrik was right.

He would have to go back and see Isabella Grå, the psychologist. And that was just the start of it. There was going to be an inquest and official reports, which meant reliving the events over and over.

He had already been interviewed about the fateful minutes in the Amager flat more times than he cared to remember. It was all he could think about, the scene showing on repeat in his mind, like frames from a horror movie.

Tone's blood on his hands.

'I'm sorry,' said Jensen. She reached across the bench and put her hand on top of his. 'I'm so sorry.'

Her hand was tiny but strong, with bulging veins. It was ice cold. He folded it inside his own. 'Do you ever ask yourself what the point is?' said Henrik.

'Why do you say that?'

'Never mind,' he said.

He looked at her, wanting to hold her, kiss her hair, run his hand down her back. 'I'll be OK,' he said. 'You don't have to worry about me.'

'I'm not,' she said. She looked at him directly with her piercing blue gaze, and he was surprised to see that she meant it. 'Why didn't you warn me about Kristoffer, Henrik?'

'I tried to. You nearly tore my head off, remember? Besides, I might have known he was a lowlife who beat his own father to death, but I had no idea of the operation he ran on Kofoed's behalf. You must trust me on that.'

She nodded meekly.

What was wrong with her? Normally she was spoiling for a fight, but here she was, actually agreeing with him.

It had never happened before.

It was unsettling.

'Kristoffer lied about everything,' she said. 'That's what hurts. The fact that I didn't see what was right in front of me because I wanted his lies to be true. Not much of an investigative reporter, am I?'

'It's OK, Jensen.'

'I'm not meant to find anyone.'

'You found me.'

'You're not available.'

'Depends on how you define available,' he said, running an illicit finger up her thigh, while keeping one eye on the party crowd inside the orangery.

She brushed his finger away and stood up abruptly, casting off his leather jacket. It landed on the gravel path between them.

'Sorry,' he said. 'I shouldn't have done that. Forgive me.'

'It's not you,' said Jensen. 'It's—'

'Look,' he said. 'Kristoffer Bro is a bastard. He didn't deserve you, but he's out of your life now. We've reopened the investigation into his father's death. I doubt if he will ever leave prison. It's over.'

'That's precisely it,' she said, with a look that sent a spike of cold fear through him. 'It's not over.'

Did he want to hear what was coming?

No.

He wanted to reach out and shake her until she was her usual self again. Even an argument was preferable to this.

'They called me from the hospital,' she said.

'No,' he said, shaking his head.

'They found something.'

'No, you can't be ill. Not you.'

'They said—'

He stood up, blocking his ears, sensing that whatever she was about to say would change everything. 'I don't want to hear it,' he said.

'Henrik,' said Jensen, gently pulling his hands away. 'I'm pregnant.'

Acknowledgements

Whilst this is a work of fiction and any mistake entirely my own, I am grateful to special consultant in the Danish police Lars Jung, and former detective chief superintendent in Counter Terrorism Policing Nick Aldworth, for answering my endless questions with patience and grace. My thanks go to the police officers around the world who, like them, have dedicated their careers to keeping others safe. Special thanks to composer and musician Mathæus Bech for taking me out on his boat in Copenhagen harbour, to my friend Helen Pike, Master and author, for reading early drafts and spurring me on, and to my son Frederik Walkden for the map that accompanies this book. Thanks also to my agent, the indefatigable Lena Stjernström, to Laura MacFarlane and Catherine Best for their hawk-eyed editing, and to Kate and Sarah Beal of Muswell Press for their continued trust in me. Last but not least, a heartfelt thanks to all you readers who have taken Jensen, Henrik, Gustav and friends to heart. Without your encouragement, and the love of those closest to me (you know who you are), this book would never have come into being.